MUSIC
A WAY OF LIFE FOR THE YOUNG CHILD

KATHLEEN M. BAYLESS
MARJORIE E. RAMSEY

MUSIC: a way of life for the young child

It is a great privilege to be permitted to search for the meaning of music in the company of a little child. If you find even a fragment of this meaning, it will add an area of beauty to your life as well as his.

Evelyn Goodenough Pitcher et al., 1974, p. 53

MUSIC

A WAY OF LIFE FOR THE YOUNG CHILD

KATHLEEN M. BAYLESS, M.A.

Associate Professor, Early Childhood Education,
Kent State University, Kent, Ohio

MARJORIE E. RAMSEY, Ed.D.

Professor, Early Childhood Education;
Assistant Dean for Student Personnel Services,
Kent State University, Kent, Ohio

with 47 illustrations

THE C. V. MOSBY COMPANY

Saint Louis   1978

Printed in the United States of America

The C. V. Mosby Company
11830 Westline Industrial Drive, St. Louis, Missouri 63141

Library of Congress Cataloging in Publication Data

Bayless, Kathleen M
  Music: a way of life for the young child.

  Bibliography: p.
  Includes index.
  1. Music—Instruction and study—Juvenile.
I. Ramsey, Marjorie E.   II. Title.
MT1.B35   372.8′7   77-14310
ISBN 0-8016-0515-6

YG/CB/B 9 8 7 6 5 4 3 2 1

To three very special "small" persons,
Matthew David Thomas, Andrew Christopher Thomas, and Richard Alva Miller, III,
for their enjoyment and appreciation.

Statement of beliefs

Music is a vital part of daily living. It becomes a part of life as opportunities are provided for experiences in singing, responding physically to different rhythms, creative expressions, playing instruments, and quiet listening. A well-organized musical environment provides for a wide range of musical activities and experiences adequate to meet the needs and interests of all children. It also supports and strengthens learning in the other areas brought into the unified experience. Music helps children understand other people and their cultures and gives increased opportunities for social and emotional development. Music also provides a means for the aesthetic enrichment and growth of every child.

WE BELIEVE

young children have a right to

- have a variety of musical experiences that will bring pleasure and enjoyment to them throughout their lives
- experience a balance of musical activities and materials that are appropriate to their age level and developmental needs
- engage in musical experiences that are based on an action art, not a performing art
- be guided to the fullest development of their musical potential
- have the opportunity for support and/or extension of content areas through the medium of music
- express themselves musically in an atmosphere of freedom and trust, where divergent and creative interpretation is encouraged
- be involved in the full gamut of musical experiences, regardless of physical, social, emotional, or intellectual limitations

adults working with children will

- provide both planned and spontaneous musical activities as a part of each child's day
- offer opportunities for listening, creating, singing, moving rhythmically, and experimenting with sound
- place emphasis on the child's enjoyment of the musical experience rather than on an expected outcome
- provide musical activities that will enhance other learning such as acquisition of language, listening skills, auditory discrimination, and social understanding
- arrange an environment in which children will feel free to explore and engage in a variety of musical experiences representative of contributions from ethnic groups and other cultures
- recognize and plan for well-balanced musical experiences for all children, adapted to physical, social, emotional, and intellectual capabilities

because

- one of the main goals for music is to make children's lives richer through musical experiences that will help develop their aesthetic senses
- a balance of musical activities can contribute to the development of all children according to their individual patterns of growth and development
- the process is more important than the product
- music can support concepts and skills that children are developing, but enjoyment of music should hold priority
- children are natural musicians and, given the opportunity, will express themselves musically in a variety of creative ways

Preface

A belief that music is a necessary and vital dimension in the lives of children from infancy through the early years led us to write this book. Encouragement from teachers, children, and friends to provide appropriate music, easily mastered, compelled us further. As the search began, it quickly became apparent that we wished to build on the many years of experience with young children, with parents, and with preschool groups, developing much of our own repertoire and selecting from other sources those melodies appealing to the young.

The Music Educators National Conference (MENC) has long been vitally concerned and interested in the musical experiences provided for the preprimary child. They have felt, as do many other educators, that a child's entire musical development is influenced by these experiences during the early years.

Recently completed reviews of the professional journals of music and early childhood indicate a paucity of literature dealing with music and the young preschool child.

Throughout the country, when individuals working with young children have been surveyed, the areas of greatest concern appeared to be:
- the need for an appropriate repertoire of suitable song and rhythm material
- the ability to guide creative rhythmic movement
- the confidence gained from possession of the skills, knowledge, and attitudes that make the musical experience mutually satisfying (the phenomenon of the "match") for child and adult

As our writing and research continued, the ideas and musical experiences that evolved and matured were "field tested." Small children sang and enjoyed, groups at national meetings participated, college students pre-

paring to teach offered to be "guinea pigs," friends and colleagues made suggestions, and we sang to one another! The music had to *work* for us.

Yet we felt it important to share the *why*. Theory and practice must go hand in hand. The reader is urged to study and consider carefully our Statement of Beliefs. The musical selections of the text are built around these beliefs. For the young child, enjoyment and appreciation of music are paramount. Thus the reader will find throughout the book suggestions and reasons for using certain approaches, ways to extend and enrich learning, and a strong developmental thread through the various age levels from infancy to age 5. At times what we say may seem repetitious or redundant. Often we intend to repeat, to emphasize, to simplify. With the young child many exposures are important and desirable.

The book has been designed for use by parents, teachers, would-be teachers, or anyone working with young children, whatever the setting, and those who believe as we do that music should be an integral part of the lives of growing children.

A wealth of resources is also offered. Listings of records, song materials, good general professional books and songbook series, arrangements of old and new songs, and instructions on how to make simple instruments are included.

We have enjoyed the search and the compiling of musical ideas and songs. The piano accompaniments have intentionally been written for ease in playing. Autoharp chording has been added for most of the songs and rhythms. It is hoped that the reader will not only delight in becoming acquainted with the materials but also will find the suggestions useful and appropriate in many situations, whether in the home or in the larger community where children gather.

Preface

The search for good musical experiences for young children continues. This volume is incomplete and only a beginning. Our own appreciation and knowledge have been stimulated and broadened. Perhaps the reader will be encouraged to *live* good music with young children and share such richness with others as we have been privileged to do.

Relating to the current concern with the use of pronouns, we have elected to use *he* and *she* in whatever manner it first occurs to us in each instance, and we hope for the understanding of the reader. Similarly, the term *teacher* refers to any adult responsible for planning programs and working with young children.

We wish to express our deepest appreciation for the interest, support, and contributions of our colleagues in the Early Childhood Education Department at Kent State University; our professional colleagues throughout the country; our many students and friends; Dorothy Gilles, E. Paul Torrance, and Jack Spelman for unselfish sharing of ideas and materials; Mazella Janecek, who very competently typed the manuscript; and, most particularly, Hal and Kim Bayless, Christine and David Thomas, Rebecca and Cynthia Ramsey, and other members of both families. Such encouragement was a very potent force in the conceptualization and completion of the book.

Every effort has been made to trace and acknowledge copyright owners. If any right has been omitted, we offer our apologies and will rectify this in subsequent editions after notification.

Kathleen M. Bayless
Marjorie E. Ramsey

Contents

Contents

1 Music making in infancy

Even very small children, in moments of quiet, and particularly when going to sleep, will hum little strains of songs they have heard; this, too, has not escaped the attention of the observant, thoughtful mother, and should be heeded and developed even more in the education of little children as the first germ of future growth in melody and song.

Friedrich Froebel

SOUNDS IN INFANCY

We believe that music is the first art form a child can enjoy. His whole world is filled with sound and music. It is everywhere. From the moment of birth and even before, the child is accommodating to sounds within his environment and relating them to his own abilities to create and explore the rhythms and tonal patterns of sound (Jacobson, 1968). Infants soon begin to use their resources for exploring the world about them. They search for the sound when voices are heard nearby. Around 3 months of age they are often awakened or quieted by the sound of their mothers' voices. Typically, they will turn their eyes and head in the direction from which the sound is coming. Even though they cannot grasp the object, they will become excited, wiggle, and smile at the sound of a bell attached to a familiar puppet as it dances before their eyes. At approximately 4 months, they may use their feet or hands to strike a favorite weighted toy that produces a pleasant "ting-a-ling" sound when it is struck. At first this happening is accidental, but if one observes closely, infants may repeat this action over and over. Piaget observed this behavior and termed it a *secondary circular reaction.*

The stage of secondary circular reactions is so called because the center of interest is not the body's actions but the environmental consequences of those actions (hence the term "secondary") and because they are repetitive and self-reinforcing (which makes them "circular"). (Phillips, 1975, p. 29.)

As Lefrancois (1973, p. 235) explains, this behavior is termed *circular* because the reactions are endlessly repeated and because the response stimulates its own repetition. "He (the child) accidentally does something that is interesting, pleasing, or otherwise amusing, and proceeds to repeat it again and again." Piaget points out that this is behavior that is designed to make sights and sounds last.

An acoustically sensitive baby may, for example, combine listening adventure with producing sounds—his own or mechanical ones. The tinkle of a bell-toy can hold him spellbound. He may even learn to turn it so that it makes different tones. If he prefers to control and produce slight changes in sound himself, the drawn-out variations of a music box may be less absorbing. This combination of extra-sensitive hearing and tone production are basics of good musicianship. . . . (Caplan, 1971, p. 120.)

1

AUDITORY STIMULATION
Young infants

Developing the sense of hearing is important to all future learning. Parents and others caring for infants should provide sound-stimulation toys and experiences that will promote auditory development. One such toy is a musical weighted apple that will produce a series of "ting-a-ling" sounds when it is shaken or struck. When an infant is a few weeks old, the parent can shake the musical toy so it can be heard. Later on, when the infant is being changed, or is lying awake in his bed, the musical toy should be placed close enough to him so that he can produce the same sound when his hands or feet strike the apple. The infant will probably continue to repeat this behavior because it is pleasing to him. Parents should be close by in order to enjoy and guide this experience with their child.

Those caring for infants under 6 months of age will find the following additional suggestions helpful in promoting auditory development:

1. Talk, hum, or sing to the baby when you change his diapers, bathe and dress him, feed and rock him, and when you take him for a ride out-of-doors.
2. Let the baby hear the ticking of a clock (ticking sound should not be harsh). As children grow older, they are fascinated by the different sounds of clocks. The cuckoo clock is one of their favorites.
3. Occasionally, let the baby hear the sound of a metronome. At first, adjust the speed of the pendulum so the ticking is not too fast. Later, increase the speed.
4. When talking to the baby, vary the tone of your voice. Always use a pleasant voice.

Older infants

1. Continue to talk, hum, or sing to the baby. Talk about his toys and play games like "Pat-a-Cake" with him.
2. Attach a mobile near the baby's crib. Many mobiles revolve and have music boxes that play delightful nursery rhyme tunes. Other mobiles contain objects that make different sounds when struck with the hand or foot.
3. Let the infant hear the radio and records. Occasionally, as you put the baby to bed, play a record containing soft music. (*Caution:* Do not play music constantly.)
4. When the infant is awake, let him listen to a record playing. Turn the volume up and down so

differences in intensity can be heard. Also, play records that contain both loud and soft music.
5. Tie a bell to the baby's bootie or shoestring.
6. Let him hear good quality wind chimes that are hung inside the house or out-of-doors.
7. Provide him with lightweight, colorful rattles producing different sounds.
8. Crumple pieces of tissue or newspaper near one ear.
9. Shake a rattle or set of keys.
10. At times, hold the telephone receiver up to the baby's ear so he can hear the voice on the other end.
11. Point to the telephone when it is ringing.
12. Let the baby hear and see water running from a faucet.
13. Clap your hands. Go from loud clapping to soft clapping. Take hold of the baby's hands. Clap them together. Sing in time to the clapping.

2

THE CHILD'S MUSICAL DEVELOPMENT

14. Show the baby how a doorbell is rung. Let him hear the sound. As the doorbell rings, try reproducing the sound with your voice.

15. When reading books containing animal pictures or objects that make sounds, reproduce the sound with your voice. As the child grows older, invite him to participate in making the different sounds. On repetition, the response from the child will generally become spontaneous.

16. When talking with a child, imitate the sounds he makes and encourage him to imitate you.

17. Play melodies on instruments such as the piano, organ, or guitar.

18. Give the child a pan and a lid or a pan and a wooden spoon; he often prefers this combination of sound makers over musical toys.

19. A restless infant can often be soothed and calmed by one's singing or playing a quiet song such as the following. While holding the baby in your arms, sing or hum this song softly. Use a gentle rocking motion.

Even though there are wide differences in children's development, "all young children have musical capacities, and all should have the opportunity to develop this potential" (Leeper et al., 1974, p. 377). One of the important things to remember is that a child's musical development is similar to the rest of his development. As he grows, he is constantly gathering all sorts of sound and movement impressions. From time to time, he will experiment with his own capacity to reproduce these impressions. Children who have had many opportunities to experiment with sound and movement will have acquired a helpful background for later musical growth and understanding. If children are sung to and have heard recordings, radio, and television, they are more likely to participate in musical activities later on. Children who come from homes and communities where music is fostered and valued will tend to reflect similar kinds of musical interest.

During the first year, a baby will coo, babble, and experiment in making sounds that are pleasing to him. Around 4 months of age, he enjoys the sound of his own

GO TO SLEEP MY BABY

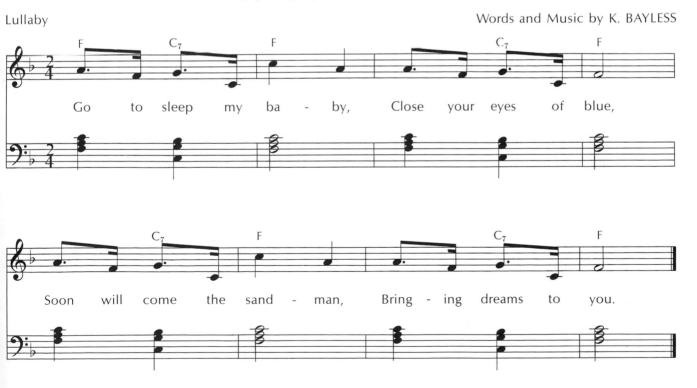

Lullaby

Words and Music by K. BAYLESS

Go to sleep my ba - by, Close your eyes of blue,

Soon will come the sand - man, Bring - ing dreams to you.

laugh and will repeat it. He is constantly communicating in his own way with those around him. Today, more than ever, child development specialists are saying that:

> The heart of early language development is building an easy, two-way give-and-take between caregiver and infant. A caregiver should speak, sing, laugh with her or his infant, encouraging him to respond to her in many ways with coos, gurgles, smiles and babbling. Soon the infant is listening to and watching conversations around him. These reactions show that he is becoming interested in words and language. The caregiver should use language with him, such as calling his name and labeling objects, people, actions and feelings. Such early exchanges, even those in which the infant does not say a word you can understand, encourage him to become involved and interested in the communication process and, as he enjoys it, motivated to seek more and more articulate ways of participating in it. (Cooper, 1976, p. 31.)

According to Shelley's research (1976, p. 207), "Bentley believes that a child sings before he talks and labels the sounds that are uttered during infancy as *lalling*. As the child begins to use words and phrases, he acquires facility in speech, his tonal inflection decreases, and the vowels become shorter; thus, he has learned to speak through singing."

As the child continues to grow and experiment with his voice, his sounds many times take on the form of singing. Usually, with some guidance, he will be able to reproduce sounds of animals, jets, machines, names of people, and the like. At this stage of the child's development, he is in almost constant motion and frequently will make sounds to accompany his play and motion. Very rarely are these beginnings of musical and bodily movement absent from the young child.

> It is almost natural for children to move to a certain beat; their own heartbeats are a first kind of rhythmic pattern for them. When they are infants, many of them move to the beat of music or nursery rhymes, suggesting they are aware of pattern beats. Their kinesthetic sense seems to guide them. (Margolin, 1976, p. 262.)

USE OF NURSERY RHYMES

During the early years, adults working with young children should share with them the many delightful

nursery rhymes, Mother Goose rhymes, and chants of early childhood. Even though young children care little about their origin and meaning, they continue to please thousands of children. According to Scott (1968, p. 140), "the memorable language of the Mother Goose or nursery rhyme has its appeal in rhythm, imagination, humor, surprise, and nonsense. Children derive untold pleasure from the primitive repetition, chanting, and suggestions for body action which these rhymes afford. The musical quality, cadence, and acceleration of these classics have prompted many musicians to write tunes for them." It is desirable to say and sing these rhymes over and over again and to include the entire family in this sharing process. If children are provided these experiences, they will soon spontaneously join in and participate in these fun-filled episodes.

Who can forget the lilting, rhythmical rhymes of the following:

HEY, DIDDLE, DIDDLE

Mother Goose

J. W. ELLIOTT
Arranged by K. BAYLESS

As the child matures and grows in strength and coordination, these rhymes can be expanded to include body movements.

Suggested movements for "See Saw, Margery Daw":

1. Rock back and forth in a one-two rhythm.

or

2. Stand facing the child. Take hold of hands. Swing arms to the right and then to the left throughout the song in a one-two rhythm.

or

3. Child and adult sit on the floor facing each other, arms outstretched, hands cupped. Rock back and forth in rhythm.

5

SEE SAW, MARGERY DAW

Mother Goose

J. W. ELLIOTT
Arranged by K. BAYLESS

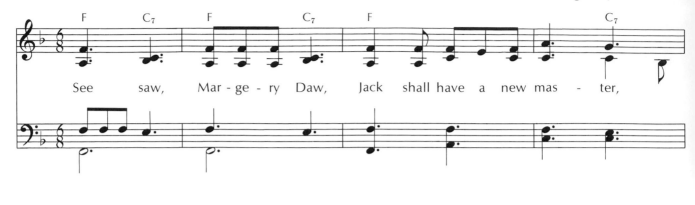

See saw, Mar-ge-ry Daw, Jack shall have a new mas - ter,

He shall have but a pen-ny a day, Be-cause he won't work an-y fast-er.

DEEDLE, DEEDLE, DUMPLING

Mother Goose

Arranged by K. BAYLESS

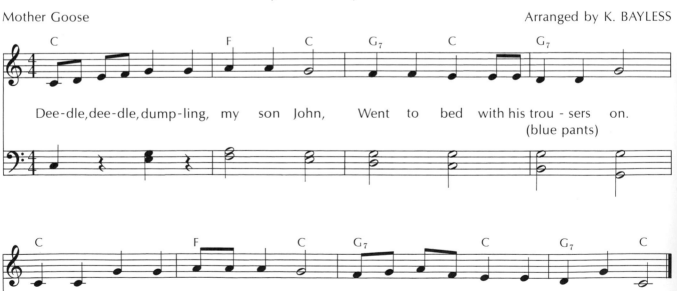

Dee-dle, dee-dle, dump-ling, my son John, Went to bed with his trou-sers on.
(blue pants)

One shoe off, the oth-er shoe on, Dee-dle, dee-dle, dump-ling, my son John.

Additional favorite rhymes of the young child

Ride a cockhorse to Banbury Cross
To see an old lady upon a white horse;
Rings on her fingers, and bells on her toes,
And so she makes music wherever she goes.

Jack be nimble,
Jack be quick,
Jack jumped over
The candlestick.

Jack jumped high,
Jack jumped low,
Jack jumped over
And burned his toe.

This little pig went to market;
This little pig stayed at home;
This little pig had roast beef;
And this little pig had none;
This little pig said, "Wee, wee, wee!"
All the way home.
(A verse for each of the child's toes)

Hush-a-bye, baby, on the treetop,
When the wind blows, the cradle will rock;
When the bough breaks, the cradle will fall,
Down will come baby, cradle, and all.

Jack and Jill went up the hill
To fetch a pail of water;
Jack fell down and broke his crown,
And Jill came tumbling after.

Higgledy, piggledy, my black hen,
She lays eggs for gentlemen;
Sometimes nine, sometimes ten;
Higgledy, piggledy, my black hen.

Little Jack Horner
Sat in a corner,
Eating his Christmas pie.
He put in his thumb
And pulled out a plum
And said, "What a good boy am I!"

Humpty Dumpty sat on a wall,
Humpty Dumpty had a great fall;
All the king's horses and all the king's men
Couldn't put Humpty Dumpty together again.

Bow, wow, wow!
Whose dog art thou?
Little Tom Tinker's dog,
Bow, wow, wow!

Bye, baby bunting,
Daddy's gone a-hunting,
To get a little rabbit skin
To wrap the baby bunting in.

Pussy cat, pussy cat, where have you been?
I've been to London to visit the queen.
Pussy cat, pussy cat, what did you do there?
I frightened a little mouse under the chair.

Roses are red,
Violets are blue;
Sugar is sweet,
And so are you!

FAVORITE SINGING GAMES

Short, rhythmical singing games also please the young child. "Peek-a-Boo" and "Pat-a-Cake," long-time favorites, have been set to music so that the family can play and sing these games with baby.

PEEK-A-BOO

Words and music by K. BAYLESS

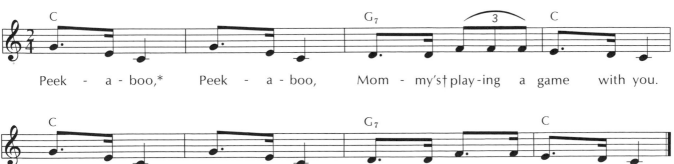

Peek - a - boo,* Peek - a - boo, Mom - my's† play-ing a game with you.

Peek - a - boo, Peek - a - boo, See if you can play it, too.

*Use appropriate actions.
†May substitute other names such as daddy's, brother's, etc.

PAT-A-CAKE, PAT-A-CAKE

Adapted by K. BAYLESS

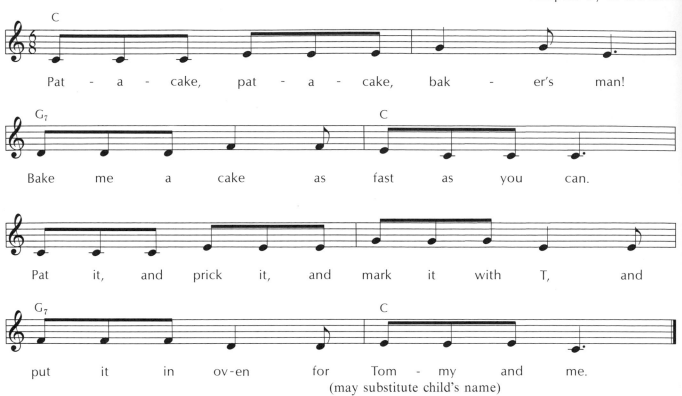

Pat - a - cake, pat - a - cake, bak - er's man!

Bake me a cake as fast as you can.

Pat it, and prick it, and mark it with T, and

put it in ov-en for Tom - my and me.

(may substitute child's name)

CHANTING: THE LINK BETWEEN SPEECH AND RHYTHM

Some authorities call the half-speaking, half-singing sounds a child makes as he goes about his play "chanting." Whether he is pounding with a hammer, pushing a wheel toy, or perhaps running with a balloon, one can hear his melodic fragments.

Chanting, the most obvious link between speech and rhythm, suggests itself immediately as a most natural response. For the child, it is as instinctive as it is delightful. For him it is a part of play, a source of interesting images and sounds. Whether he chants nursery rhymes or rhymes, he helps create about people and things with which he is intimate . . . he enters into the activity naturally and joyfully. With guidance, his chanting can open the door to all rhythmic and melodic experiences. Words can begin

to take on color; the quality of speech begins to reflect the meanings he is trying to portray. Highs and lows—both in pitch and dynamics—can develop. And, throughout, a feeling for the various kinds of meter is acquired. (Wheeler and Raebeck, 1972, p. 2.)

Children love the sound of their own voices. Parents and teachers should encourage young children to improvise and should, themselves, serve as models. When a child chants or sings word phrases, it is sound practice for the adult to repeat them back to the child. "It is common knowledge that children all over the world sing the minor third; it has been labeled the national chant of childhood" (Shelley, p. 207).

Children often half-speak, half-sing names of people, animals, and the like, using the tones of the minor third.

SOL—MI

Tones of the minor third

Sol	Mi	Mom - my	Dad - dy
		Kit - ty	Dog - gie
		Ti - ger	Bun - ny

The pentatonic scale (five-tone scale) makes use of the minor third. The most common form of this scale (in the key of C) contains the notes C, D, E, G, and A. Since these tones are so common and natural to children the world over (the scale is found in the folk songs of many countries), children should have the opportunity to sing many melodies using the pentatonic scale.

Examples using the minor third would be:

Kit - ty, Kit - ty, Come and play with me_____.

To further develop the "tie-in" between speaking and singing, it is advisable to occasionally sing requests and the like to children, such as the following:

Li - sa, bring the ball to Dad - dy. Thank you!

Tom - my, bring the cup to me.

Mat - thew, how's my lit - tle man?

9

ELEMENTS OF MUSICAL BEGINNINGS

All growth, musical or otherwise, is an active process. From birth on, in order for optimal musical development, children must be actively involved in making music. Some learning does take place through watching and listening to others, but the best learning takes place through trying out for oneself.

From infancy on, an important element in the musical development of young children is the development of perceptual awareness. This means much more than becoming aware of the visual appearance of things. It encompasses the use of all the senses, such as hearing, smelling, and touching. It is only through our senses that we learn about our environment, and it is of extreme importance that those caring for young children expose, explain, and provide guidance for rich sensory experiences. The development of a child's ability to perceive sounds, to become aware of differences and similarities, and to become involved in producing the sounds himself are of utmost importance to his future learning.

Even many 4- and 5-month-old infants are fascinated by the movement and rustling of leaves and swaying branches and are soothed by the motion of riding in a buggy or the humming of a car's engine. And, in fact, infants soon become interested in the out-of-door sounds of birds and animals, especially if attention is drawn to them. At times, babies try to reproduce similar sounds.

Early, children learn to discern differences in people's voices. It does not take infants long to discover the difference between the soft spoken words of love and happiness and the harsher words of disapproval. Eventually, they learn the difference between the sound of a barking dog and the purr of a cat. They will also begin to associate people, animals, mechanical things, and the like with their respective sounds.

Constantly be on the alert to promote perceptual awareness. Children should be taken on walks, rides, and excursions throughout all seasons of the year and at different times of the day. Care should be taken to point out different objects and sights and to give help in distinguishing the many different kinds of sounds in the environment. Repeat the sounds, if possible, for the child to hear.

On many occasions we can well remember seeing a young father carrying his little girl, sometimes wheeling her in a buggy or stroller around our village green. When we went to the village on errands, we could see them together at different times of the day—morning, midday, sometimes after sundown. The father was always talking with his child and helping her become aware of the many fascinating sounds, smells, and sights around her. For example, they would sit on the park bench and listen to the birds singing. They would also listen for the chimes to ring out the hour in the clock tower on the green. On Memorial Day they would watch and listen as the band marched down the street in the parade. This kind of "planned exposure" continued as the child grew older. One day as we conversed with the father, he said that he wanted his daughter to learn as much as she could about the beautiful world in which she would be growing up. He was a wise and sensitive father.

Growing children need plenty of time to observe, to listen, to touch, to move. Appreciate and help them cultivate the many sensory experiences that surround heir everyday living. These are the "beginnings" in vhich music can become a way of life for the young :hild.

REFERENCES AND SUGGESTED READINGS

:aplan, Frank (Ed.). The fifth month—reaching out. In *First twelve months of life*. New York: Grosset & Dunlap, Inc., 1971.

:ooper, Catherine R. Competent infants and their caregivers: the feeling is mutual. In *Understanding and nurturing infant development*. Washington, D.C.: Association for Childhood Education International, 1976.

acobson, R. *Child language*. The Hague: Mouton, 1968.

_eeper, S. H., Dales, R. J., Skipper, D. S., and Witherspoon, R. L. *Good schools for young children* (3rd. ed.). New York: Macmillan Publishing Co., Inc., 1974.

Lefrancois, Guy R. *Of children. An introduction to child development*. Belmont, Calif.: Wadsworth Publishing Co., Inc., 1973.

Margolin, Edythe. A world of music for young children. In *Young children: their curriculum and learning processes*. New York: Macmillan Publishing Co., Inc., 1976.

Phillips, John L., Jr. *The origins of intellect: Piaget's theory* (2nd. ed.). San Francisco: W. H. Freeman & Co., 1975.

Scott, Louise Binder. The wonderful world of play and make-believe. In *Learning time with language experiences*. St. Louis: Webster Division, McGraw-Hill Book Co., 1968.

Shelley, Shirley J. Music. In Carol Seefeldt (Ed.), *Curriculum for the preschool-primary child—a review of the research*. Columbus, Ohio: Charles E. Merrill Publishing Co., 1976.

Wheeler, Lawrence, and Raebeck, Lois. *Orff and Kodaly adapted by the elementary school*. Dubuque, Iowa: William C. Brown Co., Publishers, 1972.

2 Music for the toddlers plus

NEW OPPORTUNITIES FOR ENJOYMENT AND LEARNING

As children continue to grow and become more interested in their world, music can offer new opportunities for moving, listening, creating, singing, and playing instruments. Along with the enjoyment and pleasure these activities bring to children, there are certain skills and competencies that can be acquired if the person guiding these music activities selects those which are appropriate. Selection needs to be made in accordance with what can be reasonably expected of children at certain stages of their development.

A study of children between the ages of 1 and 4 will show a great amount of growth taking place in their interests and abilities. In any grouping of small children (neighborhood, Sunday school, day-care, Head Start, nursery school), there will be wide differences in their previous musical experiences. Some children will have come from homes where there has been little or no exposure to music. Others will have had many opportunities to enjoy and experience it. Since such wide variations will exist, some selected characteristics of what can be normally expected of children at certain ages should prove helpful to persons providing musical experiences appropriate for the very young.

SELECTED CHARACTERISTICS OF 1- TO 2-YEAR-OLDS

1. Babble or jabber in response to voices; may cry when there is the sound of thunder or a loud crash.
2. Enjoy listening to some sounds and imitating them.
3. In answer to questions like, "What does the kitty say?" answer by making the sound, "Meow."
4. Can point to or put hands on parts of their bodies on request.
5. Continue to reproduce sounds or combinations of sounds to explain their wants and needs; for example, may half-sing, half-say "buh-bi" for explaining that they want to go for a ride in the car.
6. Generally enjoy being held and sung to.
7. Some children are able to sing parts of songs.

RESPONSE FROM TODDLERS

Jenkins (1966, p. 60) says that "music often calls out an alert response in the toddler—he may even try to dance to a marked rhythm that appeals to him." One has only to watch young children as a band plays a lively march. If the children are in a setting where they can move, invariably most of them will begin to clap their hands and move their feet in time with the music. Their faces will show pleasure and delight. Last summer we observed this response in toddlers as they listened to our high school band playing during a bicentennial celebration on our village green. One youngster was seen parading back and forth on the lawn swinging his bottle in time to the music.

When working with children of this age, we find that music and movement are almost inseparable. Chandler (1970, p. 10) says that "music for the young child is primarily the discovery of sound; his first need is for a wide variety of sound making and the enjoyment of music for movement's sake!" Since children are so sen-

sitive to sound and movement, we will discuss some of the activities they might enjoy if given the opportunity, and where, at the same time, conceptual development can take place.

MUSIC AND WORDS: THE COMPATIBLE PAIR

As young children begin to understand the relationship between words and their meanings, adults can provide enjoyable and educational experiences that will strengthen this understanding.

Ames (1970, p. 85) says by the age of 21 months the words *up* and *down* are part of the child's vocabulary. Musical phrases or short songs that incorporate these words with movement could be introduced to reinforce their concepts.

Occasionally, as you pick up a child, sing:

Up,   up,   up,   up.

Then, as you put the child down, sing:

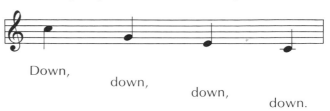

Down,   down,   down,   down.

Then sing the following tune incorporating the words *up* and *down:*

UP AND DOWN

K. BAYLESS

Up you go, up you go, Oh, so ver - y high,

Down, down, down, down, Soon we'll be on the ground.

As you do this, you are helping the child associate the meaning of the word with its direction, and you are using different levels of pitch to assist in this understanding.

Be imaginative. Make up short musical phrases and tunes such as the following:

PUT YOUR HANDS UP, UP

K. BAYLESS

Put your hands up, up, Reach them to the sky.

Let your hands come slow - ly down, Touch the floor with - out a sound.

"Hickory, Dickory, Dock" is a delightful rhyme to use in helping develop the concepts of up and down. Its marked rhythm also helps children feel the beat. When the child begins to show interest in acting out some of the words, the adult may add movement to the song. For example, when chanting or singing this rhyme, the adult can move his head up and down in a one-two rhythm. Do not force the child to participate in the rhythmic movements and words unless he shows interest. The child will probably join in the "game" spontaneously and add

actions as the song is sung. Following are suggestions:
1. Hickory, dickory, dock (swing one arm freely in rhythm with the words)
2. The mouse ran up the clock (wiggle the fingers of one hand and move it upward on the opposite arm)
3. The clock struck one (clap hands together on the word "one")
4. The mouse ran down (wiggle the fingers downward)
5. Hickory, dickory, dock (swing the arm freely in rhythm with the words)

HICKORY, DICKORY, DOCK*

Mother Goose

J. W. ELLIOTT
Arranged by K. BAYLESS

Hick-o - ry, dick-o - ry, dock; The mouse ran up the clock; The

clock struck one;† The mouse ran down; Hick - o - ry, dick - o - ry, dock.

---

*Public domain.

†On the word "one," a tone bell or triangle can be struck.

BUILDING ON CHILDREN'S NATURAL MOVEMENTS

It is important to remember that children of this age need *much* opportunity to move—to walk, run, climb, bounce, jump—not only for the purpose of increasing their muscular development, but for the sake of pure enjoyment. At first movements will be uncoordinated, but with plenty of opportunity to move and express themselves, these movements will become refined, and the children will eventually gain control of their bodies.

Children around the age of 2 like to bounce up and down on a bed or a sofa. As they do this, it is not uncommon to hear them singing words to accompany their movement. For example, they might be heard singing, "bouncy-bounce, bouncy-bounce" keeping time with their bouncing. Some adults will scold or reprimand a child for such actions without giving redirection to this type of natural behavior. Why not provide some type of "cushiony" material, such as an old mattress or gym pad for this type of activity? Have you ever noticed how many children run in complete abandon, waving their arms like birds? Have you ever watched and listened as other youngsters keep perfect time walking down the sidewalk dragging sticks behind them? Have you watched others as they teetered back and forth from one foot to another humming in rhythm to their teetering movements? At times, an appropriate record could be played, a song hummed or sung, or clapping provided to accompany these kinds of body movements. Join in with the children. Make it a game. Show your approval.

Music as a support to movement

Music should support movement. There will be times when children will ask for musical accompaniment as they move about. At other times they will not request it. A sensitive adult can encourage the child's movements by clapping or tapping on a tom tom or some similar instrument. When accompanying a child's movements, continually keep in mind to synchronize the accompaniment to the tempo of his movements. Throughout much of the preschool period one needs to accommodate the child's own rhythm rather than have the child conform to the beat. This can be done by first watching and listening to the child as he claps, walks, tiptoes, and the like, then providing accompaniment that makes the "match" to the child's own body rhythm.

> In research studies it has been found that music, phonographic or instrumental, may stimulate movement, but the children felt the desire to move first, and later asked for music. Only when the music happens to be in the child's movement tempo or he wishes to adjust his tempo to it may the two coincide. . . . It is important that the accompanist be very sensitive to the mood and the underbeat to which the child's movement relates. (Chandler, 1970, pp. 9–10.)

Since more 2½-year-olds are now attending preschools, we will discuss what they are like and what they can do at this age in relation to activities involving music and movement. Suggestions will be made for using these activities in the home or school setting.

SELECTED CHARACTERISTICS OF
2- TO 3-YEAR-OLDS

1. Can run and jump, walk on tiptoe, gallop like a pony, or clap hands to rhythm (Jenkins, p. 85).
2. Are very active and like music to which they can respond.
3. Will join in with a few words of a song; some are able to remember the words of an entire song.
4. Usually like to have someone sing songs to them.
5. Enjoy going up and down steps.
6. Can push and pull their toys.
7. Like imaginative dramatic play.
8. Speak in short (sometimes three-word) sentences (Ames, 1970, p. 75).
9. Can imitate both a vertical and a circular stroke made for them by an adult (Ames, p. 63).
10. Tend to play more by themselves or alongside others.
11. Are beginning to become interested in radio and TV commercials and jingles.

When selecting musical activities for children of this age, consider the following:

1. Large group experiences in music should be kept to a minimum. Give individual children and small groups plenty of time and space to experiment: to sing, move, make sounds, and listen to music.
2. Instruments and props such as scarves and feathers can be added when appropriate to the musical activity.
3. Spontaneous singing of musical phrases and short songs with accompaniment (by an adult) can enrich children's play activities and movement.
4. Make good use of music that promotes body movements such as jumping, running, and the like.
5. If songs are used, choose ones that appeal to the children's interests, are short, have repetition in melody and rhythm, are rhythmical, and are within the children's singing range. (Children prefer singing within the range of middle C to A, a sixth above middle C.)
6. Children like to sing familiar songs. New music material should be introduced slowly.

THE NEED FOR INDIVIDUAL AND
SMALL GROUP MUSICAL ENCOUNTERS

Many children prefer musical activities involving smaller groupings or the opportunity to try things out for themselves, yet if one were to visit various day-care programs and nursery schools throughout the country, it would not be uncommon to see that much of the musical ctivity is planned for total group participation. This type of programming is in contrast to the way in which most activities should be planned for children of this age. All too often the singing of a few songs and "dancing" to a record constitute the "daily music diet" of children in preschools or where groups of small children are gathered together. Most children enjoy group participation and should not be denied this privilege; there are values in it. But one must be on the alert not to overdo musical activities involving large groups at this age.

THE INSEPARABILITY OF MUSIC AND MOVEMENT

Music and movement remain almost inseparable at this age. With this in mind, continue to provide activities that will incorporate both. The following activities have been chosen to complement the characteristics and abilities that children of this age-group possess.

As children move about, jumping from "here to there," you might chant or sing, "Jump, jump, jump." Continue chanting this as the child jumps about. Soon the child will associate the word with the action. Try to keep the tempo of your chanting or singing adjusted to the tempo of the child's movement.

After the child seems "comfortable" with the jumping movement, musical phrases or short songs like "Jump, Jump, Jump" would be appropriate to use. Some type of accompaniment, such as clapping or tapping on a drum, could also be added.

JUMP, JUMP, JUMP

K. BAYLESS

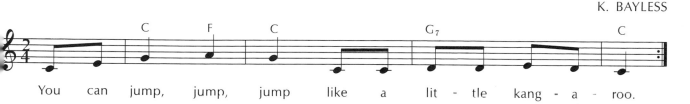

You can jump, jump, jump like a lit - tle kang - a - roo.

Note: Sing several times until the child gets the "feel" of it.

Here is a short song involving "bouncing," another favorite movement of small children.

I'M LIKE A BOUNCING BALL

K. BAYLESS

Steadily

I'm like a bounc - ing ball, I bounce with - out a fall; I

bounce and bounce and bounce and bounce, Al - though I'm ver - y small.

As children swing arms back and forth, up and down, you may find this short tune appropriate. Remember, do not hesitate to make up your own musical phrases to "match" the movement of the child. Begin with arms swinging upward.

SWING, SWING

K. BAYLES

Swing, swing, swing, swing, See how high I go.

Up, down, up, down, to and fro.

Rocking is one of the favorite movements of most 2- to 3-year-olds.

ROCKING YO HO

K. BAYLES

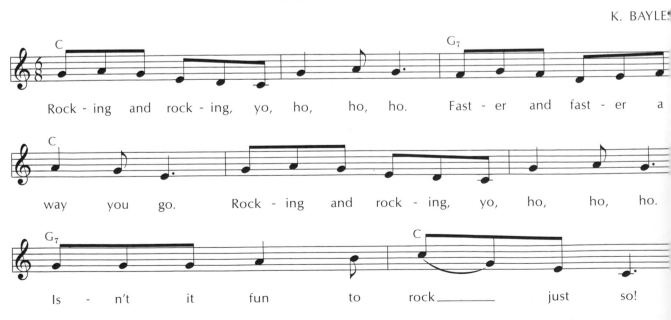

Rock - ing and rock - ing, yo, ho, ho, ho. Fast - er and fast - er a

way you go. Rock - ing and rock - ing, yo, ho, ho, ho.

Is - n't it fun to rock_____ just so!

Have you noticed how little children like to turn around in circles? This short song makes a game of it. Take hold of the child's hands. Move slowly in order to avoid dizziness. On the word "kerflop," fall to the floor or rug.

TURN AROUND

K. BAYLESS

1. Can you turn a - round with me? It's as eas - y as can be.
2. Round and round a - bout just so, Then "ker - flop," we're bound to go.

Other song suggestions are "Ring Around a Rosy" and "Here We Go Round the Mulberry Bush."

SELECTED CHARACTERISTICS OF 3- TO 4-YEAR-OLDS

1. Like to gallop, jump (can jump on both feet), walk, or run in time to music (Ames, pp. 58–89.)
2. Can build towers with blocks.
3. Are much more fluent with language.
4. Like new words, can often be influenced by such words as "surprise" and "secret."
5. Can tell how old they are.
6. Have refined notions of space: *over, up on top, under,* and *on.*
7. Have more interest in detail and direction.
8. Are able to tell on what street they live.
9. Can count two objects, sometimes up to five.
10. Can match colors with considerable success (Ames, pp. 75–90).
11. Enjoy simple versions of imaginative, dramatic play.
12. Enjoy singing games and using rhythm instruments.
13. Like to listen to stories and records.
14. Should be able to locate the source of a sound.
15. Are beginning to play cooperatively and to share and take turns.

Consider the following when planning musical activities for this age child:
1. Encourage informal singing throughout the day.
2. Continue to sing the children's favorite songs and to add new material slowly.
3. Provide plenty of opportunity for the children to dramatize songs and "act out" song stories.
4. Children of this age like to use simple props.
5. Give attention to helping children listen to and distinguish the different sounds within the environment.
6. Play simple games in which children can find sources of different sounds.
7. Rhythm and melody instruments can be introduced and used to enhance musical activities. It is usually better to introduce one instrument at a time. Choose instruments that are appropriate for the activity.
8. Children of this age may lag behind a measure or two when singing.
9. Humorous, active songs hold high appeal.

Of course, children will differ in their responses to types of music, rhyme, and suggested activities. Most 3- to 4-year-olds will enjoy acting out the following song.

JACK BE NIMBLE

Nursery rhyme

Adapted by K. BAYLESS
M. RAMSEY

Jack be nim - ble, Jack be quick, Jack jump'd o - ver the can - dle stick.

Jack jump'd high, Jack jump'd low, Jack jump'd o - ver and burned his toe!

2

Jump with one foot, then with two,
Let us see what you can do.
First with one, then with two,
Now we know what you can do.

3

Tap with one foot, then with two,
Let us see what you can do.
First with one, then with two,
Now we know what you can do.

4

Wiggle one finger, then with two,
Let us see what you can do.
First with one, then with two,
Now we know what you can do.

5

Wave with one arm, then with two,
Let us see what you can do.
First with one, then with two,
Now we know what you can do.

Children may well offer other suggestions for movement to this lively melody.
Another favorite theme is surprises. Allow time for sharing favorite surprises,
then try:

DO YOU LIKE SURPRISES?

K. BAYLESS

Do you like sur - pris - es? Then nod your head.

Do you like sur - pris - es? Then smile in - stead.

Close your eyes and lis - ten And wait so pa - tient - ly, Un -

til some - one speaks up and says, "Sur - prise, sur - prise, come see."

Most children like to be asked how old they are. Some will hold up their fingers for the number of years and then will smile and answer.

HOW OLD ARE YOU?

K. BAYLESS

How old are you? How old are you? How old are you to -

day? Three or four or five or six? Tell us right a - way.
(me)

The birthday poem "Me," suggested later in the book, might well be included here to enhance the discussion, and children may wish to chant the lines.

To encourage the learning of street names and addresses, try:

NAME YOUR STREET

Traditional tune

Adapted by K. BAYLESS

Teacher: Tell us what street you live on, you live on, you live on,
Child or I--- live on Sun - set Street, Sun - set Street, Sun - set Street,
group: Christine lives

Tell us what street you live on, (Chris - tine), please.
I--- live on Sun - set Street, Yes, I do.
Christine lives Yes, she does.

Often children will want to share telephone numbers and previous addresses. Provide time for such discussion and reinforcement of such learning.

Have you observed how often children chant and sing about what they are doing? Often one will hear them sing their words to a familiar tune such as "Here We Go Round the Mulberry Bush." This kind of spontaneous "play with words and music" should be encouraged. Following is a song that makes use of this idea:

THIS IS THE WAY

Adapted by K. BAYLESS
Here We Go Round the Mulberry Bush

Traditional English nursery rhyme tune

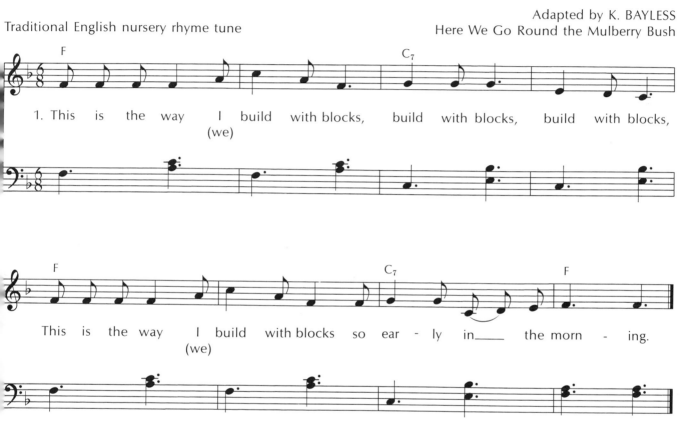

1. This is the way I build with blocks, build with blocks, build with blocks,
   (we)

This is the way I build with blocks so ear-ly in the morn-ing.
(we)

Additional suggested verses:

. This is the way we clean our room.

3. This is the way I water the plants.

Pets are always a favorite topic of conversation with children. "The Old Gray
Cat" is a song-game that young children like to dramatize. As the song is sung,
listen to the words. They tell you what to do.

THE OLD GRAY CAT

Traditional American song

Accompaniment by K. BAYLESS

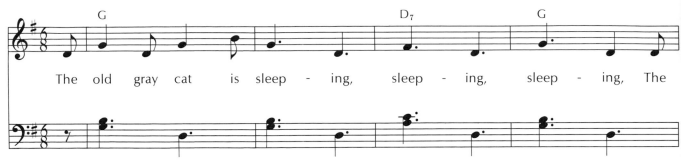

The old gray cat is sleep - ing, sleep - ing, sleep - ing, The

old gray cat is sleep - ing in the house.

2. The little mice are creeping, creeping, creeping,
   The little mice are creeping through the house.
3. The little mice are nibbling . . . in the house.
4. The little mice are sleeping . . . in the house.

5. The old gray cat comes creeping . . . through the house.
6. The little mice all scamper . . . through the house.
7. The little mice are hiding . . . in the house.

24

"Two Little Blackbirds" and "Where Is Thumbkin?," favorite finger plays of children, have been set to music for the very young.

Actions for "Two Little Blackbirds":

Two little blackbirds	(Hold up both hands,	Fly away, Jack!	(Bend down one thumb)
Sitting on a hill,	thumbs erect, fingers bent)	Fly away, Jill!	(Bend down other thumb)
One named Jack,	(Wiggle one thumb)	Come back, Jack!	(Raise one thumb erect)
And one named Jill.	(Wiggle other thumb)	Come back, Jill!	(Raise other thumb erect)

TWO LITTLE BLACKBIRDS

Traditional

Arranged by K. BAYLESS

Two lit-tle black-birds sit-ting on a hill, One named Jack, And one named Jill.

Fly a-way Jack! Fly a-way Jill! Come back Jack! Come back! Jill.

WHERE IS THUMBKIN?

Traditional

Where is thumb-kin? Where is thumb-kin? Here I am, here I am,
(put both fists behind back)   (show one thumb)   (show the other thumb)

How are you to-day, sir? Ver-y well, I thank you. Run a-way, run a-way.
(bend the one thumb)   (then bend the other thumb)   (put thumbs behind back)

Music and the young child share a special affinity. When music and movement activities pervade the daily living of young children, enjoyment and participation in future music endeavors follow naturally.

REFERENCES AND SUGGESTED READINGS

Ames, Louise Bates. *Child care and development.* New York: J. B. Lippincott Co., 1970.

Aronoff, Frances Webber. *Music and young children.* New York: Holt, Rinehart & Winston, Inc., 1969.

Chandler, Bessie E. Music. In *Early learning experiences.* Dansville, N.Y.: The Instructor Publications, Inc., 1970.

Hildebrand, Verna. *Introduction to early childhood education.* New York: Macmillan Publishing Co., Inc., 1971.

Jenkins, Gladys Gardner. *These are your children* (3rd. ed.). Chicago: Scott, Foresman & Co., 1966.

Lament, Marylee McMurray. *Music in elementary education.* New York: Macmillan Publishing Co., Inc., 1976.

3 Music for the preschool and kindergarten age child

Musical activities have traditionally been a part of the nursery-school and kindergarten programs. Friedrich Froebel, "father of the kindergarten," strongly believed in the value of musical experiences for young children and used his book, *Mother Play and Nursery Songs,* to bring this point to the attention of those who worked with children of this age. He believed that they should be given ample opportunity to sing songs and play singing games. This thought has prevailed, and today it is considered sound practice to include music as integral a part of a child's day as eating or sleeping.

By the time children are 4 or 5, they are ready for more planned musical experiences. These should include a balance of activities such as listening and appreciation, singing, playing instruments and sound making, creating songs and melodies, and ample opportunity for movement. Before discussing each of these aspects in detail, descriptions of typical 4- and 5-year-olds are offered.

SELECTED CHARACTERISTICS OF 4-YEAR-OLDS

1. Like to do things their own way; resist too many directions.
2. Are very active, can run up and down steps.
3. Enjoy activities that require good balance, such as carrying liquids without spilling them.
4. Have the ability to throw a ball overhand.
5. Are very curious and ask many questions concerning "Why?" and "How?"

6. Talk a great deal; like nonsense words, silly language, rhyming, and words that are repeated in poems or songs.
7. Love to listen to stories.
8. Are beginning to understand seasons of the year, when they occur and what takes place during a particular season.
9. Think birthdays are very important—both theirs and others.
10. Can tell the street on which they live and the name of their city.
11. On command can place a ball or rhythm instrument on, under, in front of, and in back of a chair or other object.
12. Are beginning to enjoy more group singing.
13. Like to dramatize songs and poems, as well as stories and parts of stories.
14. Should be able to carry out two simple directions in sequence.

SELECTED CHARACTERISTICS OF 5-YEAR-OLDS

1. Generally are conforming in nature; like to please and thrive on positive feedback; are sensitive to praise and blame.
2. Like to jump and climb; still need plenty of big muscle activity.
3. Some at this age can skip on alternate feet.
4. Attempt to roller-skate, jump rope, walk on stilts, "pump" on a swing, and bounce a ball.

5. Like to talk a great deal; interested in words and their meanings. By this time most of the words that adults use are a part of the child's vocabulary.

6. Very interested in calendars; can tell what day of the week it is; can name the days of the week in their proper order; are interested in holidays.

7. Know how old they are; can generally tell how old they will be in another year.

8. Are very interested in all kinds of clocks, but most cannot tell time.

9. Like to remain close to home surroundings; are primarily interested in their home and community, not distant places; are interested in different cities and states if they know someone who lives there, such as grandparents.

10. Understand and can carry out actions of such words as *forward* and *backward*.

11. Are learning the meaning of *small, smaller,* and *smallest.*

LISTENING

Listening is considered to be the foundation for *all* musical experiences. McCall (1971, p. 7) says, "the child must learn to attend before he can assimilate and use music to his own purposes." In the preceding chapters, much emphasis was placed on parents and teachers helping youngsters become more sensitive to the sounds around them and helping them translate these sounds into meaningful experiences. Efforts to continue this cannot be overestimated, since sound discrimination is vital to the musical development of the child. Unless someone has really "zeroed in" and helped a child to sharpen his listening skills, the myriad sounds that he must confront will often lead him to begin school with poor listening habits already established.

There is considerable agreement between educators and psychologists that one of the major problems of children in the elementary school is lack of good listening skills. More attention is being given to this problem by providing suggestions and ways to upgrade the whole area of "listening and attending." Music can, and should, be a "natural" in helping develop good listening skills.

A very important principle to keep in mind is that one cannot develop a *high* level of listening skill unless attentive listening is stressed. Listening is perceiving and requires thought and reasoning. When planning musical activities, careful attention should be given to arranging the environmental setting, thus maximizing the conditions for developing good listening habits. Articles that distract the children should be put away. "Listening" should be emphasized, encouraged, and expected. For example, ask that there be no talking while story records are being played. The teacher may say to the children, "I am going to sing a new song for you. After I sing it once, then you may sing with me." Be sure that they know what the word "once" means. If children join in the singing as the teacher sings it through the first time, their singing should be interrupted because directions have not been followed. The teacher can then say, "Some of you have forgotten what I asked you to do. When did I say you could sing the song?" Then the teacher should ask a child to repeat the direction. The teacher might then go on to say, "Let's try it again. I know you will remember when to sing this time." If all this is done in a nonthreatening way and in a manner of trust, children will soon learn to follow the teacher's directions. Time will be saved, and, most important of all, children will sharpen their listening skills much more quickly.

Since listening is involved in all the musical skills, much attention must be given activities that can be provided by parents and teachers to improve the children's ability to listen. Thinking and reasoning should be enhanced.

SUGGESTED ACTIVITIES

1. Adults as well as children should continue to try to cultivate awareness of sounds.

2. At times, feature listening as an activity or game, both indoors and out-of-doors.

3. Field trips offer endless ways for children to hear sounds firsthand. For example, if a train whistle blows, have the children try to match the sound with their voices.

4. Let children experiment with sounds made from their bodies by snapping their fingers, brushing with their feet, and so forth. (A detailed description of body percussion is given under the section on instruments.)

5. Make a tape of the many different kinds of environmental sounds, both those of nature and those which are man-made. Let children identify these sounds. Discuss their various tone qualities. As children gain more experience, they can begin to classify and categorize the sounds.

6. Take two containers of the same size and place different materials inside, such as rice, beans

corn, or small stones. The object is to have the children shake the containers and "match" the two that sound alike.

7. Read stories to the children about sounds. Many stories invite participation in which the children can produce the sound asked for in the story by either using their voices, parts of their bodies, or instruments that can lend the desired sound effects.

8. Arrange the children so the one speaking may be heard but not seen. Let the other children guess whose voice is being heard.

9. While playing different tones on the piano or tuned bells, play a game of having the children try to match the tones with their voices. The tones being played should not go below middle C or an octave above middle C.

10. Take a set of step bells (see illustration) and show the children that when the bell at the bottom of the steps is played, it produces a low sound. When the bell at the top is played, it produces a high sound. When playing the step bells, place the instrument in front of the children (to avoid confusion, we recommend that the lowest step bell should be at the children's left) so they can see and hear that when a low step bell is struck, it produces a low sound, and when a high step bell is struck, it produces a high sound. After the

children have had many opportunities to hear the differences between high and low sounds in this fashion, the instrument can then be removed from sight. Then see if the children are still able to tell which tones are high or low without seeing someone play the instrument.

11. While the children watch, strike three objects that produce different sounds. Have them close their eyes; strike one of the objects and have the children identify the one struck. At first, the sounds should be very different from each other. For example, a bell, a glass, and a wooden block can be used.

12. Have the children try to identify which of two, three, or four containers an object is shaken in. Containers can be cardboard, plastic, tin, or aluminum. Demonstrate the sounds each container makes before asking the children to turn their backs and give the response.

13. Ring bell. Children raise their hands when they hear the sound and lower them when the sound stops.

14. Have the children stand close together in a group. Demonstrate the difference between near and far sounds by producing identical sounds near the children, then from a far corner of the room, first with eyes open, then with eyes closed.

15. While the children close their eyes, produce

sounds from various parts of the room. Children point in the direction of the sound.

16. Ring two bells. One has the clapper taped to a side. Which is ringing? Change hands. Hold one bell high, one low. Name direction of sound, up or down.

17. One child with eyes closed pretends to be a mother cat. Three children pretend to be her kittens. As the mother cat sleeps, the kittens run away and hide in different parts of the room. The children who play kittens should not move after they hide. The mother cat wakes up and calls the kittens. They meow; she finds them from the directions of their sounds.

GAMES

Attentive listening is necessary in helping children develop musically. The following activities are enjoyable and, at the same time, help to build good listening skills.

Drummer

The adult or child taps on a drum a certain number of times as the children listen. A child is chosen to clap back the same number of taps. If his response is correct, he becomes the next drummer. Simple, uncomplicated beats should be used at first.

Variation: The adult claps hands in a given pattern. The child claps back the pattern. At first, allow children to see the person clapping. After the game is well established, do not allow the children to see the person leading the clapping. (Clapping can be done inside an enclosure.) Instead of clapping, vary the game by tapping with the foot.

Into the Puddle

A large circle is drawn on the floor. (Some classrooms have large circle designs molded into the floor covering.) The children find their own spaces around it. If possible, have the children space themselves an arm's length from each other so they will not bump each other as they jump into the puddle. When the teacher says, "Jump into the puddle," the children respond together. When the teacher says, "Jump out of the puddle," they return to their original places on the circle. (Children may take turns being the teacher.)

Variation: The teacher may tap on a drum or use a chord on the piano as the command is given.

What Do I Hear?

A child sits on a chair in the center of a circle. Children are seated on the circle's outer rim. The child sitting on the chair holds his hands over his eyes while

another youngster walks, skips, jumps, etc. around the chair. The boy or girl doing the movement then sits down. The child on the chair must get up and repeat the same movement the other child made. He then invites another boy or girl from the group to take his place.

Name the Instrument

After children have had plenty of opportunity to see and hear different instruments, make tapes or use recordings that highlight the sounds of particular ones. Have children guess which instrument is being played.

Tick, Tock, Where is the Metronome?

A child is chosen to be "it" and sent outside the room. A ticking metronome is hidden somewhere in the room. "It" tries to locate the metronome. When he does, ask him to repeat the ticking the same way he hears it. This may be done by saying the word, "tick", "tick", in the same rhythm of the metronome, or by clapping, tapping on the floor, etc. Vary the ticking speed.

DEVELOPING MUSICAL APPRECIATION

A balance of good listening activities is important for growth in musical appreciation. Children need to be exposed, to listen, and to try out different types of music so they can begin to develop musical tastes and preferences. Youngsters become acquainted and aware of some kinds of music through informal exposure as they go about their daily activities, such as listening to TV and hearing music from the car's radio. If their appreciation for music is to grow and develop, children need to be introduced to music of enduring quality. Naturally the music selected must be appropriate for their level of experience and understanding.

Children who are introduced to good musical literature through carefully selected and planned activities will begin to develop improved listening skills and a receptive, appreciative attitude toward many types of music (Smith, 1970, pp. 120–121).

SINGING

Singing can bring much joy to children. Landreth (1972, p. 108) says, "A song can lift spirits and feet." We know that most young children love to sing and love to be sung to. If one listens carefully as children go about their work and play, one will find them singing "bits and pieces" of created words that fit the rhythm of their movements. One might hear them chanting, "I'm baking an apple pie," or, "See me swing up and down." Re-

cently a small group of 5-year-olds was observed coloring with purple crayons. Suddenly, one child started to sing over and over, "Purple-durple, purple-durple." Soon the entire table joined in the singing. At times adults can sing back the chants and songs children improvise. Occasionally these ought to be written down for children to see.

As an adult sits down to play the piano or another instrument, watch the reactions of the children. Usually their faces will light up as they gather around the instrument and ask for their favorite songs. At ages 3, 4, and 5, some of the little voices will not be able to carry a tune. Above all, one must be careful not to place too much emphasis on singing in tune and building musical skills at this age. It is amazing how young children's ability to "carry a tune" will improve by their singing frequently and spontaneously. Singing should not be taught formally in the preschool. At first, short songs having three or four tones may be improvised by the parent or teacher. No accompaniment is really needed. Do not pitch the improvisations too low. Naturally, the voice or voices leading the singing should be of good quality. This does not mean the person must have a trained singing voice, but it should be accurate and of pleasing quality. It is interesting to note that young children can often match upper elementary children's singing voices better than that of adults. Some record companies are now producing song records of excellent quality using children's voices to lead the singing.

Call-and-answer songs

Call-and-answer songs, or *echo* songs, can help children as they attempt to reproduce sounds of different pitch levels. This type of song is most valuable because children must listen first, then reproduce it. There should be much singing on a one-to-one basis so that the child can hear a tone or a series of tones and attempt to match them. Examples of call-and-answer songs would be the following (first the teacher sings, then the child answers):

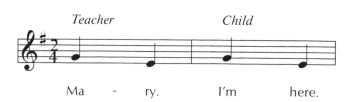

31

Teacher: What did you have for break-fast? Child: Pan-cakes.

Teacher: How are you to-day? Child: I am ver-y fine.

Teacher: Who has the glue? Child: I have the glue.

RESEARCH AND THE SINGING VOICE

Research is beginning to help us better understand the child's singing voice and to choose songs that will help develop it in a natural way. In general, 3- and 4-year-olds prefer singing in the range of middle C to A (a sixth above). Drexler found that children ages 3 to 6 could sing descending pitch intervals more easily than ascending ones (Shelley, 1976, p. 208). We have included several songs in our collection that are based on the descending scale in order to accommodate this finding.

In reference to music, it is not unusual for children to misunderstand the terms *high* and *low*. Shelley (p. 208) points out that 3-year-olds will confuse high and low with big and little. Given a choice, children generally prefer a lower starting pitch and sing more easily. Children usually prefer to use a higher range when singing spontaneously but prefer a lower range for singing songs (Shelley, p. 209).

Gould, investigating the singing problems of elementary children, concluded "that kinesthetic aspects of the discovery of the singing voice by the child and his developing skill in using and controlling this new found voice are essential to improvement in singing" (Shelley, p. 211). The study established two basic principles: "The child must learn to hear his own voice in speaking and singing and to control the high and low pitches, and he must be able to sing in unison with either another voice or instrument and to learn the sound and feeling as his voice matches the pitches he hears" (Shelley, p. 211). *These two principles are extremely important and should be kept in mind when planning musical experiences for young children.*

Suggested singing experiences based on research

Based on a review of the research pertaining to vocal development, the following list of suggestions should help adults as they plan singing experiences for young children.

1. Provide plenty of opportunity for spontaneous vocalizing throughout the day.
2. Encourage children to improvise and sing about their everyday activities at home or at school. (One kindergarten teacher we know encourages her children to sing about what they do at home in the evenings and on weekends. Some of these children sing their stories much easier than they can say them. Many get caught up in relating these events and will chant and sing delightful musical stories.) *Suggestion:* Permit the child to hold a paper in his hand as if he were reading his musical story from a book.
3. Tape children's voices. Play them back. It is es-

sential to tape individual voices so that children can hear their own. A word of caution here: use tape recorders that reproduce voices accurately. Poor reproduction of a child's voice can distort the quality and will be inaccurate. Do not tape children's voices if they seem afraid of the experience. This could result in children withdrawing from singing. In most instances, youngsters thoroughly enjoy this activity.

4. Provide many opportunities for children to make sounds using different pitches (e.g., the sound of a mewing kitten, a barking dog, a mooing cow, different siren sounds). These opportunities are essential in helping children learn to control their voices.

5. Choose as many songs as possible that are written between middle C and the A above. Children should be exposed to many songs that are easy for them if their singing voices are to be encouraged. (Sheehy, 1968, p. 60). Limited range songs should be used extensively. Scalewise songs (particularly descending ones) are good if they are not sung too rapidly. This helps develop "feeling" for tonality.

6. Use songs that have a limited number of pitch leaps—ones that do not wander all over the keyboard. Good examples would be such songs as "Deedle, Deedle, Dumpling" and "Twinkle, Twinkle, Little Star."

7. Vary the beginning pitch levels of songs. All too often adults find a comfortable starting pitch to fit their own voices and never change it for children. We believe that this "sameness" could be a contributing factor in children having such limited singing ranges as they grow older.

8. Continue to select songs that will broaden the singing range of the children. This should be done on a very gradual basis. Many adults fail to carry through this important aspect in helping youngsters develop their singing voices.

9. On occasion, recite or say poems, nursery rhymes, or songs. Encourage children to use different voice inflections to "match" the meaning and sound. The song "If You're Happy and You Know It" has unlimited possibilities. Have the children say the words using inflection in their voices. For example, "If you're happy and you know it, toot your horn. Toot, toot!" or, "If you're happy and you know it, hum out loud," etc. This approach helps children find yet another way in learning to control both their speaking and singing voices.

10. Songs that make use of repeated words, musical phrases, or repeated rhythmic patterns are good choices. Some examples of these would be "Do You Know the Muffin Man?" and "Picking Up Paw Paws."

11. Encourage children to play the resonator bells or an accurate, well-tuned xylophone. Help them learn to play short phrases so they can make up words to accompany the melody or vice versa.

12. When possible, indicate melody direction (low to high, high to low) or pitch intervals by using hand signals, body movements, or by writing dashes or picture representations on the board. Have you ever considered encouraging children to sing a scalewise song as they go up or down a stairway?

Those working with young children should find the following scalewise songs helpful.

The Snowman

Begin at bottom of scale on middle C and sing upward.

A chubby little	C
snowman	D
Had a carrot	E
nose. A-	F
long came a	G
bunny, And	A
What do you sup-	B
pose?	C

Sing down the scale starting with C above middle C.

That hungry little	C
bunny,	B
Looking for his	A
lunch,	G
Ate that little	F
snowman's nose,	E
Nibble, nibble,	D
crunch.	C

Now start up the scale again. Begin on middle C.

Nibble (C), Nibble (D), Nibble (E), Nibble (F), Nibble (G), Nibble (A), Nibble (B), *Crunch!!!* (C)

PEARL H. WATTS
(*Source unknown*)

Taking a Bath

Begin at top of the scale and sing downward. Begin with C above middle C.

Every night I	C
take a bath, I	B
scrub and rub and	A
rub.	G
Every night I	F
take a bath, I	E
splash around the	D
tub.	C

Repeat as above.

Every night I	C
take a bath,	B
Face, nose, and	A
ears,	G
Arms and hands and	F
legs and feet, E-	E
nough to last for	D
years!!!	C

M. RAMSEY

Five Little Monkeys

Substitute "puppies," "elephants," etc. for "monkeys." Begin at the top of the scale and sing downward.

Five little	C
monkeys	B
Jumping on a	A
bed,	G
One fell	F
off and	E
bumped his	D
head.	C

Repeat the scale.

Mamma called the	C
doctor, the	B
doctor	A
said,	G
"No more	F
monkeys	E
jumping on the	D
bed."	C

Repeat using "four little monkeys," etc.

Clap Your Hands

Start at top of scale and move downward.

Clap, clap,	C
clap your hands,	B
Move them in the	A
breeze,	G
Stamp your feet, then	F
turn around, And	E
sit down, if you	D
please.	C

Autumn Leaves

Start at top of scale and move downward. Begin with C above middle C.

Trees are bending	C
with the wind.	B
Leaves are falling	A
down,	G
Twirling, twirling	F
swirling, swirling.	E
Soon they're on the	D
ground.	C

Repeat the same scale starting with C above middle C.

I rake the leaves in-	C
to a pile, And	B
make it very	A
high.	G
Then I jump with	F
all my might, And	E
wheeee! I'm out of	D
sight.	C

K. BAYLESS

CONTENT OF SONGS

It is extremely important to select song material that is appropriate for the specific age level. All too often, adults do not take this into consideration when they write or choose songs for children. Careful thought should be given to the study of what children are like, what they can do, and what their interests are at certain stages of development. This should be done before writing, selecting, or presenting songs to them. There are a number of good song books on the market today for young children (Appendix B).

I WIGGLE*

LOUISE B. SCOTT

Arranged by K. BAYLESS

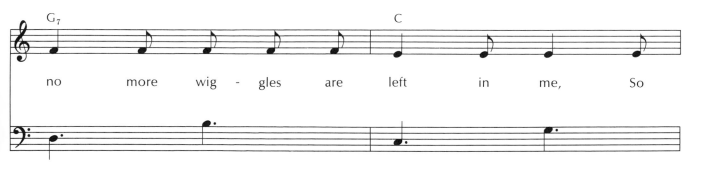

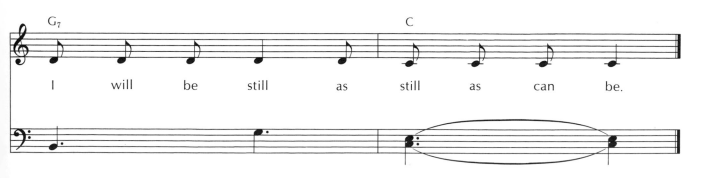

PITTER, PATTER

Very staccato

Words and music by K. BAYLESS

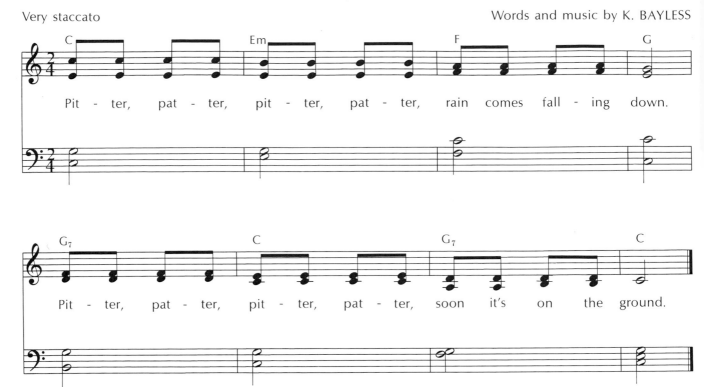

Pit - ter, pat - ter, pit - ter, pat - ter, rain comes fall - ing down.

Pit - ter, pat - ter, pit - ter, pat - ter, soon it's on the ground.

Choose songs where the subject matter and words are closely related to the child's understanding and interests. Four- and 5-year-old children particularly enjoy action songs and singing games, popular and television-related songs, and songs about:

- nature and seasons
- their own names
- birthdays and special days like Christmas, Hanukkah, and Halloween
- fun-loving and nonsense
- school activities
- flags and patriotic days
- their families and friends
- their bodies, parts of their bodies, and clothing
- feelings such as happiness
- animals and pets

PRESENTING NEW SONGS

New songs can be introduced at spontaneous times when the situation seems just right, or at a planned group time. They may be introduced to a small group of children who are informally gathered together, or to the entire class. It is important to keep the situation as natural as possible.

Almost all children are eager to learn new songs as well as to sing their favorite ones. Children like to repeat their favorites, but interest will begin to wane if songs are overworked. Variety is necessary, and the teacher should take into consideration that the same song will not appeal to the entire group. To keep interest at a high level, teachers need to have a number of songs at their "fingertips" that they know well. Hildebrand (1976, p. 332) says that, since it takes several hearings before children will be able to sing a song, they should be supplied with a number of songs in various stages of learning.

Whenever possible, one should memorize the words and melody of a song to use the nonverbal cues and eye contact that are so necessary when sharing a song with children. If the teacher's voice is accurate and of good quality, it is best to introduce the song without any accompaniment. It is easier for children to match their tones with the human voice than it is for them to match the melody played on an instrument. To support a teacher's voice that is somewhat shaky, or for the sake of variety, another instrument such as the piano, guitar, or Autoharp can be used.

Some songs will need a short introduction; others will not. Sheehy (p. 65) reminds us that "songs are made to be sung, not to be talked about. . . ." The teacher might introduce the song by showing a picture, a diorama (a three-dimensional scene showing objects and figures representative of a particular song or situation), asking a leading question, sharing a related incident, or giving some helpful background information. In presenting songs, this aspect is extremely important and must not be overlooked. This kind of motivation promotes interest and helps the children to understand the "message" of the song.

Reluctant singers

Do not be disturbed if all the children do not join in the singing. Once in a while you will find a child who will not sing with the others. He may sing freely at home or when he is alone, but not in the school setting. His reluctance to participate may be due to the fact that he is totally absorbed in watching the other children sing, or that he simply is not ready to join in. These cases are rather uncommon, since most children like to sing whether or not they can carry a tune accurately. Many children of this age are still trying to find their singing voices. In dealing with the reluctant singer, encourage but do not force the child to participate. Give him time to respond. The length of time will vary according to each child and his own personality and previous experiences.

Since children are highly motivated by action songs, we often find that those who are reticent to participate in singing will many times become involved in songs that call for action by the hands, feet, or other parts of the body. As children become involved in the physical sense, the words of the song often seem to emanate and become a part of the activity. Soon these children begin to take part.

Props for a song can also lend much interest. For example, in the song "Three Blue Pigeons," three pigeons made of construction paper or similar material and mounted on lightweight sticks for holding and carrying in acting out a song can be the motivating factor in getting children involved. There is much enjoyment and fun in holding the pigeon and acting out the song, and there is also the great sense of security that goes along with having something in one's hands. We have seen this carried out many times with youngsters at our nearby campus school.

Teaching a new song

Knowing how to present a song effectively to young children can make the difference in whether the children will like the song. Remember to sing the song slowly (not *too* slowly) and distinctly, keeping in mind the rhythmic flow.

> The teacher should not expect a response on the first day or the second. It takes time for a young child to understand and remember the words and longer still to gain a clear conception of a melody. . . . Encourage him to sing, even if he isn't singing your tune. Vocal chords need exercise, and he needs vocal expression. Drill on either words or music is harmful for preschool children. Sing the song, straight through, and let him catch what he can, even if it is only the last note. Pitch will come on the wave of rhythm (Pitcher et al., 1974, p. 47).

Smile as you sing. Rotate your head so you make facial contact with every child. Do not make the mistake of asking the children if they like the song. They may say, "No." When they like a song, children will generally say, "Let's sing it again!"

Sing the song through several times on the same day or on successive days. If interest is high, it will not be long before the children will begin to sing right along. This method, called the *whole method,* is to be encouraged. This provides children the opportunity for "chiming in" with a word or phrase that is easy for them to grasp and remember. Some phrases become cumulative, and soon the entire song is learned in a relatively short time. Songs that get children involved quickly and naturally we call *songs that invite participation*. Examples of these are "Mister Rabbit" and "Old MacDonald Had a Farm."

It is not good practice to teach a song line by line. This method, if used repeatedly, can destroy the entire effect of a song, lose meaning, and often cause children to dread learning a new song. This does not mean that a teacher should never sing a line of a song or a certain word of a song and have the children repeat it. This is, indeed, sometimes necessary for children to learn the pronunciation of a word correctly, or to fit the words and melody together as they should be. The problem stems when teachers use the "line-to-line" method in teaching every new song.

As new songs are repeated on successive days, it is not

long before you will know if the children like the song. If, after careful introduction, they do not seem to respond and like a particular song, do not use it again for a period of time. There is such a wealth of good song material, do not feel upset if children do not seem to care for a particular song. One important point to keep in mind is that once in a while, when children have learned a song well, the teacher should sing along very softly or not at all so the children can hear themselves singing and to strengthen their ability to carry the melody all by themselves.

It is not unusual for children of this age to have some difficulty in reproducing the pitch or melody of a song. The use of echo, or answer, songs, as mentioned earlier in the chapter, is extremely important to continue. Scalewise songs that are not sung too rapidly are also very helpful, since they contain words that stay on one sustained pitch for a period of time before moving on to the next pitch. We have included several scalewise songs in the book that children like and respond well to. Children who have continued pitch problems should be seated near the teacher or beside children who can help them sing with more accuracy. *In no way should a child ever be made to feel self-conscious because he cannot sing "in tune"!* We still find students at the college level who were victims of some insensitive adults who made them so self-conscious of their singing voices that they gave up early in life and refused to ever try singing again.

INSTRUMENTS

Children are fascinated by devices and instruments that produce sound. Around 1 year of age, a child's attention is quickly drawn to the movement and sound of a cuckoo clock. If one tries to divert the child's attention, almost invariably the youngster will return to watch the swinging of the pendulum and to hear the sounds of the cuckoo bird.

Children are such natural inventors! As they move through the infant stage, one of their favorite activities is taking a wooden spoon and striking it against one of mother's cooking utensils or "banging away" on a cup or cereal dish. We often hear parents say that their children prefer pots, pans, and spoons to commercial sound-making toys.

As children grow older, have you ever watched them jump mud puddles, landing on both feet? Have you watched them pound nails in rhythm, or stomp their feet to band music? This is movement and body percussion combined. This is the "stuff" on which good rhythmic experiences are built.

BODY PERCUSSION

Children delight in using different parts of their bodies to produce sounds. They soon discover, as they shuffle their feet back and forth in rhythm, that this kind of movement makes a very interesting sound. Experimentation of this kind often results in helping them express how a train starts up or slows down. Encourage children to experiment in making other sounds with their bodies, such as snapping their fingers, pounding their fists together, and tapping or clapping their hands in rhythm. Ask them to make the softest body-percussion sound they can make; the loudest; the lightest; the heaviest.

PERCUSSION THROUGH SOUND-MAKING DEVICES

After much experimentation with body percussion, percussion through use of objects can logically follow. At this point, adults and children can begin to bring together all sorts of interesting sound-making devices. Children, guided by the teacher, can begin to sort out and classify these devices according to the kinds of sounds they produce. Collecting and experimenting with "sound-making things" is a very important step in introducing instruments to children.

INTRODUCING INSTRUMENTS

There has been much controversy as to how instruments should be introduced and used with children. Many teachers have been "turned off" from using them because of initial, unpleasant experiences. This has usually been the result of handing out instruments "wholesale" to every child and letting the total group bang away. Results are often chaotic if children are allowed to use instruments in this way day after day. Many teachers readily admit they do not know how to introduce instruments. If careful thought is given to the introduction and use of instruments, much enjoyment and learning can and will take place.

When children are at an age where they can respect instruments and care for them, they should have the opportunity of using them. Both commerical and home-made instruments can be introduced. Many of these instruments can be made by the children. Others can be made by adults for use with children. Much enjoyment and pleasure can be had when whole families become involved in making some of the instruments and sharing the sound-making together. When children go through the process of making instruments, they have a much better understanding of how the sound is produced. (A section on homemade musical instruments follows shortly.)

As each instrument is introduced, it should be explained and then passed around for children to handle and explore (Nye, 1975, p. 82). At this time, it is also wise to establish a few rules for handling the instruments to prevent some of the problems that usually occur if expectations are not set. Keep the rules simple. It is sometimes helpful, until time to play the instruments, to ask the children to place their instruments on the floor in front of them or behind them.

Nye also says that:

> The teacher should establish situations in which the child can select the instrument he believes to be the most appropriate for certain music or to accompany certain songs, poems, and stories. The formalities of the rhythm band of past years, with its re-

quired conformity, have resulted in its virtual absence from the modern school. This dictatorial type of instrumental performance is in opposition to sound theories of learning and to the creative approach wherein children are involved in exploring, questioning, designing, and performing music.

There are many good songs and selections in which the instruments can be used for sound effects or for accompanying. Examples of these would be using a wood block for the ticking of the clock or using a triangle to strike the hour of one in the song, "Hickory, Dickory, Dock." In the story of "Chicken Little," an instrument such as the tone block could be struck at the point where Chicken Little thinks the sky is falling on her head.

The many nursery rhymes, folk songs, and singing games should be an integral part of every preschool and kindergarten program. Most of these songs and rhymes have definite rhythmic qualities that motivate body percussion of all kinds, such as the clapping of hands, brushing with feet, and snapping with fingers. Soon children will begin to see that some of the sound-making articles they collected will also fit a particular part of the music. They begin to evaluate, to listen, and to make choices and decisions of what sound or combinations of sounds go well together. This then becomes *their* music making, not that of the adult. If instruments are introduced in this way, children will better understand what each instrument's tone is like and how it can be played and used. Basic elements of *orchestrating* begin in this way. Soon children will be using instruments to accompany their songs and movements. "A great deal of musical value can come from the use of . . . instruments in exploring sound, discovering interesting tone qualities, and the revealing of concepts such as loud-soft (dynamics), high-low (pitch) and rhythm (duration)" (Nye, p. 82).

As children and adults explore sound-making together, there is continued need for experimentation and problem solving. For example, children can be guided to discover that if a triangle is held tightly by the hand and then struck, it will produce a dull, "dead" sound. Children are fascinated when the front of an upright piano is removed and they are allowed to see and hear what happens when the hammers strike the different strings. They can see and hear that the high sounds on the piano correspond to the short strings, and that the low, heavy sounds correspond to the long strings. Instruments like the Autoharp and guitar are also excellent for helping children become familiar with musical concepts.

It is helpful if adults can play the piano to accompany children as they use instruments, but it is not a requisite. There are many good records available for home and classroom use. Some parts of recorded classical music and folk rhythms are excellent sources to use with instruments. Some of these records introduce and explain the instruments; others tell children exactly what instruments to use and where to play them. Others encourage creativity on the part of adults and children.

Then there comes a time when the entire class plays instruments together. Hopefully, by this time, the instruments will have all been introduced, one at a time, to the children so they will know the sound each instrument makes and how that sound is produced. The total group experience should be the result of many individual and small group explorations.

The choosing or giving out of instruments often affects children's feelings about the instruments. If given a choice, children seldom choose the rhythm sticks. This is probably because there are usually more sticks available than any other instrument. Cymbals are a favorite since there is but one pair per set. Then, too, cymbals make such a "neat" sound when struck together. As a general rule, the children may be given the choice of the instrument they want to play. To make sure the less aggressive child has an opportunity to experiment with the most popular instruments, the teacher, on occasion, should pass out the instruments. To satisfy the natural curiosity of children, it is a good idea to have them exchange instruments with each other so they experience the sounds and feel of the different instruments. Teach children to care for these instruments in the same way that adult instruments are cared for. This would include establishing a method of placing the instruments in a box or on a shelf after using them (not thrown, tossed, or piled in helter-skelter fashion). With proper guidance, children can quickly learn how to use and care for rhythm and melody instruments.

Inviting resource visitors

As interest grows, musicians (older children or adults) could be invited to visit the classroom and introduce different band and orchestral instruments. In this way, children can learn firsthand what each instrument is like, how it is played, and how it sounds. The musician might encourage the children to touch the instrument, and, in some cases, play it. This needs to be done under careful supervision. In instances where the instrument's sound is produced by using the mouth, it is sound hygienic practice not to allow the children to blow into the instru-

ment. Boys and girls will be pleased if familiar melodies and songs they know are played by the musician. If songs are familiar, they will generally chime in with singing. It is also a good idea to have the visitor play a selection that is particularly well-suited to the instrument being introduced.

Many teachers make a field trip of taking their classes to the music room or the football field to provide children with the firsthand experience of seeing and hearing the band as it plays and marches across the field. We would like to encourage parents to do the same. Children also enjoy the out-of-door concert band programs. Every year the concert band of the Cleveland Symphony Orchestra gives performances at our nearby Blossom Amphitheater. Parents often bring their children to these concerts. Many bring picnic basket lunches and eat together on the grassy slopes of the hillside. It is not uncommon to see some of the little ones rolling down the hill in time to the music or marching across the grass as the band plays a stirring march.

Children's TV programs have been helpful in introducing instruments in interesting ways. There are also numerous recordings on the market that introduce individual instruments of the band and orchestra. And there are those recordings in which selected passages highlight a particular instrument. (Several of these are listed in Appendix B.)

If these suggestions for introducing instruments are used, children should enjoy their sound-making experi-ences more fully, and the teacher or parent can feel that a good foundation for appreciating instruments has been established.

Following is a list of melody, chording, and percussion instruments suitable for use with young children:

Melody instruments

piano	step bells
melody bells	xylophone
resonator bells	

Chording instruments

Autoharp	ukulele
guitar	

Percussion instruments

rhythm sticks	gong
tone blocks	drums, small and large
wood blocks	bongo drums
temple blocks	tom-tom drums
tambourines	maracas
triangles	claves
finger cymbals	coconut shells
cymbals	

COMMERCIAL RHYTHM AND MELODY INSTRUMENTS

Following is a listing of a typical commercial set of rhythm instruments. The makeup of these sets differs according to the manufacturer. They can be ordered in different sizes such as 16-pupil set, 22-pupil set, 30-pupil set, and so forth, including individual sets. Most companies take great care to ensure that each set contains the proper balance of instruments for the number of students involved. Competitive companies sometimes refer to the same instrument by different names, which can cause confusion. When in doubt, check illustrations of the instruments and write to the particular companies for complete descriptions.

30-pupil set

1 hand drum	2 jingle bells mounted on
1 bongo drum	wooden handles
6 pairs of rhythm sticks	2 triangles with holders
1 pair of wood blocks	2 castanets
2 tone blocks with mallets	2 maracas
2 sand blocks	2 pairs of finger cymbals
2 tambourines	1 pair of cymbals
2 wrist bells	

Commercial sets usually come with a baton and instructor's book. These are considered a part of the rhythm instrument set.

Descriptions of some favorite rhythm instruments and how they can be used are given in the following discussion.

Drums, the versatile instrument

A drum is a versatile instrument to have in the home and classroom. A good drum is basic to any rhythm program for young children. One can make it do ever so many things. It can be played to tell when it is time to clean up the room or to call the children in from play. The syllables of a name can also be tapped out on a drum. One can play loud or soft, fast or slow, on this "friendly" instrument.

Drums can be purchased or made, and it is recommended that a variety of sizes and kinds be made accessible. Each drum should differ in pitch so that children have opportunities to hear and distinguish different levels of pitch. If possible, at times try to arrange several different drums close together, in a semicircle for example, so that children can discover the different sounds the drums produce as they tap one, then another. Children will soon discover that the drum produces different sounds depending on how, where, and with what they strike it. In good weather, the drums can be collected and taken outside where they can be experimented with. When this kind of opportunity is provided, children can accompany their rope-skipping games and create rhythms of their own. Parents and teachers are beginning to use some of the interesting drums from different parts of the world such as the Orient, Africa, and some of the Latin American countries.

Rhythm sticks

Rhythm sticks, two slender pieces of hardwood approximately 12 inches long, are good basic instruments for keeping time when marching, singing, or accompa-

nying another instrument or a record. One stick from the pair is usually notched. A scraping sound can then be produced when the smooth stick is scraped across the stick that is notched. Sticks can be made from doweling. When making rhythm sticks, be sure the type of wood used produces a good tone quality.

Wood blocks

Two pieces of square- or rectangular-shaped wood with handles are used for this instrument. The size of the wood and the weight of the wood will depend on the age level of the children using the instrument. Some wood blocks are too heavy and large for use with the younger child. The instrument can be played by tapping or sliding one wood block against the other.

Sand blocks

Sand blocks are sandpaper attached by staples or thumbtacks to the sides of 2 wooden blocks, approximately 2½ x 4 inches. Choose size and weight according to age level of children using them. Sand blocks are much easier to use if they are equipped with handles or holders. They are played by rubbing one sandpaper block against the other.

Tone block

A small block of wood, hollowed out with a cut on each side, and a wooden mallet make up a tone block. It is played by striking the mallet above the cut opening. This produces a hollow, resounding tone. When played correctly, the instrument provides a good underlying beat for musical selections.

Wrist bells

Sleigh bells are mounted on a strap and should be of a pleasing quality. The instrument is worn on the wrist or ankle and produces an effective sleigh bell sound to accompany songs and dances.

Jingle bells on handles

Generally a single bell is mounted on the end of a handle. The instrument is held in one hand and shaken by the child in time to music.

Tambourine

Six or more pairs of jingles are usually mounted in the shell. The plastic shell head comes in different sizes. The instrument may be shaken or struck with the hand, knee, or elbow, producing an interesting jingling effect.

Triangle

The triangle consists of a steel rod bent into triangular shape, open at one corner, and struck with a small, straight, steel rod. We suggest that this instrument be purchased, since most homemade triangles have rather poor tone quality. The instrument is held by a holder and struck with a metal rod. It may also be played by placing the rod inside the triangle and striking it back and forth against the sides.

Maracas

Maracas are gourd or gourd-shaped rattles filled with seeds or pebbles. The instruments are shaken to produce rhythmic effects and can be played singly or by holding one maraca in each hand.

Castanets

Castanets are a pair of concave pieces of wood, which may be held in the palm of the hand and clicked together or attached to a handle for easier use by small children. The sound makes an interesting accompaniment for dancing.

Finger cymbals

Two small cymbals with finger holders are held with each hand and struck together. The instrument also may be played by placing the loop holder of one cymbal over the thumb and the loop of the other hooped cymbal on the middle finger. The two finger cymbals are then struck together.

Hand cymbals

Concave plates of nickel, silver, bronze, or brass produce a sharp, ringing sound when struck. Cymbals may be played in pairs by striking one against the other· or singly by striking one cymbal with a drumstick.

Autoharp

This string instrument has buttons or bars that, when depressed by the finger, dampen all the strings necessary to the chord desired. It can be played by strumming or plucking. The number of bars on Autoharps varies; the most common types have twelve or fifteen. Persons with little or no musical training can learn to play the Autoharp in a relatively short time.

Melody bells

Melody bells are arranged like notes on the piano keyboard and are mounted on a frame. The bells are played with mallets. Sets come in various ranges.

Step bells

These bells are mounted on an elevated frame, include chromatic tones, and come in various ranges. Some frames are collapsible, allowing easy storage. Children can easily see whether the melody moves up or down.

Resonator bells

Mounted individually on a block of wood or plastic, these bells are arranged in a luggage-type case. Mallets are used to play the bells. The keyboard is similar to that of the piano. Each bell may be removed from its case and played individually.

HOMEMADE MUSICAL INSTRUMENTS

Making and using simple instruments can be a real source of pleasure and satisfaction for individuals of all ages, and it offers delightful hours of wholesome, cooperative activity for children in schools and for family groups. The possibility for experimenting with materials is endless. Creating new and original instruments is fascinating and challenging. Along with the enjoyment of making the instruments, much learning through problem solving takes place. It is not uncommon for the entire family to get involved in creating and making new sound-making instruments. Some of the instruments that we suggest making in the following pages for possible use by children are just as good as, and in some instances better than, those which are commercially made.

Tom-toms, drums

Played with the hands, tips of fingers, or sticks.

Nail kegs with muslin tops
MATERIALS
1. Nail keg—may be obtained from hardware store, lumberyard, factory, drugstore, antique shop, farm sale (kegs are becoming more difficult to obtain)
2. Airplane glue—hobby shop
3. Unbleached muslin
4. Large thumbtacks
DIRECTIONS
Cut muslin about 3 inches larger than open top. Soak and stretch absolutely taut, fastening with thumbtacks or bright upholstery tacks. Do not remove rim of keg. When dry, paint top with airplane glue, giving it at least four coats. (*Caution:* Glue should be applied in a well-ventilated place, since it is highly inflammable.) Do not

paint kegs because this can affect the tone quality of the drum. A binding on the outside over the rim may be made from large rubber bands, inner tubing, or plastic tape. The sides of the keg may be decorated with cut-out figures. (See p. 45 for variations.)

Cylindrical containers of cardboard
MATERIALS
1. Large ice cream cartons, large cottage cheese cartons, oatmeal boxes
2. Airplane glue
3. Unbleached muslin
4. Large thumbtacks
DIRECTIONS
Tops for the cardboard containers are constructed like the nail keg tops.

Large tin cans
MATERIALS
1. Potato chip cans, No. 10 food cans, oil cans from filling stations
2. Inner tubing
3. Sturdy lacing if needed
DIRECTIONS
Use the best part of the inner tube for the drum head. Start cutting the tube completely around the inner edge. Find the best spot as you open it and draw around the end of the can, allowing 3 inches for overlap. Cut eight holes evenly about $\frac{3}{4}$ inch from the edge of the can. Following along the inner edge of the tube, cut strips $\frac{1}{2}$ inch wide (or just wide enough to prevent tearing when stretched), or use another type of sturdy lacing. Thread loosely all around at first. Fasten, then keep on tightening and retying until strips are taut and will snap back when pulled. These should be very tight. This type of drum will give a more mellow, softer tone than the other drums.

Small tin cans

MATERIALS

1. Empty, round tin cans—any size will do; the larger the can, the greater the volume and the deeper the tone
2. Discarded inner tube from an automobile tire; the thinner rubber gives a more pleasing tone
3. Flat paint; colored quick-drying enamel, turpentine
4. Small, round sticks, 10 to 12 inches long for drum sticks

DIRECTIONS

Select a sturdy can, free from dents, and remove one or both ends with a can opener that rolls the ends underneath so there are no sharp points. Remove the paper label with hot water, dry thoroughly, and give the can a coat of flat white paint. While this is drying, the design may be planned. Two coats of quick-drying enamel are recommended for finishing the drum.

When the finish is thoroughly dry, cut a circular piece from the inner tube to get a large rubber band ½ inch wide. One or two people are needed to help in putting the head on the drum, since the circular piece of rubber must be held tightly across the open end of the can while the ½-inch band is stretched around the can twice in a

figure-eight fashion to hold the head in place. A little patience and practice will develop the necessary skill in this process. Tighten the head by placing the hands on opposite sides of the can and pulling the circular head down by means of the part that projects below the band. Trim off uneven parts, leaving sufficient rubber to prevent slipping and to provide for later tightening.

Miscellaneous drums

1. Drums may be made also by tacking a circular piece of inner tubing over the top of a wooden bowl. The large, rather shallow type found in most homes is quite satisfactory. These offer fine opportunities for interesting decorations, and they give a nice tone.

2. More temporary, but very satisfactory and inexpensive drums can be made from round cardboard cereal boxes. Instead of using the muslin top, use a piece of inner tube for the head. The covers must be intact. A more durable drum with a better tone will result if the box is given a coat of clear shellac after it is decorated with water colors, crayons, or enamel paint. A cord or ribbon fastened through two holes in the long side of the box will enable the player to hang the drum around his neck while playing. Two lightweight drumsticks may be used.
3. True Indian drums can be made by covering a hollow log or other similar container with sheepskin that is bound or laced into place while wet. This is a more difficult operation than the others suggested. We recommend that anyone interested in this type of drum would find a book on Indian handicraft of great help.

Drumsticks

Sticks for drums can be made from any available round pieces of wood 10 to 12 inches long and ¼ to ½ inch thick. They should be sanded smooth and rounded

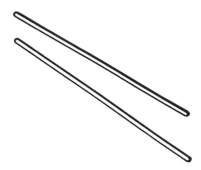

at both ends, avoiding points that might be dangerous. They may be painted to match the drum. If the drum has a head on both ends, two sticks are needed; otherwise, one is sufficient, since the player holds the drum under one arm while playing.

Other types of drumsticks
1. Tinkertoys (for muslin-top drums)
2. Wooden beads, cork fishing floats, or large spools fastened on the ends of doweling

3. Single, padded stick made by padding the end of a piece of broomstick or other round stick with cotton, felt, or wads of cloth and kept in place by means of cloth or chamois cover tied securely to the wooden handle
4. End of a wooden spoon

Rhythm sticks and blocks

Rhythm sticks
MATERIALS
1. Round sticks of varying length and thickness, doweling, chair rounds, broomsticks, etc.
2. Paint, turpentine, etc. for decoration

DIRECTIONS
The sticks should be tried out by tapping them together to find the best combination for interesting tone effects. These may then be cut to convenient lengths—12 to 15 inches—and shaped with sandpaper. Points should be avoided. They may be finished by staining, varnishing, or enameling in gay colors and design. They are especially useful for members of a large group in rhythmic play.

Rhythm blocks
MATERIALS
1. Scraps of wood of any size or thickness as long as you can get two blocks the same size; wood less than 1 inch thick easier to handle

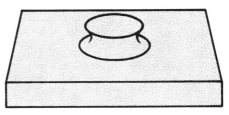

2. For the handles: such things as a pair of drawer pulls, pot-cover handles, spools or small blocks of wood that can be bolted or screwed on, or pieces of an old leather belt or other material for making strap handles
3. Small tacks, screws, or bolts, depending on type of handle
4. Paints for decorating the blocks
DIRECTIONS
Two blocks the same size and shape should be cut from the wood. Oblong, round, square, and triangular

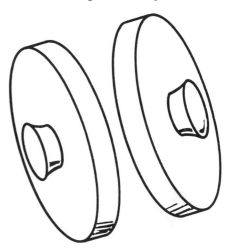

shapes are interesting. Sand the blocks until smooth, then design and paint with enamel. New wood needs a coat of flat white paint first. Attach handles so that a perfectly flat surface is preserved for playing.

Chinese wood block

MATERIALS
1. Small, oblong, lightweight wooden box such as a cheese box, cigar box, etc. (old English Leather [men's shaving lotion] box is good)
2. Braided rags, string, ribbon, or other type of cord for suspending the block
3. Walnut or dark oak varnish if desired
4. Small, round stick for beater

DIRECTIONS

In order to get that delightful hollow sound that suggests galloping horses or tramping feet, it is necessary to cut long slits $\frac{1}{4}$ inch wide on the four long sides of the box. This may be done by boring a hole in one corner of the oblong shape to be removed and then using a key-hole saw, working slowly so the wood does not split. When all four slits are made, sand the edges smooth and even with sandpaper. Drill two holes in one end of the box for the cord, which can be fastened before the cover is nailed on or maneuvered into position with the help of a nail. Finish the wood block with one coat of dark stain (not enamel, which destroys the sound) and a coat of clear shellac or varnish if desired. This improves the

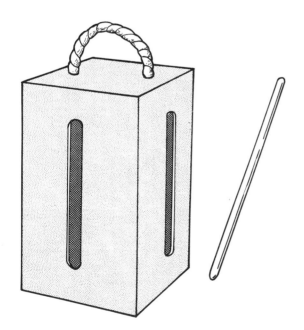

appearance but not the tone. A stick similar to a drum-stick can be used to strike the instrument.

Sandpaper blocks

MATERIALS
1. 2 oblong blocks of wood, approximately 3 x 5 inches, and at least $\frac{1}{2}$ inch thick
2. Medium grade, or fine grade sandpaper for covering bottom and sides of blocks
3. Large-headed tacks or nails
4. Materials for handles, similar to wood blocks
5. Paint for decorating the blocks

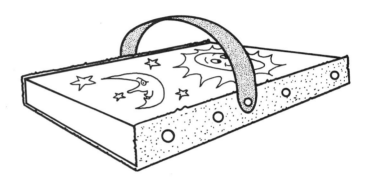

DIRECTIONS

The sandpaper should be cut to fit the bottom of the block with enough on each side to fold up and cover the edges of the block. It should be attached to the block by sufficient thumbtacks, nails, or staples along the covered-up edges to hold it securely.

Make handles by securing the ends of a 5- x $\frac{1}{2}$-inch plastic or leather strip to each side of the block. The rhythm sound may be obtained by inserting the hands through the handles and sliding the blocks back and forth.

Rattle sounds

Soap shaker rattle

MATERIALS
1. Wire soap shaker with wooden handle.
2. 4 round metal bells, miniature sleigh bell type, not the open kind with a clapper.
3. Flat white and colored enamel paint.

DIRECTIONS

Give the shaker a coat of flat white paint and then two coats of enamel. When dry, put bells in the boxlike part of shaker and fasten securely by pushing small metal ring as far down toward the box as possible, working with a hammer and screwdriver. Pinch firmly into place with pliers.

Gourd rattle

MATERIALS

1. Dry, well-shaped gourds; shells should be hard and firm
2. Small feathers or colored yarn and beans for decoration
3. Beads, sand, small pebbles, rice, seeds, or other material for inside rattle
4. Small pieces of round wood for handles
5. Large-headed nails for fastening handles
6. Glue for fastening decorations
7. Enamel paint, shellac, and turpentine

DIRECTIONS

Select well-shaped gourds—the larger the better. Remove a small part of the narrow neck with a coping saw or keyhole saw. The size of the hole depends on the thickness of the handle to be inserted. Remove the gourd seeds, unless they make a satisfactory rattle, and add a sufficient quantity of whatever hard substance is to be used to give the rattle the volume of tone desired. Corn or beans are good, and sand, fine gravel, or rice give a softer sound. Insert stick and push to the top of the gourd, leaving at least 4 inches for the handle. A single upholstery nail through the center of the top of the gourd into the end of the handle should hold it firmly. Fill the crack around the handle with glue, or plastic wood if preferred. Paint and decorate rattle if desired. Attach feathers or ribbon with glue or sealing wax.

Interesting rattles can be made of gourds that have a pleasant sound by virtue of their own dried seeds by simply decorating them and using them without handles. A coat of clear shellac often helps the tone of rattles of this kind.

"L'eggs" hose shaker

MATERIALS

1. 1 plastic "L'eggs" hose container
2. $\frac{3}{8}$-inch dowel stick 10 inches long
3. 12 dried beans, rice, or small stones
4. Plastic glue

DIRECTIONS

Cut $\frac{3}{8}$-inch hole in the long end of the "L'eggs" hose container. (Use hot instrument or a drill to cut the hole.) Insert dowel through hole. Put glue on end of dowel inside of container around the $\frac{3}{8}$-inch hole and around the center overlapping portion of the container. Place beans inside container and assemble. Make sure that the dowel is touching the inside of the container so that the glue will make the assembly rigid. Allow glue to dry overnight. Decorate. Acrylic paints work well and provide a smooth finish.

Maraca (papier-mâché)

MATERIALS

1. Light bulb (size to fit child's hand)
2. $\frac{1}{2}$-inch or narrower newspaper strips
3. Paper toweling torn in narrow strips
4. Wheat paste

DIRECTIONS

Dip torn newspaper strips in wheat-paste mixture and lay them one at a time over the light bulb, smoothing

and pressing down. Allow the first layer to dry. Then apply another layer. Allow the second layer to dry. For the third layer, use small pieces of paper toweling. Allow this to dry hard. A quick hit on the floor will break the bulb inside. This will also provide the rattle. If you wish, a hole can be drilled and the broken glass removed. Beans or rice can be placed inside the container, and the hole sealed shut. The outside may then be sanded smooth. Paint and decorate the maraca as you desire. (*Caution:* Small children should not attempt to make these because they are too difficult to put together. Also, when using the glass-bulb maracas, give the child only one to use at a time. When using two, the child might strike one against the other, causing the maracas to break and, therefore, spill out small pieces of the broken glass.)

Hand shaker

MATERIALS

1. Piece of wood 1 inch wide, 8 inches long, ¼ inch thick
2. 4 metal soft-drink bottle caps
3. 2½-inch washers
4. 2¾-inch roofing nails

DIRECTIONS

Flatten soft-drink bottle caps. Through each center, drill or punch a hole slightly larger than the diameter of the nail. Assemble bottle cap, washer, second bottle cap on nail and tack to wood paddle ½ inch from one end. Repeat second assembly 2 inches from first nail. Carve end opposite the bottle cap assemblies to fit child's hand for a handle.

Coconut shell clappers

MATERIALS

1. Coconut (should not be too large for hands of young children)
2. Saw

DIRECTIONS

Select a coconut whose rounded ends will easily fit the palms of a child 3 to 5 years old. Allow the coconut to dry for several months to dry up the milk inside and cause the solid portion to shrink away from the sides. Then place the coconut in a vise. Take a wood saw and saw through the middle. (Having another person hold the other side of the coconut while one person is sawing is helpful.) After the coconut is cut in two, take a knife and lift out the solid portion. When the shells are tapped together, they make a hollow clip-clop sound—a good imitation of horses' hooves.

Tin can rattle
MATERIALS
1. Small tin can with cover
2. Small object for inside the rattles—corks, small nails, and beans give nice tones
3. Flat white paint and enamel for decorating cans
4. Glue or plastic tape for fastening covers

DIRECTIONS
Select a can free from dents and sharp edges with a tight-fitting cover. Experiment with various kinds of material until the desired sound effect is achieved. A single small cork or nut has been found to be pleasing. Glue the cover in place if there is any possibility of its coming loose unexpectedly. Give the can a coat of flat white paint. When dry, decorate with enamel. Cardboard cans with metal ends often give interesting two-tone effects. Cardboard boxes may be used also, but they are much less durable and are not suitable for very young children.

Pie pan tambourine
MATERIALS
1. Metal pie or cake tins, either small or medium size
2. 6 or 8 round metal bells (not open kind with clapper)
3. Fine wire or cord for fastening bells
4. Flat white paint, turpentine, and enamel for decorating
5. Paintbrushes

DIRECTIONS
Make holes at equal distances around the edge of the pan, being sure no sharp points are left underneath.

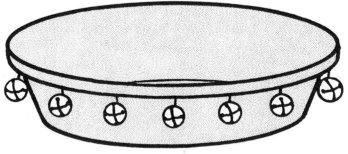

Fasten bells to pan with fine wire or cord, leaving them loose enough to ring easily when tambourine is used. Each bell may be fastened separately, or a continuous cord may be used from hole to hole. If wire is used, fasten ends in a safe manner. After a coat of flat white paint dries, the design may be put on with enamel.

Wrist bells
MATERIALS
1. 4 to 6 round metal bells (not open kind with clapper)
2. Material for making the band—knit or crocheted colored yarn or string or heavy cloth such as denim, ticking, or canvas
3. Needles and *strong* thread for fastening bells and ends of bands

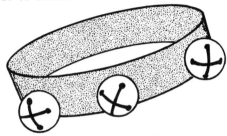

DIRECTIONS
Make a band 7 inches long and 1 inch wide, fastening the ends together securely to form a circle. Sew bells firmly to the band at even distances.

Orff instruments

Use of the Orff concept of teaching music is growing very rapidly (p. 172). Instruments for the Orff method are specially designed percussion instruments of excellent quality. They are rather expensive but excellent to use with young children.

CREATIVE RHYTHMIC MOVEMENT

Dancing*
A hop, a skip, and off you go!
Happy heart and merry toe,
Up-and-down and in-and-out,
This way, that way, round about!
Bend like grasses in the breeze,
Wave your arms like wind-blown trees,
Dart like swallows, glide like fish,
Dance like anything you wish . . .

ELEANOR FARJEON

Mimi Chenfeld (1976, p. 261) reminds us that "movement is as natural to learning as breathing is to living. We have to be taught not to move as we grow up in our inhibited, uptight society." Movement is synonymous with the growing child. Today, more than ever, we realize the great amount of learning that takes place through psychomotor activities. As indicated in earlier chapters, the young child should be free to explore and experiment with his own movements in response to stimuli. It is important that he experience these natural body movements before he is ever asked to respond to those initiated by adults.

> Movement exploration is, as the term implies, discovering how the body can move and what great movement potential the body has. It makes the child aware of his own abilities. It gives him the opportunity to understand and accept his body, to lose his self-consciousness, and to learn the joy of free movement. . . . Many times, movement exploration may lead directly into a creative dance experience or may form the basis for a folk dance. As such, it is the process, the solving of a problem, and the discovering of a new way, rather than an end product, that are important. (Clark, 1969, p. 12.)

As children's muscle coordination improves, they can begin to coordinate the rhythmic movements of their body with stimuli such as the beat of a drum, a rhythmic poem, a song, and the like.

We strongly believe, as children learn to control their body movements, they build feelings of confidence and satisfaction that will grow and carry over into mastery of other areas. Undoubtedly the child will become less fearful of trying out other activities. Have you ever seen the look on a child's face who has just found the "right combination" for skipping or who has just walked across the balance beam for the first time without falling off? Success in mastery of movements such as these help the child grow psychologically as well as physically. Prime purposes of movement programs are to help young children become more aware of what their bodies can do and to help them develop the balance and coordination needed to control all parts of their bodies.

Movement activities for the preschool and kindergarten age child vary greatly from one program to another. Ten to fifteen minutes a day of marching and skipping to music or playing rhythm band instruments is not uncommon. We feel that children should have ample opportunity to "dramatize movements" before they are required to respond to the steady beats of music played on a record or piano.

Imaginative teachers

Young children of this age move and respond so naturally with an imaginative and sensitive teacher. Teachers who are willing to experiment can develop a vital, creative rhythmic program for their children. A good movement program is developed by a teacher paying close attention to children as they move—as they

51

skip down the hall, run with the wind, pound with their hammers, twirl around in circles, or stamp their feet in puddles. *There is no set way to begin.* One way to start would be to group children informally on the rug or gym floor. Have the children lie flat on their backs or stomachs. Can they wiggle their bodies without moving from their space? Can they wiggle their bodies away from their spaces? Can they move parts of their bodies that no one else can see? Can they move two, perhaps three parts of their bodies at the same time? Can they puff up their stomachs like a cake that is rising in the oven? Keeping in mind that most children are very inventive, adults can encourage them to do all kinds of "tricks" with their bodies. It is not surprising that a child can roll up into a tiny ball, make himself so rigid that no part of his body wobbles or bends, push the clouds high into the sky, or crawl into a very, very tiny box. If motivated by a creative teacher, it won't be long before children's ideas begin to flow. Many times the whole group will pick up another child's idea and extend it. Trying out the movements of other children often encourages the more reticent youngster to try out movements of his own. Teachers can be very helpful by speaking words of encouragement. For example, if the children are discovering different ways to move across the floor, the teacher might say, "Look, Tommy is moving sideways. Let's all try to move the same way as Tommy." After the children have tried Tommy's way, the teacher might say, "Who would like to show us another way to move across the room?" Once the children have begun to share their ideas freely, the teacher can play a very important part by expanding on the ideas that children begin. The following is an example.

On a Monday following a weekend holiday, a kindergarten boy eagerly told his teacher and classmates about a trip he had just taken with his family through Pennsylvania. He told them that at times his father had to suddenly turn on the headlights of his car because it became so dark his father could not see to drive. After considerable discussion as to what that dark place was called, a child sang out, "That dark place is called a tunnel." More children then chimed in and said, "Yeah, that's what you call it, a tunnel!" The children then asked their teacher if they could darken the room and pretend that they were going through a long, dark tunnel like the ones in Pennsylvania. The teacher then asked, "What shall we use for a tunnel?" Some of the children suggested lining up a long line of tables and then crawling underneath them. Tables were quickly put

together. Each child was his own automobile. Childre crawled through the tunnel in orderly fashion. They ha captured the mood of moving through a darkened spac More discussion followed. They began to tell what it wa like to try to do things in dark places. One boy tol about his father developing pictures in his darkroon The children became so interested and asked so man questions about how a picture was developed that it wa decided to enlist the aid of the industrial arts teache since he had built a darkroom at the school. With th help of their teacher, the children took their own pi tures and developed them. Many examples like this on could be cited in which a creative movement idea deve oped into a series of expanded learning experience

The imaginative teacher uses word pictures exten sively to help create a feeling or mood to stimula children's thinking. For instance, when the time seen right, the teacher can begin to zero in on the natur movements of a child and say, "Let's walk as if a strong north wind were pushing on our backs," or, "Let's imagine we are walking through a squishy mud puddle with our boots on." If it seems appropriate, add a few simple chords on the piano or a few drum taps, making a "match" to the children's tempo. Follow the children's leads.

Moving the way the music makes you feel?

All too often children are asked to listen to a selection on a record and then told, "Now, boys and girls, move the way the music makes you feel." Unless some feeling for the music has been built into the experience, results are often chaotic and unproductive. In like manner, children are sometimes asked to move like a particular animal such as a bear. Whether using a musical background or not, a feeling about bears should be built up before children begin to respond rhythmically. Ethelouise Carpenter, early childhood teacher, says, "A child cannot be what he has not experienced in some way. Sometimes the 'experience' may need to be a vicarious one. This may come through descriptions, pictures, and discussions." For example, the teacher might ask the children, "How large are bears? What kind of feet do they have? How do they move through the woods? Do they move fast or slow? Can they climb trees?" Children need to really think before they respond. These kinds of descriptive discussions help children build up a feeling for what they are asked to become.

FUNDAMENTALS OF MOVEMENT

Since movement is such an important medium of expression for young children, it is necessary for parents and teachers to know and understand movement fundamentals in order to help children express themselves. Andrews (1954, p. 37) points out: ·

> There is no one classification of movement, or a particular sequence for presenting or developing the fundamental movements. If there were, it would not only kill creative teaching but also stifle creative expression. Nor can movement be developed in isolation without a recognition of elements of space and rhythm. As movement is developed, it is also affected by experiences, thoughts, feelings, and ideas which children continually have. The way in which these movement fundamentals, and the elements and experiences which affect them, are initiated, depends upon the teacher, the situation and the particular group of children.

Locomotor movements are those which propel the body through space. Walking, hopping, jumping, running, and leaping are all examples of locomotor movements. There are also many body movements such as crawling, creeping, scooting, sliding, and so forth. Claire Cherry in her book, *Creative Movement for the Developing Child* (1971), lists many different types of movements that young children enjoy and experience. With the introduction of each body movement such as crawling, Cherry presents a thorough description of the movement and then gives suggestions and varied activities to help develop each skill. She feels that music motivates children to respond rhythmically and suggests using familiar melodies, such as "Twinkle, Twinkle, Little Star" and "Little Brown Jug," substituting appropriate words for the original in order to help describe particular body movements. Preschool and kindergarten teachers would do well to develop movement activities similar to Cherry's to meet the special needs of their own children.

There are many excellent recordings (some with illustrated storybooks) that provide children with plenty of ideas for creative movement. Anne Lief Barlin's *Dance-a-Story* (eight recordings with illustrated storybooks) have been used very successfully with preschool- and kindergarten-age children. Bowmar's *Rhythm to Reading Series* is another excellent example of illustrated stories and records that invite movement through music. A songbook has also been written to accompany the series. (A listing of both series can be found in Appendix B.)

Many companies are producing individual story and movement records of excellent quality. Hap Palmer's records have become all-time favorites and have found their way into the hearts and lives of thousands of America's young children. His captivating melodies and rhythms seem to make up the kind of music children thrive on. They literally are caught up in the spirit of the words and rhythms. Selected classical recordings provide a great resource to enhance movement. (A suggested list of recordings will be found in Appendix B.)

Establishing the beat

Once children have had plenty of opportunity for free movement and can move about without bumping into others, more locomotor and body movements such as tiptoeing, jumping, and walking can be used. The teacher can strike up a steady beat on a drum or with chords on a piano to accompany the children's movements. As children gain more experience, the teacher

53

can then ask for response to the steady beat being played. The ability to maintain a steady beat comes easily to some children but not to others.

> Research in young children's motor development and moving to music shows that the ability to maintain a steady beat by tapping is developmental according to age and does not seem to change much after age nine. Tempo is a contributing factor to accurate motor response; and children, particularly those of nursery school age, are more successful in synchronizing their movement with fast speed than with slower ones. (Crews, 1971, p. 61.)

Skipping, for example, which is the combination of a walk and a hop, is a favorite movement of children. Yet we often find that the music being used for skipping is too slow, thus causing some children to have difficulty coordinating their skipping movements with the tempo of the music.

Folk songs and singing games also provide opportunities for children to move. These are particularly good for young children, since most of the songs are within their singing range. Ruth Seeger's *American Folk Songs for Children* is perhaps the best known collection of folk songs in America. Because of their nature, most of the songs invite participation and improvisation. Three fourths of the tunes in her collection "are accustomed to action, to being danced to, clapped to, worked to. Children listening often start clapping of their own accord, or skipping, or jumping, or kicking their feet, or trying some new motion" (Seeger, 1948, p. 24).

Children creating their own movements

Children should be encouraged to create their own movements. At first these movements could be very simple ones like showing how the leaves come falling down from trees or how cats creep when they see a mouse. Some of the very first dances are imitations and pantomimes of nature. According to Clark (1969, pp. 25–26), "As the child learns by exploration how he can move his body, he is increasing his vocabulary of skills that help him to express ideas, moods, and experiences."

Use of recordings and props

There are many fine recordings on the market that invite movement participation. These do not need to be records made especially for children. Some of the works of our finest composers, such as Grieg, Pierné, Saint-Saëns, and Mendelssohn, are excellent for stimulating free movement. At times the use of props such as scarves, long feathers, strips of crepe paper, balloons, and rhythm instruments enhance movement. Props also aid in making children less inhibited. The opportunity to hold something in their hands often gives balance to their bodies and lends variety.

As children continue to move and to sharpen their listening skills, listening for special parts in the music can begin. As music is played, adults need to help children listen for changes of tempo, mood, and dynamics. Here again, word pictures by adults working with the children help greatly in interpreting the many combinations of musical sounds.

POINTS TO KEEP IN MIND FOR ENHANCING MOVEMENT

1. Children need ample space for movement activities (enough for children to skip freely). Large spaces may present problems in controlling the group and cause difficulties in hearing.
2. If a large room, such as an auditorium, is used, prepare children in their classroom ahead of time as to where they are to go and what they are expected to do once they enter the gym.
3. Establish boundary lines.
4. Have children remove heavy clothing. Children should wear gym shoes. Some authorities advocate bare feet for certain activities.
5. Establish signals for "starting" and "stopping," for instance, the voice, a whistle, or drum.
6. Have children find their own spaces. This can be done by having them spread out their arms so they do not touch their neighbors.
7. Avoid demonstrating movements.
8. Adults guiding movement activities should have access to a good-quality drum. Children generally respond well to changes in movement when tapped out on a drum. Sometimes "drum language" commands attention more readily than the human voice.
9. Accept children's movement and interpretation to music.
10. Praise the timid child to encourage experimentation and freedom of movement.
11. Do not force the child to participate.
12. Make a thorough study of resources such as records, songs, poems, pictures, films, and the like to enhance movement. Provide variety.

Help children keep moving

Growing children need to keep moving. This is very much a part of their learning process that continues throughout a lifetime. Keep in mind that movements expressed by children are often accompanied by their innermost feelings and ideas. Wise adults will do everything within their power to find a way in which these innermost feelings and ideas can be expressed.

REFERENCES AND SUGGESTED READINGS

Andrews, Gladys. *Creative rhythmic movement for children.* New York: Prentice-Hall, Inc., 1954.

Block, Susan Diamond. *Me and I'm great.* Minneapolis: Burgess Publishing Co., 1977.

Carpenter, Ethelouise. Personal communication, 1976.

Chenfeld, Mimi Brodsky. Moving movements for wiggly kids. *Phi Delta Kappan,* November 1976, **58**(3), pp. 261–263.

Cherry, Clare. *Creative movement for the developing child* (Rev. ed.). Belmont, Calif.: Fearon Publishers, Inc., 1971.

Clark, Carol E. *Rhythmic activities.* Dansville, N.Y.: The Instructor Publications, Inc., 1969.

Crews, Katherine. Research in learning and movement. In *Music and perceptual-motor-development.* New York: The Center for Applied Research in Education, Inc., 1975.

Hildebrand, Verna. *Introduction to early childhood education.* New York: Macmillan Publishing Co., Inc., 1971.

Landreth, Catherine. *Preschool learning and teaching.* New York: Harper & Row, Publishers, 1972.

McCall, Adeline. *This is music for today—kindergarten and nursery school.* Boston: Allyn & Bacon, Inc., 1971.

Nye, Vernice. *Music for young children.* Dubuque, Iowa: William C. Brown Co., 1975.

Pitcher, Evelyn Goodenough, Lasher, M. G., Feinburg, S. G., and Braun, L. A. *Helping young children learn* (2nd. ed.). Columbus, Ohio: Charles E. Merrill Publishing Co., 1974.

Seeger, Ruth. Why American folk music for our children? In *American folk songs for children.* New York: Doubleday & Co., Inc., 1948.

Sheehy, Emma D. *Children discover music and dance.* New York: Teachers College Press, 1968.

Shelley, Shirley J. Music. In Carol Seefeldt (Ed.), *Curriculum for the preschool-primary child—a review of the research.* Columbus, Ohio: Charles E. Merrill Publishing Co., 1976.

Sinclair, Caroline B. *Movement of the young child ages two to six.* Columbus, Ohio: Charles E. Merrill Publishing Co., 1973.

Smith, Robert B. *Music in the child's education.* New York: The Ronald Press Co., 1970.

4 Music: the language builder

The growing child is a moving child and a talking child. Adults who understand these qualities can do much to foster and nurture the language development and the musical development of the young child.

MUSIC: THE PERSONAL LANGUAGE

Music is a natural and very personal language. Music is accessible to the slow learner, the gifted, the handicapped, the young, and the old—truly universal. Who has not delighted in the exuberance of the young child as he swings and chants the time-honored "See Saw, Margery Daw," enjoying the movement of his body and the fit of the words, or the child of any age who will never forget "supercalifragilisticexpialidocious" of *Mary Poppins!*

As we observe each young child, we become aware of how each interprets and integrates music within. Each is indeed unique.

The wise teacher or caregiver will capitalize on the young child's penchant for movement, rhythm, and talk. A teacher picks up the rhythmic movement of the children rather than expecting them to conform to her set tempo. She encourages the use of movement by providing opportunities for children to express themselves (Taylor, 1970, p. 67).

To further elaborate on the importance of rhythm matching, Byers and Byers (1975, p. 8), in a fascinating discussion of dimensions of nonverbal communication, say that:

> Being in synch with another person is comfortable. Being out of synch in this rhythmic way is uncomfortable. We believe that there is a biological basis for this—that rhythm matching produces psycholog-
> ical effects that are read off as "good feeling" and that rhythm mismatching produces effects that are felt as "bad feelings" or discomfort.

A good learning environment for the young child may well depend, Byers and Byers (p. 89) contend, on the acceptance that different children may look as though they are out of rhythm or synchrony with the group, while, in fact, they are only moving more of their bodies.

Body "music" may well make a difference!

EXTENDING LANGUAGE

Those who work with young children can facilitate the many kinds of language, the languages of music, of the body and of words and gestures.

Writing on the learning processes of young children, Margolin (1976, p. 263) cautions:

> Verbal facility is difficult for some children. They may not have had viable experiences prior to or concurrent with school that helped them develop verbal skills. Music provides a format for communication and the opportunity for children to express themselves. It permits them to feel a part of the total group.

Teachers need to recognize and plan for various cognitive modes and styles, using activities that enable children to move, produce, and express feelings and reactions. In addition, teachers (or caregivers) need to expose children to various tempi, the rapidity of action to which they are accustomed (Grant, 1976, p. 122).

Consider the blending of the language of music, the language of movement, and the beauty of words. What better way for the young child to experience the delight of each than building on the world of "let's pretend."

56

Many times during the day, a musical sound, rhythm, or other movement activity can build vocabulary and offer enjoyment.

Capitalize on the young child's natural movements with a strategic question such as, "What does this remind you of?" or, "Have you heard this rhythm somewhere?"

Talk about the rhythmic movement of animals as they walk. How does a duck walk? A horse? (Taylor, p. 66). Use the tom-tom to match:

Action

Horses gallop,
   Monkeys leap,
Eagles swoop,
   And possums—sleep!
Panthers pounce,
   Rabbits hop,
Bullfrogs dine,
   And donkeys—stop!

ILO ORLEANS
(*Lawrence, 1967, p. 50.*)

Or in a time of "let's pretend" use the child's own body music to imitate and to extend his understanding of movement.

Bigness compels young children. All want to be big. Build on the concept of bigness as well as rhythm with:

The Hippopotamus

What fun   to be
A Hippo   potamus
And weigh   a ton
From top   to bottamus

MICHAEL FLANDERS
(*Lawrence, p. 55.*)

Another favorite of children is:

Tiger Walk

Walk, walk, softly—slow—
This is the way the tigers go!
Walk, walk; get out of the way!
Tigers are coming to school today.
Creep, creep—softly—slow—
This is the way the tigers go!
Creep, creep, come and play,
Tigers are coming to school today.

(*Scott, 1968, p. 292.*)

Or chant together with a deepening of voice and appropriate actions:

Tiger

There's a tiger in the forest.
   Listen to him roar.
He's coming through the forest.
   Hurry—shut the door!

There's a tiger in the forest.
   He is hungry; he is thin.
He's coming through the forest.
   Run away from him!

M. RAMSEY

Just imagine:

Five Big Elephants

Five big elephants—oh, what a sight!
Swinging their trunks from left to right.
Four are followers, one is the king,
And they walk all around in the circus ring.

(*Scott, p. 294.*)

Extend movement and vocabulary further with:

The Elephants

Tail and trunk, legs and ears,
Stomp, stomp, stomp.
Tail and trunk, legs and ears,
See the elephants tromp.

Tail and trunk, legs and ears,
Stomp, stomp, stomp.
Tail and trunk, legs and ears,
Oh, so slow!

Tail and trunk, legs and ears,
Stomp, stomp, stomp.
Tail and trunk, legs and ears,
All in a row!

M. RAMSEY

Other "elephant" verses can be introduced and simple props such as cardboard ears and stuffed stocking trunks added to provide fuel for the imagination. Aileen Fisher's "The Handiest Nose" is delightful. "The Elephants," by Dorothy Aldis, and Laura Richard's "Eletelephony" will extend understanding and enjoyment.

Somehow the drum is most appropriate to portray the lumbering gait of the elephant, and the young child's body sways and stomps as he chants the verses. Notice, too, how tones of the voice will reflect mood and how freely conversation flows after "doing" several rhymes and poems.

Elaborate preparation or follow-up is not necessary with the young child. Often the impulse of the movement, the mood, or even environmental change offer a "teachable interlude" when music, movement, and words bring instant rapport for the entire group and the teacher.

Imagination and music

Adults can do much to stimulate the imagination. Many traditional poems build vocabulary, provide memory training, add a sense of excitement, and offer a stimulus for discussion and sharing.

Highlight the mystery of the unknown with this poem by John Ciardi:

About the Teeth of Sharks

The thing about a shark is—teeth,
One row above, one row beneath.

Now take a close look. Do you find
It has another row behind?

Still closer—here, I'll hold your hat.
Has it a third row behind that?

Now look in and—Look out! Oh, my,
I'll never know now! Well, goodbye.

(*Lawrence, p. 60.*)

The young child will quickly master and set to rhythm the exciting traditional rhyme:

If You Ever Meet a Whale

If you ever, ever, ever, ever,
  ever meet a whale,
You must never, never, never, never
  grab him by his tail.
If you ever, ever, ever, ever
  grab him by his tail—
You will never, never, never, never
  meet another whale.

(*Bissett, 1967, p. 45.*)

A companion verse is by Mary Austin:

Grizzly Bear

If you ever, ever meet a grizzly bear,
You must never, never, never ask him where
  he is going.
Or what he is doing.
For if you ever, ever dare
To stop a grizzly bear,
You will never meet another grizzly bear.

(*Lawrence, p. 50.*)

The sense of the macabre and the knowledge of the unlikelihood of such an encounter delight the young

child, and he will shiver with anticipation and request the lines repeatedly.

Sensory experiences

The gift of language needs to be shared. The young child delights in this sharing whenever the adult is available to listen and respond.

Scott (p. 16) tells us:

> A child has such fun putting his feelings into words. The child's world is felt, heard, seen, smelled, and tasted, for he is constantly exploring. One of his most delightful and satisfying ways of expressing these explorations and discoveries is to verbalize them.

However, a word of caution: to fully extend sensory experiences and enhance the use of language, the adult cannot afford to be a token listener. The young child quickly senses inattention and disinterest. The adult,

too, must be imaginative, sensitive to mood and opportunity.

Scott suggests the merry-go-round rhythm that makes it easy for children to participate:

Kangaroo

Teacher: Old hoppity, loppity kangaroo
Can jump much higher than me or you.
Children: Hoppity, loppity, jump one—two.
Teacher: His tail is bent like a kitchen chair
So he can sit down while he combs his hair.
Children: Hoppity, loppity, jump one—two.
Teacher: But when he jumps, he uses his tail
So he can jump high and almost sail.
Children: Hoppity, loppity, jump one—two.

(Scott, p. 289.)

Extend the visual imagery and appreciation of humor of the young child even further with this poem by Aileen Fisher:

Kangaroos

Can you picture shoes
On KANGAROOS,
On those big long jumpity feet
They use?
Can you see them hopping
easily, lightly,
breezily, brightly,
wonderfully fleet
with *shoes* on their feet?
Some jump five feet,
Some jump ten,
fifteen, twenty,
and then again
kangaroos—why, sakes alive—
have jumped as high as twenty-five!
But not in boots that cowboys use.
Only, of course,
in their "birthday" shoes.

(Bissett, pp. 34-35.)

Some children may want to measure how long 10 feet is. Provide the time to seek the answer.
And then the fascination with:

The Pocket

Today when I
Was at the zoo
I watched the mother
Kangaroo.

Inside her skin
She has a pocket.
She puts her baby
There, to rock it!

(Bissett, p. 35.)

STIMULATING LANGUAGE AND MUSIC

Awareness is the key to language and music stimulation. Throughout the day, listen and watch for cues to both.

Very often in either the home or preschool setting, we find that singing is better than talking. New words quickly become a part of the vocabulary as the teacher or parent sings:

"Mary, put the box away."
or, "Susie, now let's go to bed (jump in bed)."
or, "Tommy, you can stand up tall."
or, "Billy, let's cooperate—
eat your soup
by half past eight."

Instructions sung in good spirit are quickly followed and lead the way toward more complex communication. Torrance (undated monograph) relates the experience of working in the Sunday school setting with 4- and 5-year-olds who revealed much more about their feelings and ideas through singing than through speech.

Children are true and avid imitators. After hearing an instruction once or twice, or an ear-catching poem, they easily chant a simple melody line or create their own music to fit the message.

"Mary, Mary, brush your hair."
or, "Billy, let's pick up the toys."

There are those children for whom words have a special affinity. For them, the teacher will find that Marjory Lawrence's excellent *A Beginning Book of Poems* offers many choices of selections for movement as well as musical adaptation. Louise Binder Scott's *Learning Time* and the long-time favorite *Talking Time* are invaluable as source material.

Finger plays and nonsense rhymes

Finger plays and nonsense rhymes have an appeal of their own. Children readily chant them. The youngest can master the following traditional rhymes:

Here are mother's knives and forks,
(Fingers interwoven—palms together)
And this is father's table,
(Palms down, knuckles flat)

59

This is sister's looking glass,
  (Raise two index fingers.)
And here is baby's cradle.
  (Raise two little fingers. Rock hands.)

Knock at the door,
  (Tap forehead.)
Peep in,
  (Raise eyelid.)
Lift up the latch,
  (Touch end of nose.)
Walk in.
  (Put finger in mouth.)

Here's the church.
  (Palms together and fingers folded)
And here's the steeple.
  (Extend two index fingers.)
Open the doors,
  (Open palms.)
And see all the people.
  (Show fingers.)

Here are Grandma's spectacles,
  (Finger and thumb together for glasses)
Here is Grandma's cap,
  (Fingertips together for cap)
And this is the way she folds her hands
And lays them in her lap.
  (Fold hands in lap.)

Why Rabbits Have Bright Shiny Noses

Source unknown   Sung to the tune of "My Bonnie
                                         Lies over the Ocean"

All rabbits have bright shiny noses.
I'm telling you now as a friend,
The reason they have shiny noses—
Their powder puff is on the wrong end.

Chorus
Wrong end, wrong end, wrong end, wrong end, wrong
end, wrong end,
Wrong end, wrong end, wrong end, wrong end, wrong
end.

THE PEANUT SONG

Traditional

1. Oh, the pea-nut sat on the rail-road track, His heart was all a-

flut-ter. The choo-choo train came down the track, Toot, toot, pea-nut but-ter.

2
Oh, the bullfrog sat on a lily pad,
A-looking up at the sky.
The lily pad broke, and the frog fell in
And got water in his eye.

MISS POLLY

Unknown

1. Miss Pol - ly had a dol - ly that was sick, sick, sick. She

phon'd for the doc - tor to come quick, quick, quick.

2
The doctor came with his cane and hat.
He knocked on the door with a rat, tat, tat.

3
He looked at the dolly and he shook his head.
He said, "Miss Polly, put her straight to bed."

4
He wrote on the paper for a pill, pill, pill.
"I'll be back in the morning with a bill, bill, bill!"

EXTENDING RHYTHMIC OPPORTUNITY

Rhythm is as natural as breathing to the young child. The typical day offers many chances for participation in language building within a musical framework. The adult needs to develop a strong repertoire of simple melodies to share.

Vocabulary development, the enjoyment of participation, the rhythmic force of traditional Mother Goose, and the body action of such simple lines encourage the young child to seek further involvement.

The music of Mother Goose is striking, too. "Hey, Diddle, Diddle . . ." The words sing! The *d*s and *l*s beat out a rhythm that make the child who hears them want to say the words—words that laugh every bit as much as the boy in the rhyme. Mother Goose is a perfect vehicle for the primary child who is becoming more and more sensitive to the different sounds of language (Hennings, 1976, p. 38).

The child delights in:

Pease porridge hot,
Pease porridge cold,
Pease porridge in the pot,
Nine days old.

Can you spell that with four letters?
Yes, I can—T-H-A-T.

Or imagine the movement, musical, and memory training possibilities of:

One, two—buckle my shoe;
Three, four—shut the door;

Five, six—pick up sticks;
Seven, eight—lay them straight;
Nine, ten—a good fat hen;
Eleven, twelve—I hope you're well;
Thirteen, fourteen—draw the curtain;
Fifteen, sixteen—the maid's in the kitchen;
Seventeen, eighteen—she's in waiting;
Nineteen, twenty—my stomach's empty.

In his beautiful book *From Two to Five* (1968), Kornei Chuckovsky has much to say to us of the young child:

The child needs to be in motion either with his hands or his feet when he composes. (p. 65.)

To become a poet, the youngster must be full of animal spirits. (p. 65.)

He never isolates thinking from the rest of his activities. (p. 26.)

Young children adore nonsense rhymes. And such rhymes are very infectious. (p. 67.)

How children love the music of rhythm and rhyme!
"The little rabbit was fast and lean.
He was chased by a Magazine." (p. 66.)

All such nonsense verses are regarded by children as nonsense. (p. 95.)

Under the influence of beautiful word sequences, shaped by a pliable musical rhythm and richly melodic rhymes, the child playfully, without the least effort, strengthens his vocabulary and his sense of the structure of the native language. (p. 87.)

THE "EXPRESSIVE" ARTS

Music and language are more than avenues of communication. Children express delight they feel as well as anger and resentment. They use both without regard to any listener. By keeping many avenues of expression open in language, in movement, in the arts, we leave the child freer to grow as a person (Read, 1971, pp. 224–225).

As an emotional release, the arts for young children are unsurpassed. Fears, discomfort, and anxiety can find outlet in song and rhythm as a child verbalizes the unknown.

How much healthier than aggressive acts for the young are the expressive arts of music and language!

An important caution is voiced by Read (p. 226): "Children who use language as self-expression are not likely to be children who have been taught to recite the words of poems or songs. Self-expression is blocked by 'patterning.'"

Music and language are close relatives. The "music" of the voice is an important medium for communicating feeling (Read, p. 229). All of us quickly sense love and concern or anger and rejection in voice tones.

Watch the young child as he jumps rope, runs freely, or converses aloud with himself. The "counting out" rhymes of our childhood are ever remembered, delighting the tongue and sharpening the memory. Many are selected for the affective results.

Recall your own traditional favorites, chanted or sung:

One, two, three, four,
Five, six, seven,
All good children
Go to heaven.

One, two, three, four,
Five, six, seven, eight.
All bad children
Have to wait.

One potato, two potato,
Three potato, four,
Five potato, six potato,
Seven potato, MORE.

(Potatoes are fists extended. Leader points to fist on word "MORE"; player withdraws.)

One-ery, two-ery, zickery, seven,
Hollow bone, cracka bone, ten or eleven,
Spin, spun, it must be done.
Twiddledum, twaddledum, twenty-one.

Ibbity, bibbity, shindo,
My mother was washing the window.
The window got broke,
My mother got soak,
Ibbity, bibbity, shindo.

Fireman, fireman,
Number eight,
Hit his head against the gate.
The gate flew in, the gate flew out;
That's the way he put the fire out.
O-U-T spells out—
And out you go.

Yellow cornmeal
  Red tomato
Ribbon cane
  Sweet potato
Round melon
  Ripe persimmon
Little goober-peas.

Jean, Jean,
Dressed in green,
Went downtown
To eat ice cream.
How many dishes did she eat?
One, two, three, four, five.

Or try more contemporary ideas:

Best of All

Lollipops and gumdrops,
Choc'lets, bubble gum,
Lemon drops, and licorice,
Oh, yum, yum!

Lollipops and ice cream,
Choc'let cake and pie,
Butterscotch, vanilla,
O, yum, yum!

Choc'let chips and M & M's,
Gum balls, big and small,
Jello, pudding, sundaes, rolls,
Oh, I love them all!

M. RAMSEY

Me

Today's my birthday;
I am four;
Growing bigger, too;
Cake and ice cream, gifts, and toys.
How old are you?

Today's my birthday;
I am five;
Growing taller, too;
Cookies, ice cream, cars, and boats,
How old are you?

Today's my birthday;
I am six;
Growing stronger, too;
Ice cream, chocolate, books, and school.
How old are you?

M. RAMSEY

PLANNING FOR LANGUAGE OPPORTUNITY

For most young children language unfolds naturally as part of the growth process. Maximum development comes only through careful nurturing of language opportunity by the adult.

Remember, children often use language for the joy of it—the "feel" on the tongue—the delight of startling adults with made-up words. One writer recalls a 3-year-old, standing in her crib, chanting, "Patty say naughty word," and she did—many of them! There was no sense of meaning, just glee at the adult reaction and the music of the sounds.

Along much the same line of thought, Lewis (1975, p. 143) reminds us that there is a crucial relationship between the lively body and lively language, particularly in early childhood. Piaget has said that to silence the child's tongue is to silence his thinking. We might add, to immobilize his body is to silence his language and thought.

A very critical question is asked by Lewis (pp. 144–145:

> If vigilant senses and a lively body are related to vitality in language, why aren't we doing more in our schools to give young children daily opportunities for rhythmic, full-bodied, dramatic expression, a chance to move and jump and skip to drumbeats or other musical accompaniment? Why rhythms only once or twice a week, and in some preschools and kindergartens not at all?

Why, indeed? In many homes, in many classrooms, the sterility of the experiences denies the need for movement, for creative outlet, for the interaction with others—for the joy of being a child. The need for quality in the verbal transactions of the child cannot be overemphasized. The vitality of his language will be directly related to both quality and frequency of opportunities for interchange.

MUSIC AND READING SKILL

As the young child matures, another seeming paradox warrants attention. Often the child who cannot read language is able to read music and to then begin to read language.

This seeming contradiction led Professor Ruth Zinar of New York College, City University of New York, to say that the difficulties in learning to read music—the need for concentrated attention and memory and the understanding of abstract concepts—indicate that the degree of intelligence required to read music is at least as great as that required to read language (Zinar, 1974, p. 8).

Zinar and others have noted that often a child who does poorly in regular schoolwork learns to read music, and the child who studies music seems to improve in language. Researchers theorize that perhaps it is the multisensory approach—through movement, eye, ear, and body coordination—coupled with the improvement

in self-concept that make the difference. It is the *whole* child who learns!

How then can we rationalize the lack of music teachers in the elementary school, the poor quality of many musical programs, and, in many schools *and* homes, the absence of musical experiences of all kinds in the everyday life of the child?

The creative instinct is the essence of the child and the adult. The power of language and the other expressive arts cannot be overlooked or denied.

Young children delight in language play and language games and respond intuitively to the fascination of music.

SUGGESTIONS FOR ADULTS

We know that music offers unique possibilities to expand and extend vocabulary. A rich vocabulary is a necessary skill for the young child as he grows to adulthood. Adults can play a significant role in structuring the environment that fosters and facilitates music and language growth through:

1. Increasing their own awareness of the range of musical opportunities.
2. Providing a wealth of musical experiences for the young child.
3. Making music an integral part of the total day.
4. Building a strong and varied repertoire of rhythms, finger plays, poetry, and movement exercises.
5. Fostering a sharing, "talking" atmosphere surrounding the young child.
6. Recognizing the individual differences reflected in each child's musical preferences.
7. Enjoying with the young child the delight of music.
8. Interacting with the child as he sings or speaks by repeating or adding side comments:
   "More candy, please."
   "May I have more candy, please?
   Candy is sweet."
9. Helping the young child put to music his own nonsense rhymes, riddles, and verses.
10. Using music to expand memory. (Why is it that young children and indeed adults never seem to forget certain refrains or even television commercials?)
11. Playing a supportive role as the young child experiments and discovers music.

The possibilities of music as a language builder for the young child are infinite and irresistible!

REFERENCES AND SUGGESTED READINGS

Bailey, Charity. Music and the beginning school child. *Young Children,* March 1966, **21**(4), 201–204.

Bissett, Donald J. Poems and verses about animals. In Book 2, *Poetry and verse for urban children.* San Francisco: Chandler Publishing Co., 1967.

Bissett, Donald J. Poems and verses to begin on. In Book 1, *Poetry and verse for urban children.* San Francisco: Chandler Publishing Co., 1967.

Byers, Happy, and Byers, Paul. Dimensions of nonverbal communication. In Charlotte B. Winsor (Ed.), *Dimensions of language experience.* New York: Agathon Press, Inc., 1975, pp. 79–94.

Chukovsky, Kornei. *From two to five.* Berkeley: University of California Press, 1968.

Cleveland Association for Nursery Education. *Fingerplays and rhymes for children.* 1958.

Corcoran, Gertrude B. Activities to enhance language needs of young children. In *Language experiences for nursery and kindergarten years.* Itasca, Ill.: F. E. Peacock Publishers, Inc., 1976.

Grant, Barbara M. " 'Cold' media victims" in the early and middle childhood years of schooling. *Theory Into Practice,* April 1976, **15**(2), 120–125.

Hennings, Dorothy Grant. Waddle away with Mother Goose. *Early Years,* March 1976, **6**(7), 38–39.

Kuhmarker, Lisa. Music in the beginning reading program. *Young Children,* January 1969, **24**(3), 157–163.

Lawrence, Marjory. *A beginning book of poems.* Menlo Park, Calif.: Addison-Wesley Publishing Co., Inc., 1967.

Leight, Robert L. (Ed.). *Philosophers speak of aesthetic experience in education.* Danville, Ill.: The Interstate Printers & Publishers, Inc., 1975.

Lewis, Claudia. Our native use of words. *Dimensions of language experience.* New York: Agathon Press, Inc., 1975.

Margolin, Edythe. *Young children: their curriculum and learning processes.* New York: Macmillan Publishing Co., Inc., 1976.

McCall, Adeline. *This is music for kindergarten and nursery school.* Boston: Allyn & Bacon, Inc., 1971.

Mother Goose melodies. New York: Dover Publications, Inc., 1970.

O'Bruba, William S. Mother Goose remembered. *Early Years,* March 1976, **6**(7), 40.

Read, Katherine H. *The nursery school: a human relationships Laboratory* (5th. ed.). Philadelphia: W. B. Saunders Co., 1971, pp. 224–235.

Scott, Louise Binder. *Learning time with language experiences for young children.* St. Louis: Webster Division, McGraw-Hill Book Co., 1968.

Scott, Louise Binder. *Talking time.* St. Louis: Webster Publishing Co., 1951.

Scott, Louise Binder, and Thompson, J. J. *Rhymes for fingers and flannelboards.* St. Louis: Webster Division, McGraw-Hill Book Co., 1960.

Steiner, Violette G., and Pond, Roberta Evatt. *Fingerplay fun.* Columbus, Ohio: Charles E. Merrill Publishing Co., 1970.

Taylor, Barbara J. *A child goes forth.* Provo, Utah: Brigham Young University Press., 1970.

Torrance, E. Paul. Creativity in communication with young children. Undated monograph, University of Georgia Press.

Vernazzo, Marcelli. What are we doing about music in special education? *Music Educators Journal,* April 1967, **53**(8), 55–58.

Winsor, Charlotte B. (Ed.). *Dimensions of language experience.* New York: Agathon Press, Inc., 1975.

Withers, Carl (Collector). *Counting-out rhymes.* New York: Dover Publications, Inc., 1970.

Worstell, Emma Vietor. *Jump the rope jingles.* New York: Collier Books, 1961.

Zinar, Ruth. Reading, writing and music. *Education Summary,* January 1974, **26**(13), 8.

5 Music and the exceptional child

The greatest need of the exceptional child is to be treated like other children.

Todd and Heffernan, 1970, p. 149

Music with its integrating and organizing power can provide the oneness all children need. Music cuts through all age levels, all groups, all differences in children. It can provide a truly unifying and rewarding experience.

Music may be unique in the way it permits the child to be easily drawn into a group and still feel a heightened sense of individuality (Smith, 1970, p. 211). Every child, regardless of the type or severity of exceptionality, can participate and enjoy music as a natural mode of expression.

Schneider (1968, p. 143), speaking to the same point, reminds us that one of the particular problems of such a child is the difficulty of belonging to a group and making a positive contribution to it. Many exceptional children tend to live much of their lives on a one-to-one basis with adults, be they parents, teachers, or others. For many, the opportunities to associate with the peer group are limited. Kondorossy (1965), too, agrees that in music many children find their only cooperative venture, since they are often withdrawn or shielded.

Kirk (1962, p. 4) defines the exceptional child as that child who deviates from the average or normal child in mental, physical, or social characteristics to such an extent that he requires a modification of school practices, or special educational services, in order to develop his maximum capacities.

With several million children having special needs, there is much to be done. We are concerned here with the values of music and musical opportunities for these "special" children.

MUSICAL GOALS

The goals of music for special children are much the same as those for all children: to have opportunity to experience and participate in music in all its forms, to learn to appreciate music, and to the best of ability develop musicianship. For the exceptional child there are many individual goals based on extreme differences and needs (Vernazza, 1967, p. 56).

For some, music can provide a nonverbal means of expressing feelings—a springboard for oral communication for those who cannot or will not communicate, a nonpunitive and nonthreatening medium (Purvis and Samet, 1976, foreword).

In music for special children there is a constant shifting of emphasis. Goals are modified so that they are attainable by the handicapped child. Very often, music is the means of fulfilling goals other than musical ones (Vernazza, p. 56).

The key to working with any child, be he fast or slow, is to know his area of strength and build on it.

Cruikshank, writing in 1952, stipulated "in music, do not give him (the exceptional child) a separate program—if possible bring him into the musical experience of normal children where the exceptional child can cease to be exceptional" (Graham, 1968, pp. 79–80).

The current trend toward placement with normal children in regular classrooms (mainstreaming) and in social groups augurs well for the exceptional child deriving the benefits of music in a natural setting. Music can offer the potential for growth that recognizes no handicap.

NEEDS

The needs of the exceptional child are not unlike those of the normal child, including the need for:
1. Security
2. Self-respect and self-gratification
3. Love and affection
4. Movement
5. Positive interpersonal relationships
6. A sense of belonging, worth, and acceptance
7. A feeling of accomplishment and contribution

These needs are common to all. Music can play a major part in satisfying these needs for the exceptional child. However, specific uses of music must be determined for individual children.

Deno (1971, p. 44) advises, "Every child fits into a category of one—*his own category.* The handicapped is not so much of a problem to a teacher (adult) who recognizes that every child is different and who, therefore, uses an individualized approach. . . ."

We need the reminder that it can be easy to become so caught up in the differences of an exceptional child that we lose sight of the fact that he is largely like other children and should be treated as much like them as possible (Van Osdol and Shane, 1974, p. 259).

VALUES OF MUSIC

Music speaks to all children and elicits strong responses from each. Thus the values of involvement with music are still untapped. For many exceptional children, music plays a primary role:
1. Sheer pleasure and enjoyment
2. Opportunity for individualistic expression and sense of identity
3. Potential for language development and speech clarity
4. Development of attentive listening
5. Therapeutic value of contributing to emotional stability, lessening of aggressive action
6. Increased attention span

7. Lessening of distractibility and hyperactivity
8. Better muscular coordination and control and rhythmic movement
9. Release of tensions, anxieties, and inflexibility
10. Modification of unconventional behavior

Musical activities, carefully selected, can provide a satisfying dimension in the life of the exceptional child.

Common to all children are the basic areas of singing, rhythms, informal use of instruments, and music listening experiences. For the exceptional child, the differences are reflected in the techniques and philosophies used in the basic areas. Whatever the method, working on a one-to-one basis or in small groups is strongly recommended. Determine what works, then adapt and refine.

EXCEPTIONALITY AND MUSIC

There are healthy, normal, creative aspects of every child, regardless of the type of severity of his handicap (Purvis and Samat, foreword). The guidelines and approaches that follow are illustrative of the possibilities music offers to the exceptional child. Most of the songs and rhythms suggested for the normal child can easily be adapted to meet the needs of the special child.

THE PHYSICALLY HANDICAPPED CHILD

Orthopedically handicapped children must cope with lack of, or restriction of, mobility. Again, the physical handicap is just another variable degree. Singing offers relaxation for the tight muscles of the spastic and an opportunity for sharing, participating, and enjoying.

Pearl S. Buck, long a champion of the special child, felt that a handicapped child singing intently is deeply committed to his singing. The musical instrument he uses is his body, his voice, and he experiences his singing as a direct extension of himself (Nordoff and Robbins, 1971, foreword).

Mrs. Buck advised, "The most effective kinds of songs for handicapped children are those about activities that happen within the songs themselves, or about things or events the children know, or can imagine, or can grow to understand" (Nordoff and Robbins, p. 22). Many old favorites, Mother Goose and nursery rhymes, and simple verses are appropriate.

Rhythms, too, can be enjoyed if the child can manage lightweight, simple instruments such as sticks, bells, sand blocks, tambourines, or drums. Sometimes body rhythms such as nodding, swaying, moving the upper body, a kind of ballet, and tapping fingers and hands are possible. Some physical therapists do mat exercises with music. Simple finger plays set to music offer opportunities for appreciation, enrichment, and release of pent-up feelings. Coordination and control will also often improve and muscles strengthen through use of rhythms.

Children with multiple handicaps often withdraw into themselves and operate within a small radius. Problems with laterality and directionality (up, down, over, under, around) are confusing. Music can be used quite successfully to stimulate mastering these concepts.

The multiply handicapped may take part peripherally, but music has no right or wrong, no competition; thus security soon builds.

An excellent discussion of the benefits of movement in music is offered by Matteson in *The Music Educators Journal* for April, 1972.

Schneider reports that the largest single group of physically handicapped children in our society today is comprised of those suffering from cerebral palsy.

Clinical studies indicate that music and musical activities have a beneficial influence on the tension levels, proper breathing, destructibility, hypersensitivity, and affective tone of many children with cerebral palsy. For these children, music has the added benefit of attracting attention; building sensitivity and imagination; increasing concentration span, relaxation, and self-control; adding to feeling of belonging; and enhancing interpersonal relationships (Schneider, p. 136).

The *blind* or *partially seeing child* gains particular benefits from music, since other art forms are closed to him. Music can be a strong morale builder and satisfy the need for social recognition. Music has an instantaneous effect on internal status, it affects individuals in mood, temperament, and motivation (Margolin, 1976, p. 266). Often mobility is restricted because the blind child, isolated, hesitates to venture out. Because of the absence of visual stimuli, the blind child is characterized by bodily inaction and a retarded organization of physical faculties (Fraser, 1971, p. 115). Blind children usually have a distorted awareness of space and need reinforcement of spatial boundaries. Their limbs are usually bent and pulled in protectively. There is also fear of falling. Elevation is frightening and balance is difficult (Weisbrod, 1972, p. 68). Circle games are particularly well suited to building feelings of security and associations with peers. "Looby Lou," "Mulberry Bush," "Go In and Out the Window," "London Bridge," and "Farmer in the Dell" are excellent. Musical performance helps to get rid of "blindisms." There is discipline involved in performing music. Perhaps one of the most important aspects is that it can give something to someone else. When a blind child must accept favors most of the time, it is gratifying to him to be able to do something for others (Vernazza, p. 57).

Many blind children are now being exposed to keyboard instruments as well as rhythm instruments. Contemporary piano music is becoming available in Braille. Cascia's study of the status of general instrumental programs for the blind indicates that considerably more emphasis is being placed on music in schools for the blind than in other schools (Josepha, 1968, p. 114).

The sensory world of the blind and partially seeing child can be immeasurably extended through music.

The *deaf* or *hearing-impaired child* can enjoy and become more aware of the world about him through music. Deaf children often have a tendency to move with rather stiff, tense, and rigid motions. Superficial breathing patterns are common, with poor voice development and language problems the result. Musical activities help promote flexibility and relaxation.

Deaf children can participate in rhythmic activities, folk dances, and keyboard experiences. Ballet and simple folk dances are recommended as well as the use of piano, cymbals, records, accordion, guitar, and chord organ. The harp could offer an unusual experience; touch the vibrating strings and put the ears against the instrument to "hear" the music! Headsets can be used to amplify music to develop concepts of loud and soft, near and far, and high and low.

Encourage hearing-impaired and deaf children to play and feel the different instruments. Let a deaf child *feel* the vibrations. Have him clap along with other children at song time (Gramato, 1972).

Playing musical instruments also increases muscular strength and joint motion and develops coordination.

The deaf child can be helped to "learn" nursery rhymes by emphasizing the tactile sense, placing fingers on the lid of the piano to get vibrations or sitting on the floor near the piano or hearing the drum. Much repetition is necessary to feel the rhythm. Strong rhythmic actions such as marches, hopping, and skipping can make music a personal experience for the deaf child as well as improve bodily coordination and speech rhythm.

Although use of music with the deaf is mentioned as far back as 1802, little research has been reported on music and hearing-impaired children. Wecher's study of twelve profoundly deaf children found an increase in response and appreciation of music and progression from simple to more complex melody through the use of headphones with individual volume controls (Josepha, p. 118). When we consider the magnitude of the handicap of deafness, we see why music is not always emphasized. The child who is born profoundly deaf must have several years of highly specialized training before he has acquired the ability to communicate using language comparable to that of a normal 5-year-old child.

Since the development of clear speech is of paramount importance to all deaf children, speech is incorporated into all musical activities (Fahey and Birkenshaw, 1972, p. 45). Further investigation should encourage expansion of musical opportunities for the deaf. For an expanded discussion of music for the deaf, the reader is referred to Fahey and Birkenshaw.

The *speech-deficient child* needs the stimulus of music in his daily life. Both speech and songs have phrasing, rhythm, and emphasis; both may have rhyme and repetition (Kuhmarker, 1969, p. 157). Music sharpens the ear and aids in the development of *focused* listening skills, which in turn produce better speech. Learning to sing also sets up kinesthetic patterns in the throat that serve as clues for the child in a way that we do not fully understand (Kuhmarker, p. 160). These patterns then serve to develop effective speech. Listening to the sounds of words orients the child to hear accent, or stress, on certain syllables, loud and soft tones, tempo, and patterns that repeat themselves (Margolin, p. 268).

Nearly two thirds of children who are speech impaired suffer from articulation defects. When speaking or singing, sounds are distorted, substituted, or omitted, the most common being the *d*, *l*, *r*, and *s*. Songs that incorporate these sounds in a kind of speech game are useful.

Sing, sing, sing,	Ring around the rosy,
Say your name.	Sing your name.
Sing, sing, sing,	Ring around the rosy,
All the same.	Play the game.
Sally, Sally, Sally,	La, la, la,
Sing your name.	Ding, dong, ding.
Sally, Sally, Sally,	La, la, la,
Say your name.	Sing, sing, sing.
La, la, la,	M. RAMSEY
Sing, sing, sing.	
La, la, la,	
Ring, ring, ring.	

Cleft-palate speech, delayed speech, and stuttering are other defects in which music may help alleviate distress through relaxation of the muscles and vocal chords. In many cases, severe stutterers can sing with no evidence of defect yet stutter when speaking.

Many of the traditional, simple songs of early childhood offer excellent memory and speech training opportunities. The repetition, lively movement, and humor of such rhymes as "Three Blind Mice," "Row, Row, Row Your Boat," "Baa, Baa, Black Sheep," "This Old Man," "Pop Goes the Weasel," "Old MacDonald Had a Farm," "Ten Little Indians," "One, Two, Buckle My Shoe," and "Shoo, Fly" are favorites and particularly good with nonverbal children. In fact, the adult working with speech-deficient children might deliberately select songs that promote strong language and speech development. Even television commercials, jingles, and popular songs are appealing. Watch a group of young children enjoying and participating in "Sesame Street" or Saturday morning cartoons. Even the youngest quickly learns the sprightly tunes, and increased speech production is encouraged.

Taping the child's voice in speaking and singing and then using the playback also offer incentive to speech improvement. Louise Emery (1966, p. 266) reports the case of a nonverbal child with a strong response to music who was frustrated into speech by unfinished lines of his favorite song. The teacher sang these songs but stopped before the last word of the line. The child had to hear the line completed and supplied the omitted word himself! Thus singing stimulates speech.

Autistic children, as reported in the literature, appear to show unusual interest, and often talent, in music. Such children tend to come from very intelligent families and are most intolerant of direct human contact. Rhythmic activities and the pleasurable stimuli of music may lure the autistic child out of his shell (Euper, 1968, p. 184).

Aphasics, children with loss or impairment of the power to use or understand speech, seem to find new interest and strengthening of morale through singing and rhythms. The same simple repetitive songs with strong emotional appeal to the young child should be selected for the autistic and aphasic. From infancy on, participation in music builds good speech habits and patterns and provides the exceptional child a comfortable and enjoyable means of learning to alleviate deficiencies. Aphasics often reveal extreme physical rigidity, depression, and withdrawal. Movement and rhythmic activity will tend to relax and add vitality to these children.

THE INTELLECTUALLY "DIFFERENT" CHILD

The slow learner, the gifted, the culturally different, the perceptually handicapped, and the severely retarded can all profit from musical activities. Early identification of these special children can facilitate planning of appropriate programs for each. Many of these children are resistant to involvement. Guidance and support from adults provide the close contact, security, and encouragement so necessary to the intellectually handicapped.

For these children, music seems to have unique value as a teaching tool. Through song, the child is helped to recognize himself as a person, taught acceptable play contacts with other children, introduced to academic readiness, and given an opportunity to contribute to group activity (Emery, p. 266). Music develops self-confidence and opens up channels of communication.

Slow learners and *mentally retarded children* possess a minimum of ability to generalize and conceptualize. They do not, as a rule, initiate activities necessary for development (Happ, 1967, p. 33).

Graham (1972, p. 25) summarizes the musical achievement expectations of preschool mentally retarded children (0 to 5 years) as follows:

Trainable mentally retarded
- have poor motor development
- have minimal speech
- cannot learn "basic repertory" of rhythmic movements
- are likely to be completely unmusical
- apparently have little or no ability to sing
- have general reluctance to "experiment" with voice
- show little evidence of being able to listen to music for any length of time

Educable mentally retarded
- can learn to sing simple songs shortly after fourth birthday
- have pitch problems that are quite prevalent
- might listen to music that interests them for brief periods

Graham, as well as other authorities, believes that in the vast majority of cases the trainable child must be taught to enjoy music. In the teaching process, the adult must himself respond in a manner of excited, enthusiastic interest. The child then learns to value music by anticipating enthusiasm and excitement, thus growing musically as well as socially.

The retarded have fewer means for gratification from performance success and consequently suffer from lack of self-esteem. While enjoying a familiar tune, the retarded child is taught to pay attention, develop coordination through rhythms, discover innate abilities, improve in self-concept, and develop listening ability, spontaneous interest, and a desire to participate. In music, the child's rate of progress or lack of it is not aimed at comparison with others (Cameron, 1970, p. 32).

Sometimes the attitude of the adult caregiver restricts what these children can do and experience. Given a chance, the retarded can enjoy music.

There are many monotone singers among these special children. This may be due to slow development of the muscles governing the vocal chords and a weakness of muscular coordination. It is more apt to be a result of prolonged lazy listening, lack of perception, and an inability to understand what is required (Cameron, p. 33).

With slow learners, adults need to sing simple songs *directly* to the child, find songs appropriate to the age level, and use many illustrative and repetitive materials.

Old favorites such as "I'm a Little Teapot," "Humpty Dumpty," "Hickory, Dickory, Dock," "Sing a Song of Sixpence," "Little Miss Muffet," and "Little Bo-Peep" can be introduced with colorful illustrations and movement to facilitate learning.

Isern (1958, p. 164), reporting on a study of the influence of music on the memory of 104 mentally retarded children, stated that the feeling state of music apparently helped to reinforce, organize, and focus the attention of the children on the learning experience. For the very young slow learner, music can strengthen memory and concentration and train him to achieve.

Richard Weber, in a research project at Columbia, found that he could teach severely retarded children to play hand and orchestra instruments by giving them individual lessons. Using materials developed from only six tones, the children performed according to their own standards. Added respect, prestige, and lengthened attention span, as well as transfer to other areas, were other values (Vernazza, p. 57).

Levin and Levin (1972, pp. 31–34) report that the school district of Philadelphia has experimented with a team approach to music experience for the trainable mentally retarded. Drums, resonator bells, cymbals, zithers, and Autoharps have been used. Music with phrases or short phrases consisting of repeated tones in the same sequence is emphasized. Selections are brief, the length varying with the age and ability of the children. Music has proved a great ally in building on the learning potential of the retarded and extending emotional growth.

Listening is an important skill for the retarded. Many tire easily and have poor eye-hand coordination. Try wrist bells, sticks, wood blocks, and triangles, but do not mix rhythm instruments with singing (Ginglend and Stiles, 1965, p. 135).

With the retarded, rate of development is uneven, background is acquired at a slower pace, and musical experiences need to be repeated more often and in many different ways. Never be discouraged in working with the retarded child, since he may be absorbing and learning more than the responses reveal.

Almost all retarded children are either emotionally disturbed or emotionally immature. Songs that are happy, purposeful, and thoughtful can educate the emotions (Nordoff and Robbins, p. 32). Music, because it is nonverbal, may be a "magic wand" with the mentally retarded.

Rocking the body to music, clapping, and brisk stepping can be demonstrated by the adult and enjoyed by slow-learning children. A song such as "Row, Row, Row Your Boat" has strong appeal and coupled with movement invites participation. When a song is an action song, large muscle movements are additional reinforcement to memory (Kuhmarker, p. 260).

"Jack Be Nimble" can be chanted and acted out. Short phrases, familiar topics, strong rhythm, and repetition are most successful. Many authorities suggest that singing be the focal point for these children. Give ample opportunity to sing, particularly emphasizing enjoyment. The record player, piano, Autoharp, and chord organ have found a place in the lives of retarded children.

The musical achievement of the handicapped child is necessarily related to his condition, and very often he may not be able to achieve much in any field. Nevertheless, the musical results he achieves always reach deeper and wider than the standard of his performance would indicate (Cameron, p. 34).

During the last decade, another group of children having special needs has been identified—those with *learning disabilities* or *perceptually handicapped children.*

A learning disability (L.D.) is a subtle problem not as easily discovered as a physical handicap. Found usually in a child with a normal or higher IQ, it is a malfunctioning or immaturity of the central nervous system that affects the child's ability to receive, organize, store, and transmit information (Gilles, 1973, p. 1).

Such a child may show deficiencies in auditory or visual learning, have difficulty with concentration, coordination, directionalism, memory, and shutting out details, and may display inconsistent performance. Often L.D. children do not develop language and communication skills as rapidly as their peers.

Many children labeled hyperactive, hypoactive, immature, or unstable may, in fact, have perceptual problems. Often the behavior of this child is misunderstood, and the child may exhibit aggressiveness, withdrawal, or other social maladjustment.

The child with learning disabilities may well experience difficulty with music—performing with instruments, maintaining attention, or remembering melody lines. However, emphasis on enjoyment of music provides a common ground and basis for success.

Music can be a good background modifier for an L.D. child, but each child may need a special kind of music (Campbell, 1972, p. 39). The same music may not soothe all individuals. Some children will respond favorably, others adversely. The problems of each child are unique.

Make it possible for the child to experience music with his whole body whenever possible. Talk through all activities to be sure there is no misunderstanding. Demonstrate actions and new vocabulary when feasible. Watch carefully the activity level and the total room environment for distractors. Pace activities and use simple lyrics to help participation build slowly with less frustration. Proceed from the concrete to the abstract. With perceptually disabled children, adults need to be prepared for a slower rate of progress, a multifaceted approach to learning, and the need to develop broad general skills such as listening, attending, and speaking. Enjoyment, humor, simplicity, and repetition should characterize musical activities. The area of rhythm and time offers productive avenues for research in the learning characteristics of L.D. children (Campbell, p. 39).

The *neurologically handicapped child* is often described on the basis of his actions, and his disorder is confused with many other deficiencies. Behaviors are nearly always exaggerated, extreme, and persistent:

1. Rigidity—wanting everything to be as always: the same song, the same way, the same key and tempo; change disturbs and disorients
2. Hyperactivity—irritable attention; paying too

much attention to everything; unable to distinguish between important and less important

3. Emotional lability—inappropriate and extreme expressions, laughter

Those working with the neurologically handicapped report that such children often respond strongly to music. For many, music is the first medium that holds their attention and, until communication is established, sometimes the only one (Welsbacher, 1972, p. 27).

The *culturally different child* often brings with him a rich heritage of music and a budding appreciation of music. It behooves adults working with such a young child to explore and capitalize on the musical heritage and find ways of sharing the richness with all ethnic groups.

Perhaps of greatest importance is the reminder that most of the behavior patterns children learn are culture and family related. Thus the adult, well informed of the backgrounds of children in the group, will understand passivity on the part of some, nonverbal responses from others, fear of failure, bilingual exchanges, and the fact that some will seldom volunteer and others will not look directly at adults: the gamut of family expectations children bring with them.

Music is universal, and therein lies the appeal. It can cross boundaries, separating cultures, nationalities, and emotional differences. There is some form of musical expression attractive to each child. We need to develop awareness of both cultural differences and similarities. Often adults of the community can be used as resource persons to share the folk music, the dances, the musical instruments, and, yes, even some of the rhythms of the language "strange" to the ears.

The young child learns quickly, is eager for new experiences, will usually, if made to feel comfortable, participate willingly in small group situations, and strives to please. The culturally different young child can thrive and blossom in the nonpunitive, nonthreatening atmosphere music provides.

For some different children, music seems to be the first, and sometimes the only, group participation experience that can *consistently* interest them (Foster, 1965, p. 376).

Gifted children have needs common to all children. According to Passow, "There are no unique methods of teaching gifted children" (Leeper, 1965, p. 425). Enrichment offers the most for able children with stress on independent thinking and action.

Pitcher et al. (1974, p. 52) caution, "Never exploit a talented child; if he is made self-conscious, he may never try again." It is a temptation for any adult, on "discovery" of the musically talented child, to display that child and often expect more, forgetting that the child also has other needs.

The gifted child will usually seek out more activities, be stimulated toward more complex rhythms and lyrics, and often can be quite precocious with melody and instrumentation, enjoying keyboard activities and, in some cases, composing. However, the musically talented young child should enjoy his talent and participate fully in the normal activities of any young child.

Music for the gifted child must above all be geared to meet him at a level of complexity appropriate to his superior abilities; otherwise the child may grow up unaware of both his own and of music's capacity for mature expression. Vaughn (1972, pp. 70–72) suggests guidelines:

1. Do not view creative activities as substitutes but as alternative ways of expanding horizons.
2. Do not abandon all old procedures—use every approach.
3. Do not be afraid to structure things.
4. Do not be afraid to stand back and let things out of your personal control—stress quality.
5. Soak up all kinds of musical experiences yourself.
6. Be prepared for the fact that gifted children will outstrip you time and again, and more power to them.

Most important, parents and other adults need to be directed to whatever resources and enrichment opportunities exist within the community that will expand the musical interests of the gifted child. Often area libraries theater and dance groups for children, church groups and civic groups have much to offer. Remember, the child first, talent second.

ACTIVITIES FOR THE "SPECIAL CHILD"

We have said in many ways that the needs of exceptional children are similar to those of normal children. In music, most exceptional children will respond readily to the situation offered where enjoyment, participation, and self-esteem are paramount.

With the special child as with the normal child, the caregiver might structure:

1. Songs of identification—names, family, pets, etc.
2. Favorite songs—"Happy Birthday," "Good Morning," "I'm Pleased to See You," television jingles, rhymes, and family favorites

3. Action songs involving specific body parts and motions—clapping, rocking, hopping, and nodding
4. Circle games inviting participation with others
5. Music with humor or an element of surprise
6. Songs for special days or seasons
7. Songs that can incorporate rhythm instruments such as tone blocks, drum, sand blocks, and bells
8. Songs that are enhanced by props—balls, scarves, and puppets
9. Songs with definite rhythm, emotion, and repeated word phrases
10. Songs that require listening to directions

Very often the child will show the way in selecting and extending musical activities. Rhythmic activities make working together easier for child and adult because no words are needed; rhythm is the common bond. It is the wordless meaning of music that provides its potency and value (Gaston, 1968, pp. 18–23).

GENERAL GUIDELINES FOR HELPING "SPECIAL" CHILDREN

Although the same general guidelines for musical activities pertain to both normal and special children as discussed throughout the volume, authorities suggest some additional cautions and suggestions for the "special" child (Gramato, 1972).

1. Teach through activity.
2. Teach through many senses.
3. Teach at the appropriate *level* and *pace*.
4. Use repetition.
5. Avoid drastic changes of "gears."
6. Reduce distractions. Be aware of total environment.
7. Give directions in small steps.
8. Provide success-assured activities.
9. Do not overstimulate with too much loud and/or rhythmic music.
10. Keep in mind the child's level of language development and his social age.
11. Remember the short attention span of many of these children and/or other handicapping conditions.
12. Repeat songs taught in the *same* way until children are very familiar with them before trying variations.
13. Expect small successes, anticipate changes, be flexible.
14. Do not use rhythm instruments with a song until children know it well.
15. Exchange ideas with others who work and care for the special child. Find out "what works."

Be patient, be tender. For many exceptional young children, music can provide a beginning, an entrée into the world of other young children—a first opportunity to be with and be like others.

REFERENCES AND SUGGESTED READINGS

Alvin, J. *Music for the handicapped child.* London: Oxford University Press, 1965.

Bailey, Charity. Music and the beginning school child. *Young Children,* Washington D.C.: National Association for Education of Young Children, March 1966, **21**(4), 201–204.

Cameron, Rosaline. The uses of music to enhance the education of the mentally retarded. *Mental Retardation,* Albany, N.Y.: American Association on Mental Deficiency, February 1970, **8**(1), 32–34.

Campbell, Dorothy Drysdale. One out of twenty: the L.D. *Music Educators Journal,* April 1972, **58**(8), 38–39.

Chinn, Peggy L. The mentally retarded child during infancy and early childhood. In Philip C. Chinn, Clifford J. Drew, and Don R. Logan (Eds.), *Mental retardation: a life cycle approach.* St. Louis: The C. V. Mosby Co., 1975, pp. 115–135.

Coleman, Jack L., et al. *Music for exceptional children.* Evanston, Ill.: Summy-Birchard Co., 1964.

Cultural diversity. *Exceptional Children,* Washington, D.C.: The Council for Exceptional Children, May 1974, **40**(8). (Entire issue.)

Deno, Evelyn. Strategies for improvement of educational opportunities for handicapped children: suggestions for exploitation of the EPDA potential. In Maynard C. Reynolds and Malcolm D. Davis (Eds.), *Exceptional children in regular classrooms.* Minneapolis: Department of Audio-Visual Extension, University of Minnesota, 1971.

Diggs, Ruth W. Education across cultures. *Exceptional Children,* May 1974, **40**(8), 578–581.

Dobbs, J. P. B. *The slow learner and music: a handbook for teachers.* London: Oxford University Press, 1966.

Dunn, Lloyd M. (Ed.). *Exceptional children in the schools.* New York: Holt, Rinehart & Winston, 1963.

Emery, Louise. Use of standard materials with young disturbed children. *Exceptional Children,* Washington, D.C.: The Council for Exceptional Children, December 1966, **33**(4), 265–266.

Euper, Jo Ann. Early infantile autism. In E. Thayer Gaston (Ed.), *Music in therapy.* New York: The Macmillan Co., 1968.

Fahey, Joan Dahms, and Birkenshaw, Lois. Bypassing the ear:

the perception of music by feeling and touch. *Music Educators Journal,* April 1972, **58**(8), 44–49, 127.

Foster, Florence P. The song within: music and the disadvantaged preschool child. *Young Children,* Washington, D.C.: National Association for Education of Young Children, September 1965, **20**(6), 373–376.

Fraser, Louise Whitbeck. Music therapy as a basic program for the handicapped child. In Paul Nordoff and Clive Robbins (Eds.), *Music therapy in special education.* New York: The John Day Co., Inc., 1971.

Gaston, E. Thayer (Ed.). *Music in therapy.* New York: The Macmillan Co., 1968.

Gearheart, Bill, and Weisbahn, Mel. *The handicapped child in the regular classroom.* St. Louis: The C. V. Mosby Co., 1976.

Giacobbe, George A. Rhythm builds order in brain damaged children. *Music Educators Journal,* April 1972, **58**(8), 40–43.

Gilles, Dorothy C. Music and disabled children. *Lyons Teacher News,* Elmhurst, Ill.: Lyons Band, Spring 1973, **21**(3).

Gilles, Dorothy C., and Kovitz, Valerie. Helping learning disabled music students (Reprint). Evanston, Ill.: The Cove School, 1973.

Ginglend, David R., and Stiles, Winifred E. *Music activities for retarded children.* Nashville, Tenn.: Abingdon Press, 1965.

Graham, Richard M. Music therapy for the moderately retarded. In E. Thayer Gaston (Ed.), *Music in therapy.* New York: The Macmillan Co., 1968.

Graham, Richard M. Seven million plus need special attention. Who are they? *Music Educators Journal,* April 1972, **50**(8), 22–25.

Graham, Richard M. Special music education. In R. M. Graham (Ed.), *Music for the exceptional child.* Reston, Va.: Music Educators National Conference, 1975.

Gramato, Sam (Project manager). *Day care: serving children with special needs* (DHEW Publication No. [OCD] 73–1063). Washington, D.C.: U.S. Department of Health, Education, and Welfare, Office of Child Development, 1972.

Hamilton, Lucy. *Basic lessons for retarded children.* New York: The John Day Co., Inc., 1965.

Happ, F. William. Teaching aids for the mentally retarded child. *Mental Retardation,* Albany, N.Y.: American Association on Mental Deficiency, August 1967, **8**(1), 33–35.

Hendrick, Joanne. Working with exceptional children. In *The whole child: new trends in early education.* St. Louis: The C. V. Mosby Co., 1975, pp. 252–270.

Hildebrand, Verna. Creative music activities. In *Introduction to early childhood education.* New York: The Macmillan Co., 1971, pp. 230–259.

Hoem, Jean C. Don't dump the students who "can't do." *Music Educators Journal,* April 1972, **58**(8), pp. 29–30.

Isern, Betty. The influence of music upon the memory of mentally retarded children. In *Music therapy,* Parsons, Kan.: Parsons State Hospital and Training Center, 1958.

Josepha, Sister M., O.S.F. Music therapy for the physically disabled. In E. Thayer Gaston (Ed.), *Music in therapy.* New York: The Macmillan Co., 1968.

Kirk, Samuel A. *Educating exceptional children.* Boston: Houghton Mifflin Co., 1962.

Kondorossy, Elizabeth Davis. Music speaks for the handicapped. *The Oberlin Alumni Magazine,* April, 1965.

Kuhmarker, Lisa. Music in the beginning reading program. *Young Children,* Washington: National Association for Education of Young Children, January 1969, **24**(3), 157–163.

Leeper, Sarah Hammond, et al. *Good schools for young children* (2nd. ed.). New York: The Macmillan Co., 1965.

Levenson, Dorothy. Aesthetic education in the classroom. *Teacher,* December 1976, **94**(4), 31.

Levin, Herbert D., and Levin, Gail M. Instrumental music: a great ally in promoting self-image. *Music Educators Journal,* April 1972, **50**(8), 31–34.

Margolin, Edythe. A world of music for young children. In *Young children: their curriculum and learning processes.* New York: Macmillan Publishing Co., Inc., 1976.

Matteson, Carol A. Finding the self in space. *Music Educators Journal,* April 1972, **58**(8), 63–65.

Mills, S. R. *A source guide for the special child: learning activities and music and fun with instruments,* 1976. Sherry R. Mills, 2220 Glenwood Circle, Colorado Springs, Colorado 80909.

Nordoff, Paul, and Clive Robbins. *Music therapy for handicapped children.* Blauvert, N.Y.: Rudolf Steiner Publisher, 1965.

Nordoff, Paul, and Clive Robbins. *Music therapy in special education.* New York: The John Day Co., Inc., 1971.

Painter, Genevieve. The effect of a rhythmic and sensory motor activity program on perceptual motor spatial abilities of kindergarten children. *Exceptional Children,* October 1966, **33**(2), 113–136.

Pitcher, Evelyn Goodenough, et al. Learning problems in the classroom. In *Helping young children learn* (2nd. ed.). Columbus, Ohio: Charles E. Merrill Publishing Co., 1974, pp. 167–185.

Purvis, Jennie, and Samet, Shelley. *Music in developmental therapy.* Baltimore: University Park Press, 1976.

Reynolds, Maynard C., and Davis, Malcolm D. *Exceptional children in regular classrooms.* Minneapolis: Department of Audio-Visual Extension, University of Minnesota, 1971.

Schneider, Erwin H. The cerebral palsied: music therapy for the cerebral palsied. In E. Thayer Gaston (Ed.), *Music in therapy.* New York: The Macmillan Co., 1968.

Todd, Vivian Edmiston, and Heffernan, Helen. *The year before school: guiding preschool children* (2nd. ed.). New York: The Macmillan Co., 1970.

Torrance, E. Paul. *Encouraging creativity in the classroom*

Dubuque, Iowa: William C. Brown Co., Publishers, 1970.

Van Osdol, William R., and Shane, Don G. Trends in the field of special education. In *An introduction to exceptional children.* Dubuque, Iowa: William C. Brown Co., Publishers, 1974.

Vaughn, Margery M. Music for gifted children: a bridge to consciousness. *Music Educators Journal,* April 1972, **58**(8), 70–72.

Vernazza, Marcelle. What are we doing about music in special education? *Music Educators Journal,* April 1967, **53**(8), 55–58.

Weisbrod, Jo Anne. Shaping a body image through movement therapy. *Music Educators Journal,* April 1972, **58**(8), 66–69.

Welsbacher, Betty T. The neurologically handicapped child: more than a package of bizarre behaviors. *Music Educators Journal,* April 1972, **58**(8), 26–28.

Witty, Paul A. (Ed.). *The educationally retarded and disadvantaged.* The Sixty-sixth Yearbook of the National Society for the Study of Education. Chicago: University of Chicago Press, 1967.

6 Music through the day

Children's musical learning is inseparable from other learnings in that they all take place at the same time and also follow the same general pattern of development.

Chandler, 1970, p. 9

We know that music is an integral part of children,
and we know that we strive to develop the total child.
Thus music becomes a natural part of the young child's
environment wherever experiences to stimulate learning
occur. The adult working with the young child has
countless opportunities to integrate music as a daily
event. Music at any age cannot be relegated to *only*
special times. Awareness is the key.

THE TOTAL ENVIRONMENT

Whether the young child is in the home, a day-care
center, a preschool, or with a group of other young
children in an informal setting, music can be part of the
environment.

A caring, understanding adult is perhaps the most
significant factor in promoting an environment condu-
cive to musical growth and experiences. Knowledge of
the children, a love for and strong acquaintance with a
variety of music, flexibility, sensitivity, alertness, and a
belief in the creative potential of children are desirable
characteristics.

The physical setting, too, is important. A warm, colorful, attractive space in which the young child can feel at
home frees each one to enjoy, to discover, and to try out
music in all its forms. Ample space promotes easy
movement, dance, and rhythmic activity. Light, color,
and access to the out-of-doors influence mood and emotions.

"Children who feel secure are more likely to venture forth, try new experiences, and express themselves in creative ways than are children who are using up their energy by worrying or being frightened or anxious" (Hendrick, 1975, p. 151).

Accessibility of materials—simple rhythm instruments, a record player with a good stock of records, a piano or Autoharp, or, in the home, materials to make instruments—will encourage music as part of the child's day.

The home is the beginning of music for the infant, the toddler, and the young child. We have discussed the early months and years and the impact of the mother and other adults on musical development. Attitude is all-important. Does the mother sing and hum to the child when they are together or working? Do the parents or caregivers enjoy music in all its forms? Is music valued? Is listening to music encouraged? Does the child have a corner for a record player and records? On occasion, does the family participate in musical events, fairs, or festivals? Is there a receptivity and enthusiasm for melody, and is the young child applauded for early attempts to "make" music?

Taylor (1970, p. 21) says, "There isn't anything quite so delightful as seeing a young child wholly absorbed in expressing himself creatively."

One of us (M. R.) shared the delight of all onlookers at a Romanian wedding when, as a professional singer was entertaining the bridal couple and about a hundred guests, a small, curly-haired Romanian moppet about 3 years old, in all her beruffled wedding finery, advanced to center stage, danced and clapped in perfect rhythm before all, and, of course, upstaged the singer! Applause and merriment followed the child as she skipped back to her parents. She had added her good wishes in her own best way.

Chandler (p. 9) echoes this child's efforts as she writes, "The roots of children's earliest music are their rhythmic bodily movements and the sounds which they make or which come from their surroundings. These beginnings of music and of movement are never absent from the child."

Hildebrand (1971, p. 231), too, states that enjoyment is the first requirement. Any demand for perfection has no place at this young age. Music for these years is an action art, as opposed to spectator or performing art.

The young dancer at the wedding responded to the environment and moved out naturally to the music. She expressed joy in being alive.

As the child ventures out into the setting of the day-care center, the preschool, or the kindergarten, again the sensitive, aware adult must provide the opportunities for growth and participation in music. From the well-known "Good Morning, Good Morning" to perhaps "Happy Birthday" to "Lullaby, and Good Night," music and sound permeate the day.

Many educators strongly believe that music should be a daily event in every preschool—that only through the inclusion of music can the total capacity of the child be known.

Think of ways music can be added to the day. Listen as children talk and work together. Do the children chant as they work?

> When children sing as they finger paint, rock a doll, hammer at a carpenter's bench, or build with blocks, you know they are happy and that music is an expression of their sense of well being. When they experiment with drums, sticks, cymbals, bells and other instruments, you realize that they are exploring different kinds of sounds and patterns, discovering the basic elements from which music is made (McCall, 1971, p. 6).

The boundless enthusiasm and spontaneity of the preschool child in reaction to exciting sounds and music is a distinct advantage. Adults can build on these qualities to enrich the daily living of the young child.

Sheehy (1968, pp. 12–13) believes that children have unlimited imagination. They continually use sound to make their play more realistic. They do not imitate, they *become.* Sheehy feels that we are blind and deaf to the vigor and vitality of the music children have within themselves.

In the many suggestions offered by Pitcher et al. (1974, p. 45), we find the phrase, "Everyone who has worked with young children knows that, at the preschool level, music is better caught than taught!" Included in the suggestions are the following:

- action songs
- personal songs
- transition songs
- songs of dramatic play
- humorous songs
- singing games
- original calls
- chants
- narrative songs

What a wealth of opportunity for the imaginative adult to provide music throughout the day!

There is no limit to the themes that appeal to children:

- other children
- the family
- the home and pets
- machines
- holidays
- food
- birds
- friends
- growing things
- seasons and weather
- shopping
- "me"

However, in planning music for young children, we must think first of the child and his interests and needs, and then we must study each child as an individual. Sheehy (p.21) also cautions that children use music functionally and, unless we have a broad understanding of it, we are likely to "educate it out of them."

GUIDED, PLANNED MUSICAL EXPERIENCES

Informal, spontaneous musical moments are to be valued as the young child grows. Coupled with such "serendipity" are those guided, planned experiences throughout the day when definite effort is made to extend and enhance other learning. There are few academic areas that cannot be enriched through music.

Music has an integrity of its own. There should be nothing contrived, nothing artificial, no "stretching" to make a point in whatever the academic area. Select only musical experiences that enhance the concepts being presented. A child will quickly sense what is false. Above all, remember that, for the young child, enjoyment and appreciation should be uppermost.

Let us consider then some possibilities in the respective academic areas that might comprise part of the day's activities for the child in a preschool or kindergarten setting in which music might naturally occur.

MATHEMATICS

Every young child enjoys numbers and counting. They are part of the adult world to be mastered; a feeling of power results. Order and categorization appeal to the child; sequence builds memory. Listen to and observe the young child singing and learning the following:

"One, Two, Buckle My Shoe"
"This Little Pig Went to Market"
"Ten Little Indians"
"This Old Man"
"Three Blind Mice"
"Three Little Kittens"
"Baa, Baa, Black Sheep"
"Sing a Song of Sixpence"
"As I Was Going to St. Ives"
"Hot Cross Buns"
"One for the Money"

Each of the following songs provides an exciting way to develop the concept of numbers.

ONE, TWO, BUCKLE MY SHOE

Traditional
Arranged by K. BAYLESS

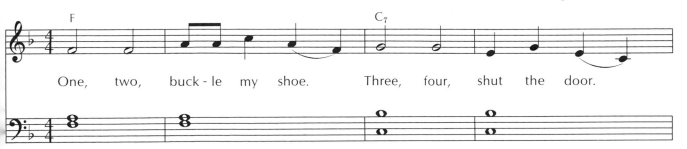

One,   two,   buck - le   my   shoe.   Three,   four,   shut   the   door.

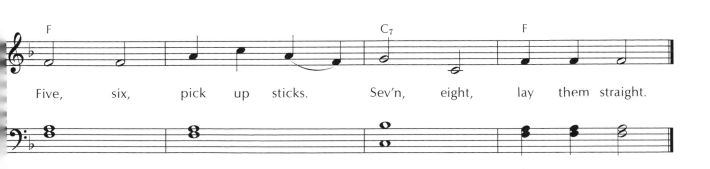

Five,   six,   pick   up   sticks.   Sev'n,   eight,   lay   them   straight.

ONE, TWO, THREE, FOUR, FIVE

M. RAMSEY

K. BAYLESS

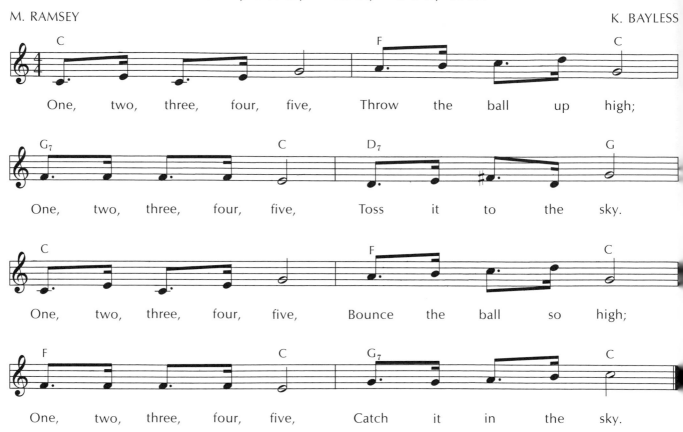

One, two, three, four, five, Throw the ball up high;

One, two, three, four, five, Toss it to the sky.

One, two, three, four, five, Bounce the ball so high;

One, two, three, four, five, Catch it in the sky.

(As the song is sung, children do the actions.)

TEN LITTLE INDIANS

American folk air

Arranged by K. BAYLESS

1. One lit - tle, two lit - tle, three lit - tle In - dians,

Four lit - tle, five lit - tle, six lit - tle In - dians,

Seven lit - tle, eight lit - tle, nine lit - tle In - dians,

Ten lit - tle In - dian boys.

en little, nine little, eight little Indians,
even little, six little, five little Indians,
our little, three little, two little Indians,
ne little Indian boy.

ACTIVITIES

1. This is an action-type song. It may be sung as a finger play. The child holds up both fists, fingers and thumbs tucked in and the backs of the hands toward the body. The corresponding number of fingers and thumbs are held up as the count goes to ten. As the second verse is sung, one finger at a time is tucked away.

2. When the children are old enough to count from one to ten, the song may be sung as an action game. Choose ten children. Number them from one to ten. As each numeral is sung, the child representing that numeral stands up until all are standing. Sing the second verse and have each child sit down in order.

3. Children or teacher writes the numerals from 1 to 10 on pieces of cardboard. As each child's numeral is sung, the cardboard showing that numeral is held up. On the second verse, the order is reversed and the cardboards are put down.

ONE ELEPHANT

Singing game

Arranged and adapted by K. BAYLESS

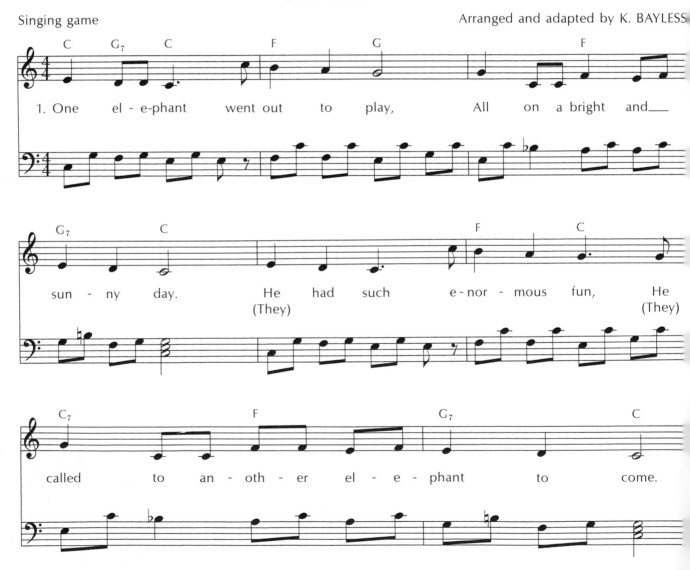

2. Two elephants went out to play

3. Three elephants went out to play, etc.

SUGGESTIONS

After each verse is sung, have the children call out in singing fashion for the next elephant to come. Have them sing "éléphant" (French word for elephant). Sing the syllables of the word "éléphant" as follows:

él - é - phant

One could also use the Spanish, Italian, etc. words for elephant. Children love calling out for the next elephant in different languages.

ACTIONS ("Johnny Works with One Hammer")

Verse 1: Pound on right knee with right fist in time with music.
Verse 2: Add left fist; pound on left knee.
Verse 3: Add right foot; tap on floor.
Verse 4: Add left foot; tap on floor.
Verse 5: Add head; nod up and down. On words "goes to sleep," stop pounding, drop head, or lie down on floor and rest.

JOHNNY WORKS WITH ONE HAMMER*

Folk song

Arranged by K. BAYLESS

John - ny works with one ham - mer, one ham - mer, one ham - mer,

John - ny works with one ham - mer, Then he works with two.

2

Johnny works with two hammers,
two hammers, two hammers,
Johnny works with two hammers,
Then he works with three.

3

Johnny works with three hammers,
three hammers, three hammers,
Johnny works with three hammers,
Then he works with four.

4

Johnny works with four hammers,
four hammers, four hammers,
Johnny works with four hammers,
Then he works with five.

5

Johnny works with five hammers,
five hammers, five hammers,
Johnny works with five hammers,
Then he goes to sleep.

Music: a way of life for the young child

SCIENCE

Involvement with science is active. Few children remain uninterested when we deal with the world about us. Science learning can be extended in many ways through music. Consider these possibilities:

- animal songs
- seasons
- color
- plants

- the child
- the body
- growing up
- food

- indoors and out-of-doors
- senses
- weather

In fact, the adult will have a difficult time delineating the uses of music with science. The world about is an exciting and mysterious place to the young child. His curiosity is ever present, and the need to know, imperative. Everything must be done and learned—*telling* the child will not suffice. (For excellent ideas and suggestions, review Barbara Taylor's *A Child Goes Forth* and *When I Do, I Learn*.)

Music and science go hand in hand. Awareness of the world about us can be greatly extended through song.

COLOR GAME

Words and music by K. BAYLES

If you have on red, touch your head. If you have on green, blink your eyes in-stead. If you have on yel-low, wave your hand. Is-n't it a fun game? Let's do it a-gain.

Work with children to add extra verses.

84

ECHO GAME

Words and music by K. BAYLESS

Hoo - hoo-hoo, Hoo - hoo-hoo, Do you hear me call - ling you?

Hoo - hoo-hoo, Hoo - hoo-hoo Is our ech - o game for two.

HEAR THE RAIN

M. RAMSEY

K. BAYLESS

Staccato

Drip, drip, drip, drip, drip, drip, Hear the rain come down.

Drip, drip, drip, drip, drip, drip, All_____ o - ver town.

THE NORTH WIND

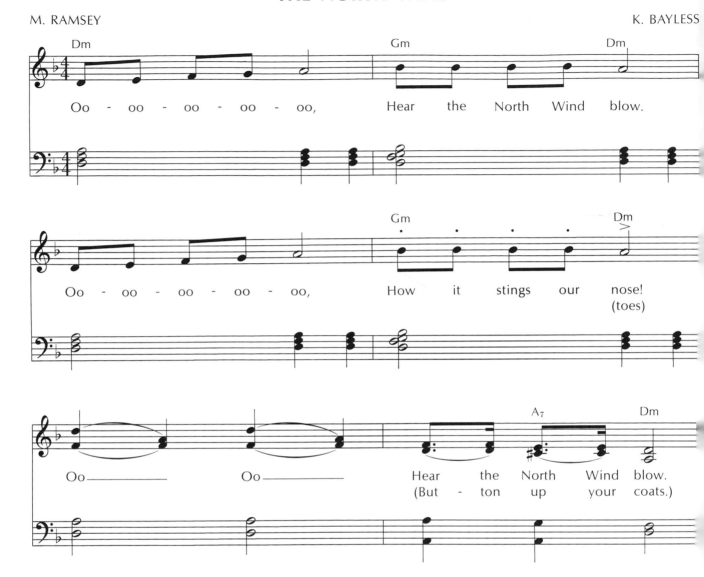

M. RAMSEY

K. BAYLESS

Oo - oo - oo - oo - oo, Hear the North Wind blow.

Oo - oo - oo - oo - oo, How it stings our nose!
(toes)

Oo ———— Oo ———— Hear the North Wind blow.
(But - ton up your coats.)

Snow

Sung to tune of "Row, Row, Row Your Boat"

Look, look, see the snow,
  See it falling down;
Swirling, swirling, swirling, swirling
  All around the town.

Look, look, see the snow,
  Cold and very white;
Swirling, swirling, swirling, swirling
  All through the night.

M. RAMSEY

Many of the traditional nursery rhymes extend sc:
ence learning and discussion:

"Pussy Willow"   "Kitty"
"Little Miss Muffet"   "Beehives"
"Eensy, Weensy Spider"   "The Animal Store
"My Turtle"   "My Shadow"

Following is a traditional song with a tinge of scienc
that children enjoy:

EENSY, WEENSY SPIDER

Traditional   Traditional

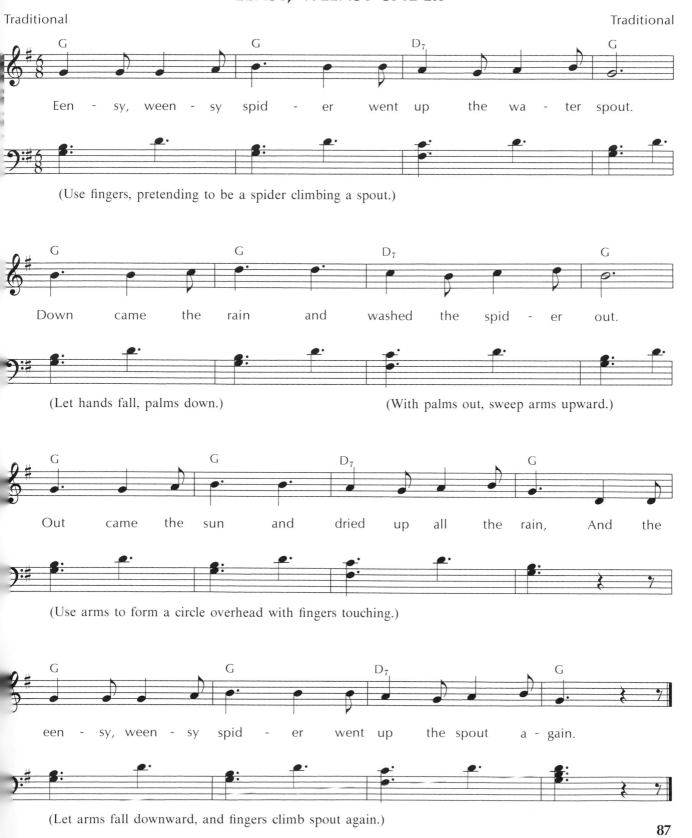

Een - sy, ween - sy spid - er went up the wa - ter spout.

(Use fingers, pretending to be a spider climbing a spout.)

Down came the rain and washed the spid - er out.

(Let hands fall, palms down.)   (With palms out, sweep arms upward.)

Out came the sun and dried up all the rain, And the

(Use arms to form a circle overhead with fingers touching.)

een - sy, ween - sy spid - er went up the spout a - gain.

(Let arms fall downward, and fingers climb spout again.)

Music: a way of life for the young child

Pussy Willow

Key of C   Traditional song

Sing each line on the letter of the scale indicated. Begin on middle C and sing upward, until "Meow," then sing downward.

I know a little pussy, Her	C
coat is silver gray, She	D
lives down in the meadow, Not	E
very far away, Al-	F
though she is a pussy, She'll	G
never be a cat, For	A
she's a pussy willow, Now,	B
what do you think of that?	C
Meow C	
Meow B	
Meow A	
Meow G	
Meow F	
Meow E	
Meow D	
Meow C (middle C)	

SCAT!!!

(The word "SCAT" is sung an octave above the last "Meow.")

Leeper, in *Good Schools for Young Children* (1963: 361–368), provides an excellent developmental sequence of musical activities for young children that gives us a yardstick for selection.

Animal themes reflected in poetry and song can be used to extend science learnings.

My Puppy

I'm looking for my puppy;
He is lost, you see.
I'm looking for my puppy.
Where can he be?

I need to find my puppy;
He's my friend, you see.
Have you seen my puppy?
Bring him back to me.

I'm looking for my puppy;
Freddie is his name.
Help me find my puppy.
Bring him home again.

Oh, he's home again!

M. RAMSEY

Mouse

I saw a little furry mouse
Hiding by the door.
He was the nicest little mouse
To come into the store.

I liked the little furry mouse,
But Mama said, "Now scat."
"Don't let him get into the cheese
Before I get the cat!"

I saw the little furry mouse
Hide behind the door.
He could have been a friend to me,
But Mama said, "No more!"

M. RAMSEY

Cat

My cat is furry,
All in black,
Golden eyes that shine,
Purring, purring,
Silky, soft.
Gee, I'm glad he's mine!

M. RAMSEY

BARNYARD FAMILY

American folk song

Arranged by K. BAYLESS

1. I have a lit-tle roost-er by the barn - yard gate, And that lit-tle roost-er is my play-mate, And that lit-tle roost-er goes cock - a-doo-dle-doo, Doo - doo,____ doo - doo,____ doo - doo - dle doo.

2.
have a little hen by the barnyard gate,
And that little hen is my playmate,
And that little hen goes cluck, a-cluck-a-cluck,
cluck-cluck, cluck-cluck, cluck-cluck-a-cluck.

3
I have a little duck by the barnyard gate,
And that little duck is my playmate,
And that little duck goes quack-a-quack-a-quack,
Quack-quack, quack-quack, quack-quack-a-quack, etc.

MAMMA KANGAROO

M. RAMSEY

K. BAYLESS

I am Mam-ma Kang-a - roo, Like to see me jump? I can take a great big leap

up a - bove this hump. I am Mam-ma Kang - a - roo, Peek in - to my pock - et____.

This is ba - by Kang - a - roo, Sleep - ing in my pock - et____.

OLD MACDONALD HAD A FARM

Traditional

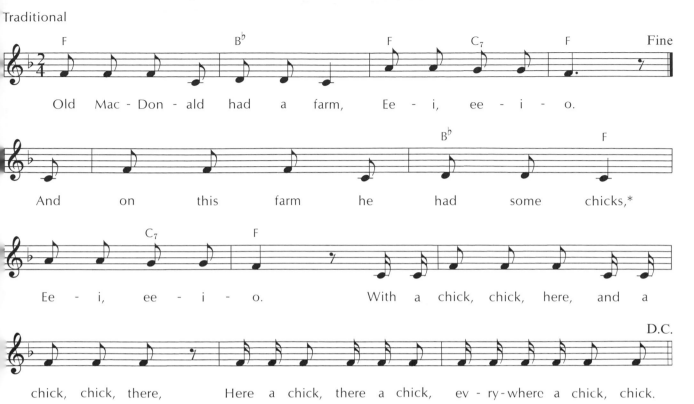

Old Mac - Don - ald had a farm, Ee - i, ee - i - o.

And on this farm he had some chicks,*

Ee - i, ee - i - o. With a chick, chick, here, and a

chick, chick, there, Here a chick, there a chick, ev - ry - where a chick, chick.

*With other verses, add ducks, pigs, cows, etc.

MY FARM FRIENDS

Words and music by K. BAYLESS

One day I went to vis - it a farm and walked and walked a -

long the way. I looked and saw a friend - ly (duck), and then I heard it

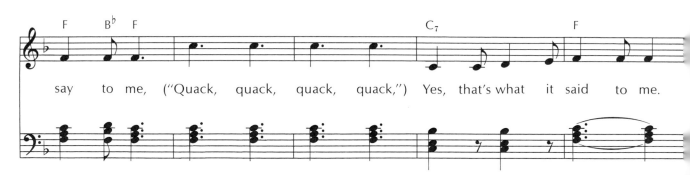

say to me, ("Quack, quack, quack, quack,") Yes, that's what it said to me.

Additional verses may be sung by using names of other farm animals and the
sounds they make.

SIX LITTLE DUCKS*

Folk song from Maryland

Arranged by K. BAYLESS

1. Six lit-tle ducks that I once knew, Fat ones, skin-ny ones, fair ones too. But the

one lit-tle duck with a feath-er on his back, He led the oth-ers with a

quack, quack, quack! quack, quack, quack! quack, quack, quack! He led the oth-ers with a quack, quack, quack!

Down to the river they would go,
Wibble, wabble, wibble, wabble to and fro.
Refrain

3
Home from the river they would come,
Wibble, wabble, wibble, wabble, ho, hum, hum.
Refrain

MY DOG RAGS

Unknown

I've got a dog, his name is Rags, He eats so much that his

tum - my sags. His ears flip - flop and his tail wig - wags, and

when he walks he zigs and zags. Flip - flop, wig - wag, zig - zag.

Flip - flop, wig - wag, zig - zag. He does - n't have an - y

ped - i - gree, But I love him, and he loves me.

Flip - flop, wig - wag, zig - zag. Flip - flop, wig - wag,

zig - zag. Flip - flop, wig - wag, zig - zag.

HAND MOTIONS

On words "flip-flop," flip left hand over head, then right hand over head.

On words "wig-wag," put hands together in back of you. Flip them to the left and then to the right of the body.

On words "zig-zag," bend over, hands on hips. Bend the body to the left and then to the right.

94

SOCIAL STUDIES

Music and the social studies go hand in hand. Special days and holidays are celebrated with music. People and their activities are studied, as is the community. The present is more important than the future to the child. What is nearby attracts and holds his attention. People and events that touch the life of the child hold most appeal. Family groups and community groups build meaning into observances and festivals of all kinds. The young child can find his own ways of knowing and celebrating through music.

Halloween, jack-o'-lanterns, and witches; Indians, turkeys, and Thanksgiving; birthdays; the country's Bicentennial; Christmas and the magic surrounding that day; Easter; valentines; Hanukkah; patriotic music, stirring marches, and the music of the many ethnic groups that inhabit the nation; the world of work—all speak in the language of music to the young child as horizons expand.

The following themes are dear to the heart of a young child:

Clowns

Here come the clowns.
See all the fun,
Shiny red noses,
Big tummy tums.
Here come the clowns.
See how they run.
Maybe my mother
Would let me be one!

M. RAMSEY

Or try the same poem in song on p. 96.

HERE COME THE CLOWNS

M. RAMSEY

K. BAYLESS

Here come the clowns. See all the fun, Shin-y red nos-es, Big tum-my tums.

Here come the clowns. See how they run. May-be my moth-er would let me be one!

New Shoes for Me

My daddy bought me new shoes,
   New shoes, new shoes.
My daddy bought me new shoes.
   I'm so proud!

Now I'll learn to tie them,
   Tie them, tie them.
Now I'll learn to tie them,
   And *he'll* be proud!

M. RAMSEY

New Wagon

My new wagon has four wheels.
It has a handle too.
There is a place for us to sit,
Just for me and you.

My new wagon has four wheels.
I got it just today.
There is a place for us to sit,
So hurry, come and play.

M. RAMSEY

Toys

When Mom and I go shopping,
I only look at toys.
She always says, "Now, Mary,
Those are for the boys."

But cars and trains and missiles
Are really lots of fun;
It does seem a bit unfair
I can't buy every one!

M. RAMSEY

Shopping

What would you buy,   What would you buy,
What would you buy,   What would you buy,
What would you buy   What would you buy
At the store?   At the store?
Ice cream and candy   Puppies and kittens
And peppermint sticks.   And goldfish and snai
What would you buy   *That* I would buy at
   at the store?   the store!

M. RAMSEY   M. RAMS

SHINY NEW SHOES

Words and music by K. BAYLESS

(Tom) has new shoes all shin-y and bright, One for his left foot, One___ for his right. He can run and
(Substitute children's names)   (her)   (her)   (She)

jump with them, hop and skip and leap,   Then at night he puts them by his bed and goes to sleep.
(she)   (her)

97

IF YOU'RE HAPPY

Traditional

Arranged by K. BAYLESS

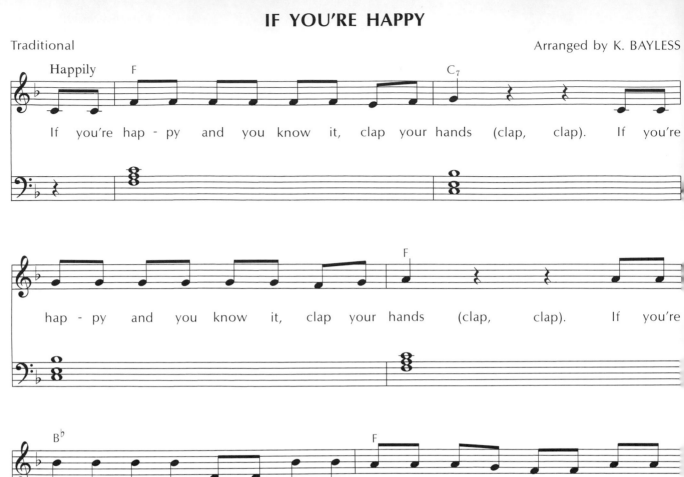

2. If you're happy and you know it, stamp your feet.
3. If you're happy and you know it, nod your head.

4. If you're happy and you know it, swing around.
5. If you're happy and you know it, shout out loud!

Have children create their own verses.

BROWNIE SMILE SONG*

HARRIET E. HEYWOOD

Melody by Ms. Heywood's Brownie
Girl Scout troop

1. I've some-thing in my pock - et. It be - longs a - cross my face, And I
2. I'm sure you could-n't guess it If you guessed a long, long while, So I'll

keep it ver - y close at hand in a most con - ve - nient place.
take it out and put it on-- It's a great big Brown - ie Smile!

(May substitute "happy" for "Brownie")

THEODORE

M. RAMSEY

K. BAYLESS

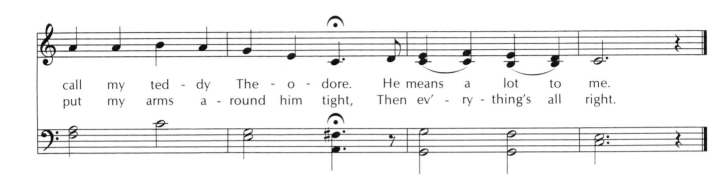

1. I have a fuz - zy ted - dy bear, As cud - dly as can be._____ I
2. I take my ted - dy bear to bed,_____ Each and ev' - ry night._____ I

call my ted - dy The - o - dore. He means a lot to me.
put my arms a - round him tight, Then ev' - ry - thing's all right.

GUESS WHO?

Words and music by K. BAYLESS

Hel - lo, lis - ten, tell us, please,

Whos' lost a front tooth, let_____ us_____ see.
dee - dle, dee - dle dee.

GOOD MORNING, BOYS AND GIRLS

M. RAMSEY

K. BAYLESS

Good morn - ing, boys and girls, Good morn - ing, boys and girls. We're

here to work, we're here to play, Let's have a hap - py day.
(see your smil - ing face.)

AMERICA, WE LOVE YOU

Words and music by K. BAYLESS

Proudly

A - mer - i - ca, A - mer - i - ca, We are so proud of you. We'll

give a cheer for our coun - try's flag, The red, white, and the blue!

Spoken cheer optional: America, America, *We - love - you* !!!

BATTLE HYMN OF THE REPUBLIC

JULIA WARD HOWE

Music attributed to WILLIAM STEFFE
Arranged by K. BAYLESS

Glo - ry, glo - ry, hal - le - lu - ia! Glo - ry, glo - ry, hal - le - lu - ia!

Glo - ry, glo - ry, hal - le - lu - ia, His truth is march - ing on!

HAPPY BIRTHDAY

K. BAYLESS

German folk tune
Arranged by K. BAYLESS

Hap - py birth - day, Hap - py birth - day, Hap - py birth - day to you, Hap - py

birth - day, Hap - py birth - day, A - mer - i - ca we LOVE YOU!

JACK-O'-LANTERN

Words and music by K. BAYLESS

Happily

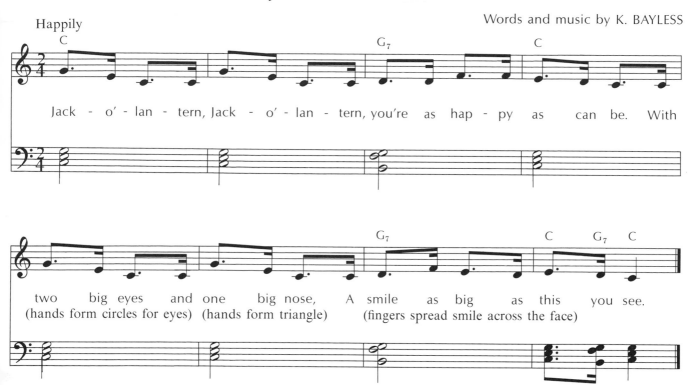

Jack - o' - lan - tern, Jack - o' - lan - tern, you're as hap - py as can be. With

two big eyes and one big nose, A smile as big as this you see.
(hands form circles for eyes) (hands form triangle) (fingers spread smile across the face)

BOO! BOO!

Words and music by K. BAYLESS

I'll scare some folks on Hal-lo-ween night, and this is what I'll do, I'll

run and hide be-hind the gate, And then I'll shout, "BOO!! BOO!!"*
(bush)

*Help children discover that the melody in the second line is like the first.

BLACK CAT

M. RAMSEY

K. BAYLESS

Black cat's eyes are shin - y; Black cat's eyes are green;

Black cat's tail is snap - ping, 'Cuz it's Hal - lo - ween!

HIYAH, HIYAH

Words and music by K. BAYLESS

Hi - yah, hi - yah, Hi - yah, hi - yah, beat up - on our drums.

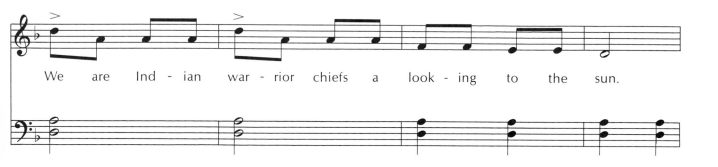

We are Ind - ian war - rior chiefs a look - ing to the sun.

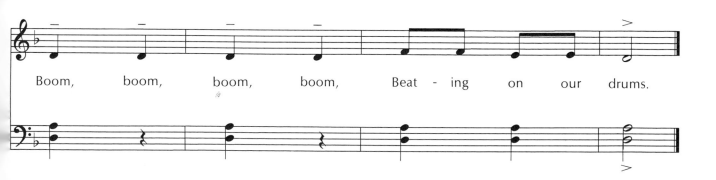

Boom, boom, boom, boom, Beat - ing on our drums.

*Left-hand chords may be played an octave lower.

MR. TURKEY

Words and music by K. BAYLESS

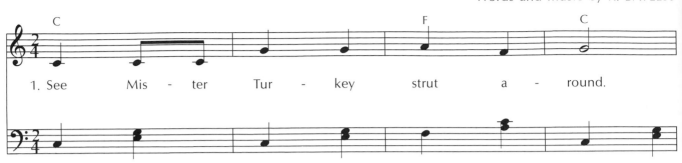

1. See Mis - ter Tur - key strut a - round.

Gob - ble, gob - ble, gob - ble, gob - ble is his fun - ny sound.

2
See Mister Turkey, he's so fat.
Wibble, wobble, wibble, wobble, round he goes like that.

SANTA'S HELPERS

Children's song

Arranged by K. BAYLESS

(First line use rhythm sticks.)

(Second line use bell instruments.)

(Rhythm sticks)

(Rhythm sticks and bell instruments)

UP ON THE HOUSETOP

Traditional

Arranged by K. BAYLESS

1. Up on the house-top the rein-deer pause. Out jumps good old

San-ta Claus; Down through the chim-ney with lots of toys,

All for the lit-tle ones'___ Christ-mas joys. Ho, ho, ho! who would-n't go!

Chorus

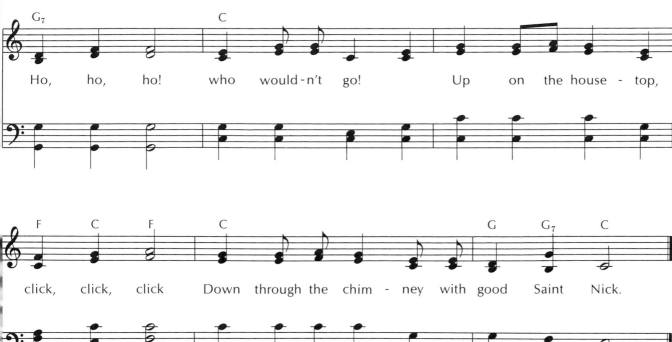

Ho, ho, ho! who would-n't go! Up on the house - top,

click, click, click Down through the chim - ney with good Saint Nick.

2
First comes the stocking of little Nell.
Oh, dear Santa, fill it well;
Give her a dolly that laughs and cries,
One that can open and shut its eyes.
Chorus

3
Look in the stocking of little Bill.
Oh, just see what a glorious fill!
Here is a hammer and lots of tacks,
Whistle and ball and a whip that cracks.
Chorus

Our Snowman

Source unknown

Sung to the tune of "This Old Man"

Our snowman
Stands so tall.
We just made him from snowballs
With a big black hat to shade him from the sun.
Making him was so much fun!!

VALENTINE, VALENTINE, WON'T YOU BE MINE?

Words and music by K. BAYLESS

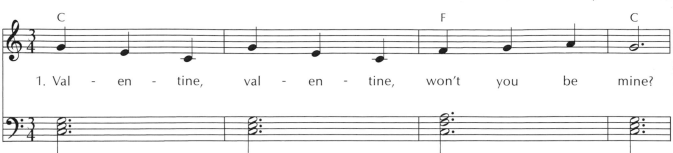

1. Val - en - tine, val - en - tine, won't you be mine?

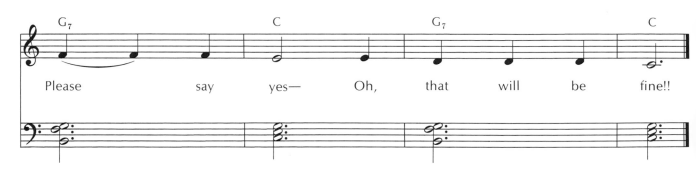

Please say yes— Oh, that will be fine!!

2
Valentine, valentine, won't you be mine?
This is the way you make the sign.
   (Make the shape of a heart by placing knuckles together with thumbs touching to form the shape.)

THE EASTER BUNNY IS COMING SOON

Words and music by K. BAYLESS

HOT CROSS BUNS

Nursery rhyme
Adapted by K. BAYLESS

Traditional
Arranged by K. BAYLESS

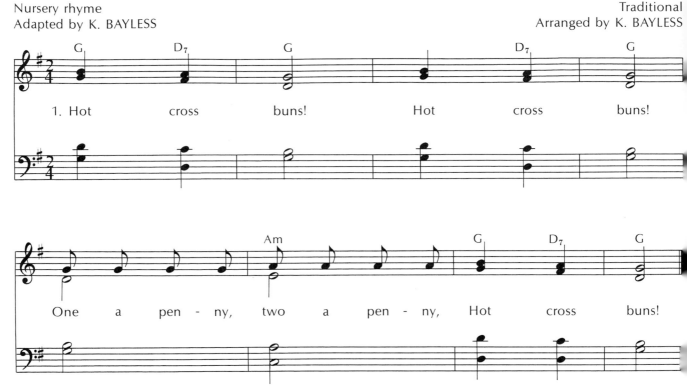

Have the children help suggest additional verses such as: 2   Clap, clap, clap, Tap, tap, tap,
Jog in place, jog in place, How about that?

LANGUAGE ARTS

The language arts and music are natural partners. Music may be used in an effective manner to acquire facility with words and phrases—overall language development. We have discussed in some depth in Chapter 4 the many ways in which music and language are interrelated.

Oliphant, writing in the *Music Educator's Journal* (1972, p. 63), states that music and language, together with mathematics, form a triad of uniquely human accomplishment. They offer structure, order, pattern, and relationship. They make up the basic materials of civilized existence.

Going on with the discussion, Oliphant feels that we have long recognized that there is a relationship between musical development and general cognitive growth. Indeed, it has often been pointed out that good music programs and good reading programs go together.

We might find that a grasp of musical language would strengthen a child's understanding of natural language and use of verbal skills.

Kuhmarker (1969, p. 157), too, states, "When his beginning reading vocabulary is introduced through music, the child's psychological involvement in the experience is intensified. When the child sings words, the rhythm and phrasing of the text emerge with greater clarity than when the words are spoken."

According to Kuhmarker (p. 160), songs have the advantage of patterned drill without its deadly monotony. The advantages of introducing beginning reading activities through music include the following:

(1) Reading becomes a multi-sensory experience.
(2) There is high interest and involvement even among children for whom English is a second language.

Poetry set to music for the purpose of language development is suggested by Garretson (1976, pp. 281–282).

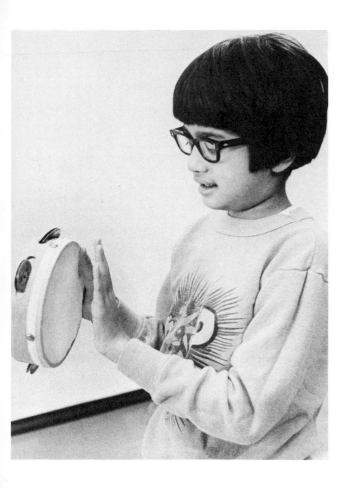

1. The rhythm of poetry is similar to that of music in that it has meter, accent, and various phrase lengths.
2. Use background music for poetry reading or dramatization.
3. Set poetry to music.
4. Pretend to be a particular animal or workman—select music to portray.
5. Dramatize heavy things, light things, fast—slow—quiet—noisy.
6. Dramatize favorite songs—Old MacDonald, etc.

The teacher who is really dynamic and imaginative in the teaching of music will most certainly provide the children with an ideal background for experiences that result in the creation of the completely new and original (Garretson, p. 36).

Sheehy (pp. 8–10) believes that poetry is music, that children revel in the clash and repetition of words, and that poetry is basically *sound,* not *sense,* music in words; that is, children attend more to the sound, not the sense, of poetry; the musical element is the appeal.

Naming objects, classifying, devising rhymes, responding to questions, word repetition, vocabulary, plurals, and awareness of rhyme are other language skills practiced in song.

Memory for words and language is developed through old favorites:

"The Alphabet Song"	"Billy Boy"
"Twinkle, Twinkle, Little Star"	"Frog Went a-Courtin'"
	"Marching to Pretoria"
"Shoo, Fly"	"Blue-Tail Fly"
"Yankee Doodle"	

PEASE PORRIDGE HOT

Traditional   K. BAYLESS

Pease_____ por - ridge hot, Pease_____ por - ridge cold,

Pease_____ por - ridge in the pot, Nine days old.

Music: a way of life for the young child

ACTIONS

Pease[1] porridge[2] hot,[3]
Pease[1] porridge[2] cold,[3]
Pease[1] porridge[2] in the[4] pot,[2]
Nine[5] days[2] old.[3]

Some[1] like it[2] hot,[3]
Some[1] like it[2] cold,[3]
Some[1] like it[2] in the[4] pot,[2]
Nine[5] days[2] old.[3]

On (1) clap hands on lap.
On (2) clap hands together.
On (3) clap hands with partner's hands.
On (4) clap right hands together.
On (5) clap left hands together.

THE ALPHABET SONG

Nursery rhyme

French folk tune
Arranged by K. BAYLESS

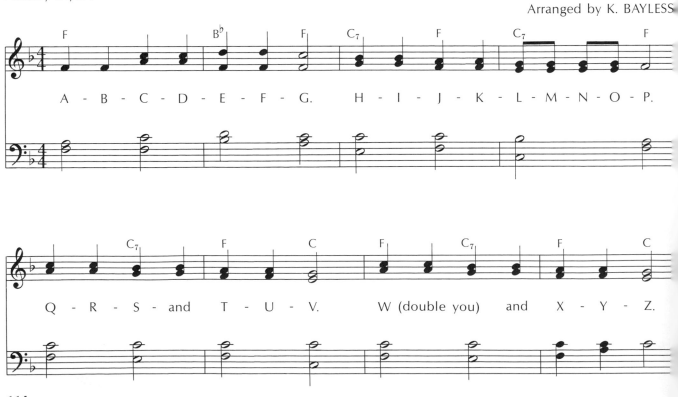

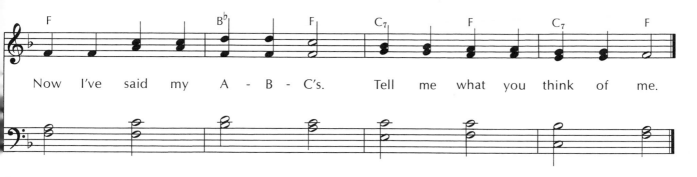

Now I've said my A - B - C's.   Tell me what you think of me.

SWEETLY SINGS THE DONKEY

Traditional   Arranged by K. BAYLESS

Sweet - ly sings the don - key   at the break of day.

If you do not feed   him,   this is what he'll say: He -

haw!   He - haw!   He - haw, he - haw, he - haw!

Children will enjoy the opportunity to create nonsense-type verses that rhyme.

A-HUNTING WE WILL GO

English folk tune

Arranged by K. BAYLESS

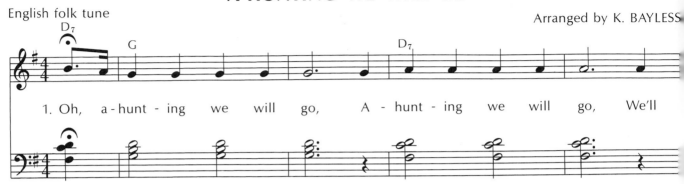

1. Oh, a-hunt-ing we will go, A-hunt-ing we will go, We'll

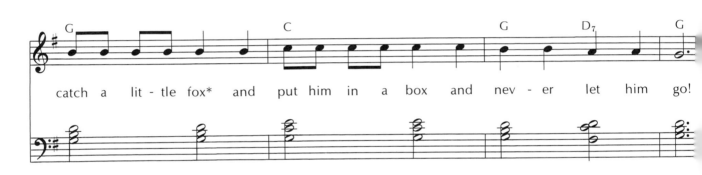

catch a lit-tle fox* and put him in a box and nev-er let him go!

2
Oh, a-jogging we will go,
A-jogging we will go,
We'll jog in place
And get a red face,
A-jogging we will go.

3
Oh, a-riding we will go,
A-riding we will go,
We'll ride our horse "Ned"
And put him to bed,
A-riding we will go.

4
Oh, a-singing we will go,
A-singing we will go,
We'll sing a little song
The whole day long,
A-singing we will go.

---

*Other animal names may be substituted for "fox" and corresponding rhyming words for "box."

Encourage the children to bring their favorite records. Make sure of a broad sampling including Latin American and African rhythms, waltzes, opera, rock, blues, country, and folk music. Each will contribute to language.

Many authorities agree with Zinar, whose research was reported earlier, that speech and song are alike in so many ways that children can use their musical vocabularies as a beginning stage of learning to read. For many children, learning to "read" music precedes learning to read words. Children who have experienced failure with reading and have enjoyed music are often led through the medium of music to success with reading. Perhaps the order of music, the relaxing qualities, the sequence, the movements that often accompany favorite songs, and the spontaneity ease the anxiety and tension often coupled with reading and permit a smooth flow and transition to verbal fluency.

The opportunities for music, language arts, and reading are many all through the preschool years. Each day presents interludes for musical and language growth.

MUSICAL TRANSITION ACTIVITIES

Transition activities flow naturally from music. Often in the preschool or kindergarten environment the adult may wish to effect a smooth flow from one activity to another; thus the need for many and varied transitions.

Today, much study and emphasis are being placed on movement activities. The following songs and rhythms stress movement and actively invite participation. They also provide excellent transition activities.

WIGGLES

M. RAMSEY

K. BAYLES

I can wig - gle my fing - ers, I can wig - gle my toes,

I can wig - gle my el - bows, I can wig - gle my bones,

I can wig - gle my tum - my, I can wig - gle my head, Bu

oh, I would much rath - er Wig - gle my nose in - stead.

THREE BLUE PIGEONS

American folk song

Arranged by K. BAYLESS

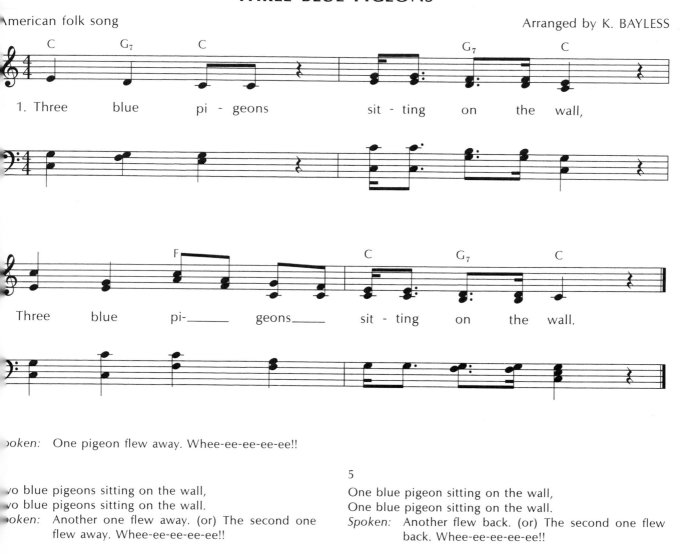

1. Three   blue   pi - geons   sit - ting   on   the   wall,

Three   blue   pi-_____ geons_____   sit - ting   on   the   wall.

Spoken: One pigeon flew away. Whee-ee-ee-ee-ee!!

Two blue pigeons sitting on the wall,
Two blue pigeons sitting on the wall.
Spoken: Another one flew away. (or) The second one
   flew away. Whee-ee-ee-ee-ee!!

One blue pigeon sitting on the wall,
One blue pigeon sitting on the wall.
Spoken: Another one flew away. (or) The third one flew
   away. Whee-ee-ee-ee-ee!!

No blue pigeons sitting on the wall,
No blue pigeons sitting on the wall.
Spoken: One flew back. (or) The first one flew back.
   Whee-ee-ee-ee-ee!!

5
One blue pigeon sitting on the wall,
One blue pigeon sitting on the wall.
Spoken: Another flew back. (or) The second one flew
   back. Whee-ee-ee-ee-ee!!

6
Two blue pigeons sitting on the wall.
Two blue pigeons sitting on the wall.
Spoken: Another flew back. (or) The third one flew back.
   Whe-ee-ee-ee-ee!!

7
Three blue pigeons sitting on the wall,
Three blue pigeons sitting on the wall.
Spoken: And now the pigeons *are all home!!*

FOLLOW, FOLLOW*

GLADYS ANDREWS
Adapted by K. BAYLESS

GLADYS ANDREWS

1. Fol - low, fol - low fol - low me. Fol - low, fol - low fol - low me.

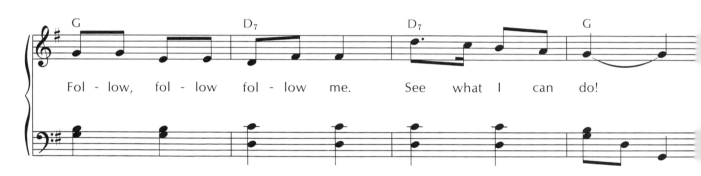

Fol - low, fol - low fol - low me. See what I can do!

2
This is what I can do,
See if you can do it, too.
This is what I can do,
Now I'll pass it on to you.

*From Andrews, Gladys. *Creative Rhythmic Movement for Children*, 1954, pp. 48–49. Adapted by permission of Prentice-Hall, Inc., Englewood Cliffs, N.J.

OPEN, SHUT THEM

Traditional

Arranged by K. BAYLESS

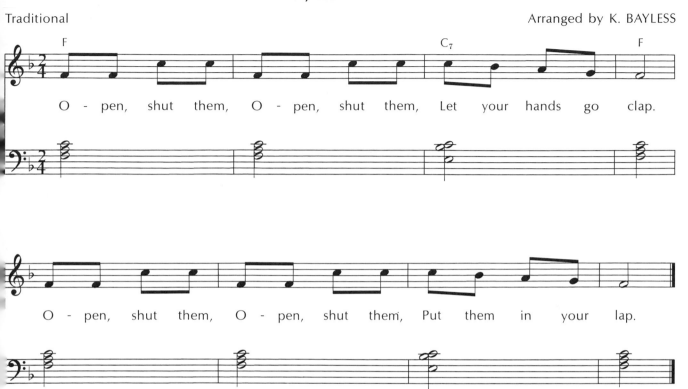

O - pen, shut them, O - pen, shut them, Let your hands go clap.

O - pen, shut them, O - pen, shut them, Put them in your lap.

COME, WALK WITH ME

Words and music by K. BAYLESS

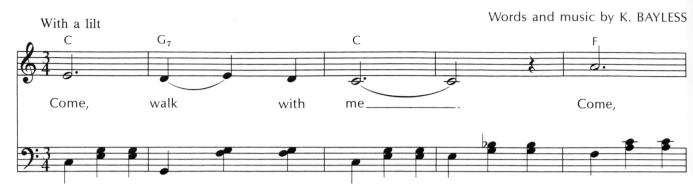

Come,   walk   with   me_____ .   Come,

walk   with   me_____ .   Let's take   a   look   at our pret - ty

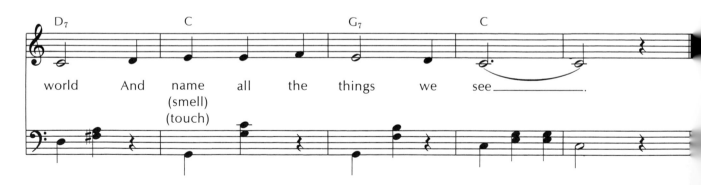

world   And   name   all   the   things   we   see_____ .
        (smell)
        (touch)

2. Come, skip with me.
3. Come, skate with me.
4. Come, run with me.

5. Come, tiptoe with me.
6. Come, swing with me.

SKIP SO MERRILY

Adapted and arranged
by K. BAYLESS

Happily

Skip so mer - ri - ly, skip so mer - ri - ly, all a-round the cir - cle.

Skip so mer - ri - ly, skip so mer - ri - ly, all you hap - py chil - dren.

Choose a part - ner quick as a wink. Take a hand, now don't you think

Skip - ping is fun, skip - ping is fun, All a - round the ring.

HOP SE HI

Words and music by K. BAYLESS

With a hop se hi and a hop se ho, With a

hop se hi and a ho, ho, ho, With a hop and a "bop" and a-

way we go, Hop se hi and a ho! ho! ho!

FLY LITTLE BIRD

Words and music by K. BAYLESS

Fly   lit - tle bird, fly,_____   Fly,   lit - tle bird, fly._____
Flap,   flap__ your wings,_____   Flap,   flap__ your wings._____

Fly,   lit - tle bird, fly,_____   Through   the   air._____
Flap,   flap__ your wings,_____   As   you (we)   sing._____

MAKE A LITTLE MOTION

American folk song   Arranged by K. BAYLESS

Make a lit - tle mo - tion, yes, in - deed, Make a lit - tle mo - tion, yes, in - deed,

Make a lit - tle mo - tion, yes, in - deed, Rise,   sug - ar,   rise.

THE BUS SONG*

Play song

Arranged by K. BAYLES

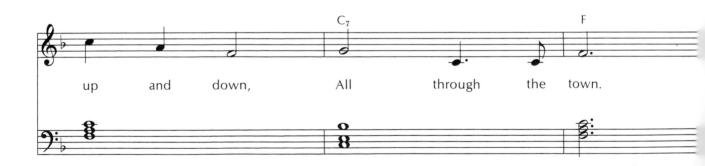

2
The wheels on the bus go round and round,
  Round and round, round and round.
The wheels on the bus go round and round,
  All through the town.

3
The horn on the bus goes toot, toot, toot,
  Toot, toot, toot, toot, toot, toot.
The horn on the bus goes toot, toot, toot,
  All through the town.

---

*"The Bus Song" originally entitled "The Bus" from *Singing on Our Way* of OUR SINGING WORLD series, © Copyright, 1959, 1957, 1949,
Ginn and Company (Xerox Corporation). Used with permission. Verses 7–10 by Kathleen M. Bayless.

4
The money in the box goes ding, ding, ding,
  Ding, ding, ding, ding, ding, ding.
The money in the box goes ding, ding, ding,
  All through the town.

5
The wiper on the glass goes swish, swish, swish,
  Swish, swish, swish, swish, swish, swish.
The wiper on the glass goes swish, swish, swish,
  All through the town.

6
The driver on the bus says, "Move on back,
  Move on back, move on back."
The driver on the bus says, "Move on back,"
  All through the town.

7
The lights on the bus go flash, flash, flash,
  Flash, flash, flash, flash, flash, flash.
The lights on the bus go flash, flash, flash,
  All through the town.

8
The brakes on the bus go squeak, squeak, squeak,
  Squeak, squeak, squeak, squeak, squeak, squeak.
The brakes on the bus go squeak, squeak, squeak,
  All through the town.

9
The signal on the bus goes click, click, click,
  Click, click, click, click, click, click.
The signal on the bus goes click, click, click,
  All through the town.

10
The children on the bus just like to sing,
  Like to sing, like to sing.
The children on the bus just like to sing,
  All through the town.

Most of the rhymes, poetry, rhythms, and songs suggested throughout the chapter and the book can be used successfully with many ages of children.

From the use of simple musical phrases using the child's name to a stirring march or folk song, the adult can make the total day an exciting and worthwhile learning environment. Instead of chaos or disarray in the room, enjoyment, humor, and even nonsense can be interjected through the wise use of musical transition activities.

Two writers add their voices for the values of music throughout the young child's day. Campbell (1972, p. 39) takes a strong position.

> It is now time for all who are interested in children and their optimum development to combine forces into an honest team effort. Instead of having reading taught here, music there, and arithmetic somewhere else at another time, all can be combined to produce a milieu totally conducive to learning, to growing, and to developing the skills that the children will need in the years ahead.

Hoem (1972, p. 30), too, feels strongly that "mathematics and science may teach children how to earn their bread and butter, but it is in the sphere of the aesthetics that they truly learn how to live."

Music enhances the quality of living for the young child and for the adult. Find ways to enjoy and appreciate music together whatever the time of day.

Music is an integral part of all creative effort. Paul Torrance, a well-known authority in the field of creativity, offers suggestions (1970, pp. 39–40) to parents or adults concerned with young children:

1. Provide materials that develop imagination and enrich imagery.
2. Permit time for thinking and daydreaming.
3. Encourage children to record their ideas.
4. Accept and use the tendency to take a different look.
5. Prize rather than punish true individuality.
6. Be cautious in editing children's productions.
7. Encourage children to play with words.

And particularly to parents, Torrance adds:

1. Respect the curiosity of children.
2. Encourage explanation, experimentation, fantasy, testing and developing creative talent.
3. Prepare children for new experiences.
4. Emphasize growth rather than punishment.
5. Find creative ways of resolving conflicts.
6. Find opportunities for the child to make a contribution.
7. Supplement and reimburse the efforts of the school.

Torrance goes on to say that concerned adults need to ask themselves (of their children):

1. What kind of persons are they becoming?
2. What kind of thinking do they do?
3. How resourceful are they?
4. Do they consider their ideas important?
5. How do they handle problems and disappointments?

Torrance's exciting record, *Sounds and Images,* might well be a beginning to stimulate awareness and perception of sound (Appendix B).

Hayes (1971, p. 161), speaking of expanding the child's world through drama, music, and movement, states, "You want to help children develop bright, clear, compelling images—to feel growing strength and expansion within themselves—simple hulas as warm-ups—imagine places and people with eyes closed 'watching what is behind your eyelids'—'talk with your body'—'talk with a guitar'—use music to furnish atmosphere, improve oral language."

Music, whatever the time of day, can add yet another dimension. In her beautiful book, *The Arts in the Classroom,* Cole (1940, p. 70) says:

> We like to believe that all children are happy within themselves—free to act joyously. Such is wishful thinking. For years, the child has been taking

on the tensions of the family, the schoolroom, of life all about him. We are not even right in believing the very young child to be free.

Music frees the spirit, lets us share beauty and emotion, helps rid us of tension and anxiety, gives us common meeting ground, provides pleasure and relaxation. "The appeal of music is universal and axiomatic" (Bailey, 1966, p. 204). Music has a truly integrating power.

PLANNING MUSICAL EXPERIENCES FOR YOUNG CHILDREN

As an aid to those working with young children to extend musical learnings, the following plans have been developed. You will note that the concept to be taught is stated first, followed by anticipated learnings, materials and possible approaches. These plans are merely guides and can be used either where music might be taught separately or as a part of the child's day.

"Ten Little Frogs"

CONCEPT
Numbers as they apply to objects
LEARNINGS
After hearing the song, the children will:

1. Identify the numerals 5, 4, 3, 2, and 1 as they correlate them with objects or persons
2. Subtract 1 from each number as the song is sung
3. Imitate frogs by jumping into a pool

MATERIALS
1. Song: "Ten Little Frogs" by Scott and Wood, which contains ten frogs; in this lesson the number is reduced to five for use with younger children. *For variation:* Teacher or children can remove a felt frog from a feltboard each time the song is sung.
2. 5 felt frogs, 1 felt log, 1 felt pool, 1 feltboard

APPROACH
Teacher: "I am going to sing a song for you about frogs. When I finish, let's see if you can tell us how many frogs there are altogether in the song."

PROCEDURE
1. Sing the song.
2. Ask children how many frogs are in the song.
3. "If we used children instead of frogs to act out the song, how many children would we need?"

4. Discuss with the children what could be used for a make-believe log, a make-believe pool.
5. Ask for five "frog" volunteers.
6. Tell the children they may sing with you this time. Many of them will not join in. At first, they will be too absorbed in the action and in trying to remember what number comes next as each verse is sung. (*Suggestion:* At the end of each verse, count the number of remaining frogs on the log. Do this until children get accustomed to "taking away" one frog each time.) Encourage those who are not frogs to help sing.

Songs using the subtraction concept should not be used until children have had many experiences with songs using the addition concept.

EVALUATION
1. Did the children enjoy singing the song and acting it out?
2. Could the children remember to reduce a number each time the song was sung?

TEN LITTLE FROGS*

LOUISE B. SCOTT   Adapted by K. BAYLESS

1. Ten lit - tle speck-led frogs, Sat on a speck-led log, Catch-ing some
2. Nine, etc.

most de - li-cious bugs, yum, yum. One jumped in - to the pool,

where it was nice and cool, Then there were nine green speck-led frogs, glub, glub.

Last verse
One little speckled frog, Sat on a speckled log,
Catching some most delicious bugs, yum, yum.
He jumped into the pool, Where it was nice and cool,
Then there were no green speckled frogs, glub, glub.

"Jack-in-the-Box"

CONCEPT

The power of springs to make sudden and bouncy movements

LEARNINGS

The children will:

1. Discover that a mechanical spring, after being compressed and released suddenly, will produce a bouncy movement
2. Duplicate the same kind of springing action with their bodies
3. Discover that the muscles in their legs serve as springs to their bodies

MATERIALS

1. Jack-in-the-box toy that plays the tune "Pop Goes the Weasel"
2. A spiral gravy mixer, a "Slinky," or other objects having springs
3. Scalewise song: "Jack-in-the-Box" by Scott and Wood

APPROACH

Show the children the jack-in-the-box toy. Allow one of them to turn the handle and play the tune (Jack pops up at the end of the song).

Teacher or *parent:* "What do you think makes Jack pop up? Let's find out."

PROCEDURE

1. Permit each child to push Jack down in the box with his hand and then let him jump up again. (Do not put lid down each time because that will take up too much time.) Each child can feel the springing movement. "What do you think is inside Jack that makes him pop up?" Some child will probably guess that Jack has something inside his body that makes him spring up.
2. Show the children different kinds of springs. A gravy mixer composed of a spiral spring on a handle (which takes lumps out of gravy) is a good example to use. Children can push down on the handle and let loose suddenly. They can then see the springing action.
3. Sing the song "Jack-in-the-Box."
4. Have children pretend that they are jack-in-the-boxes.
5. Have them spring up on the words, "Yes! I will!"

FOLLOW-UP

1. "What did you do to make your body spring up like a jack-in-the-box?"
2. "Why did some of you go higher than the other boys and girls?"

ENRICHMENT

Poem

Do you have something well hidden from view
That helps you jump when you tell it to?
Sometimes it helps you jump so high
You think you'll almost reach the sky!

131

JACK-IN-THE-BOX*

LOUISE B. SCOTT

LUCILLE F. WOOD
Adapted by K. BAYLESS

*"Jack-in-the-Box," from SINGING FUN by Louise Binder Scott and Lucille Wood, copyright 1954 by Bowmar Publishing Corp. and used with their permission.

"Pairs"

CONCEPTS
1. Pairs
2. Set of two

LEARNINGS
The children will:
1. Identify a set of two and discover that a pair is a set of two things
2. Apply the concept of pairs and discover that a pair is two similar items
3. Apply the story of *One Mitten Lewis* to their own experiences

MATERIALS
1. Book: *One Mitten Lewis* by Helen Kay, published by Lathrop, Lee, and Shepard

2. Song: "Pairs," The Upstarts, Inc. Arranged and adapted by K. Bayless
3. Felt characters from the story of *One Mitten Lewis*
4. Feltboard
5. Paired felt mittens (different sizes and colors)
6. Paired items in a box: earrings, shoes, child-size mittens, socks, scissors, etc.

APPROACH
Teacher or *parent:* "I have a story to tell you about a little boy whose name is Lewis. Lewis had a big problem. Perhaps some of you have had the same kind of problem that Lewis had. Let's find out."

PROCEDURE
1. Tell the story of *One Mitten Lewis,* placing the fel

characters on the feltboard as the story is told.

2. After telling the story, discuss with the children some of their experiences of losing mittens.

3. Ask the children how many mittens it takes to cover both hands.

4. Tell the children there is a special word to describe two mittens that are alike and that it is used in a song they are going to learn. "Listen to the song while I sing it for you."

5. Sing the song. Encourage the children to participate in singing the song after you have sung it a few times.

6. Ask the children if they can think of another pair of something.

7. Continue to add new verses.

8. Remove feltboard figures. Take the small felt mittens from the box and place them in random fashion on the feltboard.

9. Choose children to come to the feltboard and find two mittens that make a pair.

10. Continue to do this until all the mittens are matched in pairs.

EVALUATION

The children will demonstrate their understanding of a pair and a set of two by:

1. Recalling pairs of things they are familiar with

2. Matching the felt mittens

The children may recall experiences of losing their own mittens and will understand how other people feel when they have lost something that belongs to them.

ENRICHMENT

Poem: "The Mitten Song" by Marie Louise Allen

PAIRS*

Words and music by NANCY MACK
Arranged by K. BAYLESS

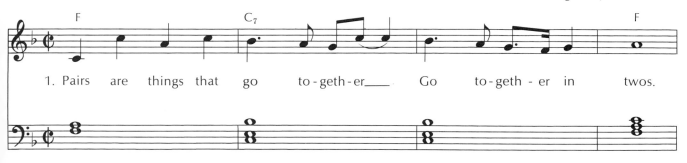

1. Pairs are things that go to-geth-er___ Go to-geth-er in twos.

Pairs are things that go to-geth-er___ Just like a pair of shoes.

2. Eyes are things that go together   3. Twins are things that go together   4. Mittens are things that go together

"Hello, Hello, and How Are You?"

CONCEPT

Being friendly and caring for others, helping to bring happiness into our lives

LEARNINGS

The children will:

1. Learn that friendliness is promoted through greetings
2. Discover that the word *hello* is used as an expression of greeting
3. Relate how they care about the feelings and health of others
4. Be able to understand that people can express their feelings through music

MATERIALS

1. Song: "Hello, Hello, and How Are You?"
2. Pictures of people shaking hands and greeting each other

APPROACH

Teacher or *parent:* "Why do people sometimes shake hands with each other?" Show children picture of people shaking hands, smiling, and greeting each other. Talk about how other cultures express greetings. "Today we are going to learn a greeting song called 'Hello, Hello, and How Are You?'"

PROCEDURE

1. "Boys and girls, what do you think the word *hello* means?" Explain that it is a word that many people use when they greet someone.
2. Ask the children how a dog says "hello" and shows that he is friendly.
3. Sing the song through several times. Have children join in the singing as soon as they can.
4. "Now smile and shake hands with the person beside you as we sing our 'Hello' song again."
5. Discuss the importance of caring how another person feels.

EVALUATION

1. Were the children able to understand how and why people exchange greetings?
2. Did the children mention ways in which they care about the feelings and health of others?

HELLO, HELLO, AND HOW ARE YOU?

Words and music by K. BAYLESS

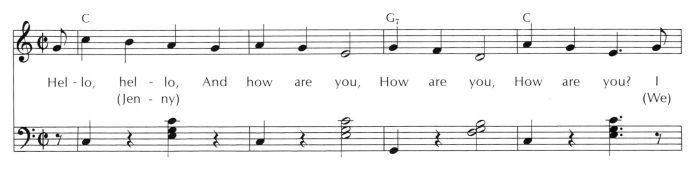

Hel - lo, hel - lo, And how are you, How are you, How are you? I
(Jen - ny) (We)

hope you're feel - ing fine to - day, So how___ do you do?

"Mister Wind"

Rhythmic movement

CONCEPTS

Wind:
1. Is air set in motion
2. Has the power to carry and push things
3. Can be felt and heard but not seen

LEARNINGS

The children will:
1. Discover that wind is air set in motion, has the power to carry and push things, and can be felt and heard but not seen
2. Use their imaginations to create their own movements stimulated by discussions about the wind

MATERIALS

1. Pictures showing "winds" of different strengths at work and play. Include flying kites, wind blowing against an umbrella, storms, sailboats sailing in the water, branches of trees bending in the wind, etc.
2. Poem: "Who Has Seen the Wind?" by Christina G. Rossetti.
3. Rhythmic participation record: "My Playmate the Wind," Young People's Records. (This record, which is presently out of production, is a valuable resource.)
4. Song: "Mister Wind" by K. Bayless and M. Ramsey

APPROACH

Teacher or *parent:* Read or say the poem "Who Has Seen the Wind?"

PROCEDURE

1. Show and discuss pictures of wind scattering milkweed seeds, a flag flying in the wind, leaves blowing to the ground, storms, kites flying in the sky, etc.
2. Have children blow on their hands. Help them discover that by using their mouths they are making a small wind.
3. Play activity record, "My Playmate the Wind." Have children find their own spaces and move to the words and music.

4. At another time, permit children to find their own spaces and create their own movements stimulated by "word pictures," music, visuals, poems, records, etc. about the wind.

Teacher or *parent*

1. "Pretend that you are a tree. Your arms are the branches. How would you move your branches if the wind were blowing slowly and gently? If it were blowing very hard?
2. Now pretend you are holding onto an umbrella. Suddenly a gust of wind comes along. How would you hold your umbrella so it wouldn't get away from you?
3. The wind is strong and pushing hard on your back. How would you walk?
4. If you were a kite, use your arms and hands to show how the wind might blow you about in the sky."

EVALUATION

1. Were the children able to create their own rhythmic movements illustrating the effect of wind on people and things?
2. Did the children give examples of feeling and hearing the wind?

ENRICHMENT

Poems
    "Wind Song"—Lilian Moore
    "The Wind"—Robert Louis Stevenson
    "Clouds"—Christina G. Rossetti
    "The North Wind Doth Blow"—Unknown
    "To A Red Kite"—Lilian Moore

Songs
    "The North Wind"—K. Bayless
    "The Autumn Leaves"—Words and music by
      A. Harwood, *The Spectrum of Music*

Records
    "Rustle of Spring"—Christian Sinding
    "Autumn Leaves"—Mercer et al.

MISTER WIND

Words and music by K. BAYLESS

1. Mis - ter Wind, you seem to be So mys - te - ri - ous to me.

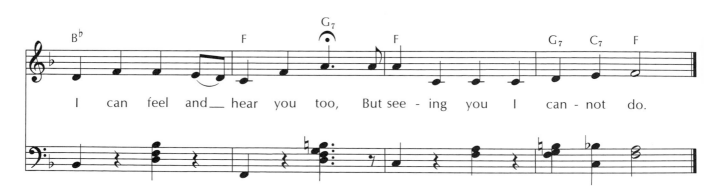

I can feel and— hear you too, But see - ing you I can - not do.

2
You are like a funny clown,
Twirling up and sometimes down,
But you help me fly my kite,
So Mister Wind, you are all right!!

Loud and soft

CONCEPT
Musical tones played soft or loud (dynamics)

LEARNINGS
The children will:
1. Understand that music can be played using differ-ent dynamics, such as soft and loud
2. Be able to recognize and distinguish parts of music that are played soft and loud
3. Understand the following words: concerts and or-chestra conductor
4. Gain an appreciation for fine music

MATERIALS
1. Record player
2. Record: *Symphony No. 94 in G Major* by Franz

Josef Haydn, *Surprise Symphony,* second movement
3. Piano
4. Tape recorder (Previous to the lesson, tape sounds that are played softly and then loudly. For exam-ple, play a drum softly. Wait a few seconds and then play it loudly. Tape other sounds in the same manner.)

APPROACH
Play the tape. Have children distinguish when the drum is played softly and when it is played loudly. Do the same with chords on the piano. Ask the children to touch their heads with their hands when the sound is soft. Ask them to raise their hands very high when the sound is loud.

PROCEDURE

1. Tell the story of why Mr. Haydn wrote the music. (It is not certain that this story is factual.) "Mr. Haydn was a very famous composer. He also conducted an orchestra that played concerts for people. These concerts were often attended by the King. Sometimes the King would fall asleep and snore while the music was being played. This made Mr. Haydn very unhappy. So he decided to write some music that would make the King wake up. Let's listen to the music and find out how Mr. Haydn did it."
2. Play Haydn's *Symphony No. 94 in G Major.* (Play only the part where the theme begins softly and ends with a loud, abrupt chord.)
3. Play it again. Discuss which part is soft, which is loud. Have the children clap once on the very loud, surprise chord.

EVALUATION

1. Were the children able to identify the soft part and the very loud chord?
2. Did they remember to clap once on the loud, surprise chord?
3. Could they explain the following words: concerts and orchestra conductor?

ENRICHMENT

I Love Music

Sometimes the music gets so loud
I feel my heart just pound
And then it gets so very soft
I hardly hear a sound.

I like to open and close my eyes
While pretty music plays,
Right away my feet join in
They tap, tap, tap this way.

Then before I know it
My hands are clapping too,
My whole self seems to feel it
I love it so, don't you?

BETH FRAZIER

Toy Symphony

CONCEPT
Children becoming appreciative and discriminative listeners by exposure to good music throughout the early years

LEARNINGS
The children will:

1. Have the opportunity to listen to and appreciate an appropriate piece of musical literature
2. Enjoy the unusual "toy" sounds produced with traditional orchestral instruments
3. Experience hearing music that is full of gaiety and happiness
4. Become acquainted with the word *composer*

MATERIALS
1. Record player
2. Record: *Toy Symphony* by Franz Josef Haydn

APPROACH
Teacher or *parent:* "Today we are going to listen to some music that is played by an orchestra." (If children are hearing the word *orchestra* for the first time, explain what the word means.) "You will be surprised when you hear some of the sounds the instruments make."

PROCEDURE

1. Play the recording. Expect the children to smile and laugh at some of the unusual "toy" sounds.
2. If the children are not too young, play it again so they can begin to identify some of the "toy" sounds.
3. Help them understand that certain kinds of music, like this piece, are written to make people feel happy and joyful.
4. Explain to the children that the composer (explain the word, *composer*) wrote the music for people to enjoy, particularly for boys and girls like themselves.

EVALUATION

1. Were the children able to identify some of the "toy" sounds?
2. Could they recognize parts of the music that delighted them?

ENRICHMENT

1. *Visuals:* Show illustrations of instruments that were highlighted in the selection.
2. *Resource visitor:* Invite a resource visitor to the room to play some of the instruments. Show children how a musician plays some of the unusual sounds heard in the selection.
3. *Musical recording: March of the Toys* by Victor Herbert, played by the Philadelphia Orchestra, Eugene Ormandy conducting

Skating movement

CONCEPT
Sliding feet alternately and smoothly over the floor (ice-skating motion)

LEARNINGS

The children will:

1. Make movements with their bodies as if they were skating on ice
2. Have the opportunity of hearing music in ¾ rhythm and adjusting their gliding movements to the rhythm
3. Be careful to use their own spaces and not bump into their neighbors
4. Hear that the first beat in ¾ rhythm is accented more than the second and third beats

MATERIALS

1. Record player
2. Record: *The Skater's Waltz* by Emil Waldteufel
3. Pair of ice skates

APPROACH

Visual: Show picture of children skating on ice. Have children tell what is happening in the picture.

PROCEDURE

1. Hold up a pair of ice skates. Discuss such things as: "Why are ice skates difficult to stand on?" "What is the name of the part of the ice skate you stand on?" (blade)
2. *Teacher* or *parent:* "We are going to pretend that we are skating on ice. Instead of using real ice skates, we are going to use pretend ones. Before we skate we are going to listen to some skating music."
3. Play the record.
4. After hearing the selection, have children glide to the music in skating fashion. The waltz has such a pronounced rhythm that it should not take the children long to be able to glide smoothly in rhythm.

"Head, Shoulders, Knees, and Toes"

CONCEPT

Learning to name and identify parts of the body.

LEARNINGS

The children will:

1. Identify and name parts of their bodies as each part is mentioned in the song

2. Relate the parts of a doll's body to their own
3. Experience fast and slow tempi

MATERIALS

1. Feltboard
2. Doll character, miniature boy or girl, plus body parts made of felt
3. Song: "Head, Shoulders, Knees, and Toes"—action song

PROCEDURE

1. Make up a short descriptive story about a doll or boy or girl figure, naming the parts of the body as you assemble them on the feltboard. (Body parts mentioned in the song are head, shoulders, knees, toes, eyes, ears, mouth, and nose.)
2. Sing the song, pointing to the doll's body parts as they are mentioned in the song.
3. Block the board and remove one part of the body. Have the children guess the part that is missing and name it. Continue to take turns. A child may help remove a body part.
4. Sing the song again, and have the children point to their own body parts.
5. As the children become familiar with the song, increase the tempo. They will enjoy singing the song faster and faster as they point to their body parts mentioned in the song.

EVALUATION

Were the children able to identify the parts of their bodies mentioned in the song? Were they able to name each part?

ENRICHMENT

Poem

I look in the mirror and guess what I see,
My head, my ears, they're a part of me.
And every day I wiggle my toes,
And sometimes you'll find me wiggling my nose.

Song: "Boa Constrictor"—Peter, Paul, and Mommy record

HEAD, SHOULDERS, KNEES, AND TOES

Action song

Head, shoul-ders, knees, and toes, knees, and toes. Head, shoul-ders, knees, and

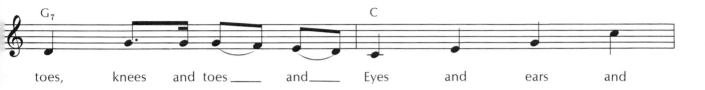

toes, knees and toes ___ and ___ Eyes and ears and

mouth ___ and ___ nose, Head, shoul-ders, knees, and toes, knees, and toes.

REFERENCES AND SUGGESTED READINGS

Andress, B. L., Hermann, H. M., Rinehart, C. A., and Talbert, E. G. *Music in early childhood.* Washington, D.C.: Music Educators National Conference, 1973.

Bailey, Charity. Music and the beginning school child. *Young Children,* March 1966, **21**(4), 201–204.

Bereiter, Carl, and Englemann, Siegfried. *Teaching disadvantaged children in the preschool.* Englewood Cliffs, N.J.: Prentice-Hall, Inc., 1966.

Bloom, Kathryn, and Remer, Jane. A rationale for the arts in education. *The National Elementary Principal,* January/February 1976, **55**(3).

Campbell, Dorothy Drysdale. One out of twenty: the L.D. *Music Educators Journal,* April 1972, **58**(8), 38–39.

Chandler, Bessie E. *Early learning experience.* Dansville, N.Y.: The Instructor Publications, Inc., 1970, pp. 9–18.

Clark, Carol E. Creative rhythms. In *Rhythmic activities for the classroom.* Dansville, N.Y.: The Instructor Publications, Inc., 1960.

Cleveland Association for Nursery Education. *Fingerplays and rhymes for children.* 2084 Cornell Road, Cleveland, Ohio.

Cole, Natalie Robinson. *The arts in the classroom.* New York: The John Day Co., Inc., 1940.

Garelick, Mae. *Where does the butterfly go when it rains?* New York: Scholastic Book Services, 1961.

Garretson, Robert L. *Music in childhood education* (2nd. ed.). Englewood Cliffs, N.J.: Prentice-Hall, Inc., 1976, pp. 281–282.

Hayes, Eloise. Expanding the child's world through drama and movement. *Childhood education,* April 1971, **47**(7), 141.

Hendrick, Joanne. *The whole child: new trends in early education.* St. Louis: The C. V. Mosby Co., 1975.

Hildebrand, Verna. *Introduction to early childhood education.* New York: The Macmillan Co., 1971.

Hoem, Jean C. Don't dump the students who "can't do." *Music Educators Journal,* April 1972, **58**(8), 2.

Hurwitz, Irving, Wolff, Peter H., Bortnick, Barnie D., and Kodas, Klara. Nonmusical effects of the Kodaly music curriculum in primary grade children. *Journal of Language Disabilities,* March 1975, **8.**

Krevitsky, Nik. Errand into the maze. *Childhood Education,* March 1973, **49**(6), 283–287.

Kuhmarker, Lisa. Music in the beginning reading program. *Young Children,* January 1969, **24**(3), 157–163.

Lawrence, Marjory. *A beginning book of poems.* Menlo Park, Calif.: Addison-Wesley Publishing Co., Inc., 1967.

Leeper, Sarah Hammond, et al. The creative arts: art and music. In *Good schools for young children* (2nd. ed.). London: The Macmillan Co., Collier-Macmillan Ltd., 1969.

Leight, Robert L. (Ed). *Philosophers speak of aesthetic experience in education.* Danville, Ill.: Interstate Printers & Publishers, Inc., 1975.

Levenson, Dorothy. Aesthetic education in the classroom. *Teacher,* December 1976, **94**(4), 31.

Margolin, Edythe. A world of music for young children. In *Young children: their curriculum and learning processes.* New York: Macmillan Publishing Co., Inc., 1976.

McCall, Adeline. *This is music for today—kindergarten and nursery school.* Boston: Allyn & Bacon, Inc., 1971.

Michel, P. The optimum development of musical abilities in the first years of life. *Psychology of Music,* June 1973, **1**, 14–20.

Milne, A. A. *Now we are six.* New York: E. P. Dutton & Co., Inc., 1955.

Oliphant, Albert. Music and language: a new look at an old analogy. *Music Educators Journal,* March 1972, **58**(7), 60–63.

Pitcher, Evelyn Goodenough, et al. *Helping young children learn* (2nd. ed.). Columbus, Ohio: Charles E. Merrill Publishing Co., 1974.

Purvis, Jennie, and Samat, Shelley. *Music in developmental therapy.* Baltimore: University Park Press, 1976.

Scott, Louise Binder. *Learning time with language experiences for young children.* St. Louis: Webster Division, McGraw-Hill Book Co., 1968.

Sheehy, Emma D. *Children discover music and dance.* New York: Teachers College Press, 1968.

Smith, R., and Leonhard, C. *Discovering music together: early childhood.* Chicago: Follett Publishing Co., 1968.

Taylor, Barbara. *A child goes forth.* Provo, Utah: Brigham Young University Press, 1970.

Taylor, Barbara. *When I do, I learn.* Provo, Utah: Brigham Young University Press, 1974.

Torrance, E. Paul. *Encouraging creativity in the classroom.* Dubuque, Iowa: William C. Brown Co., Publishers, 1970.

Young, William T. Music development in preschool disadvantaged children. *Journal of Research in Music Education,* Fall 1974, **22**(3), 155–169.

7 Music: the cultural heritage of children

Children can implement their understanding of history and geography with music. The backgrounds, customs, tradition, and emotions of all the peoples of the world are mirrored in their songs.

Landeck, 1958, p. 126

Music is a powerful force in bringing a child and his heritage together. All of us need a sense of belonging, of continuity, and of history. To the young child, the cohesiveness of family can be a bulwark against fears, intrusions to security, and inroads in self-esteem and positive image.

Music is also essentially a social activity, thus cementing relationships with a family group or community group.

From the very first stage of his development, a child finds himself in the matrix of cultural values, and growth is buttressed by his awareness of increasing social stature. Although the patterns of child-rearing are quite varied among different societies and at different times, every culture provides a sense of security and continuity and also offers a full array of models and experiences (Minturn and Lambert, 1964, p. 3). Wherever we travel—to an Appalachian family, an Oriental home, the homes of black Americans, Scandinavians, Creoles, or native Americans—the young child absorbs the patterns of his culture and models that which is most valued by the adults within the immediate environment.

The songs of extended family and the past can create a feeling of pride and of contribution as well as delight. Todd and Heffernan (1977, p. 514) say it well: "Music for preschool groups is like the bluebird of happiness—it is to be found at home."

THE ROLE OF MUSIC IN SOCIETY

John Blacking, in his highly interesting book, *Venda Children's Songs,* describes the relationships between the lives of children and adults in Venda society and the role of music in all levels of that culture. His writing, a documentary of traditional children's songs of the Northern Transvaal, clearly shows a phenomenon easily observed in all cultures. "Each social group has its associated style of music, its audible badge of identity, and it never seems to occur to people that music can be appreciated as sound divorced from a social context" (1967, p. 29).

In the Venda society are songs for boys, songs for girls, songs for nursing babies, songs for evening, and music suited to particular social functions. One age group does not intrude on the music of the other. How familiar is this phenomenon!

Here, in the United States, the young child continues to hum and chant nursery rhymes, nonsense verses, jump rope jingles, and television commercials, as well as popular music. Often, too, children will be singing songs without necessarily knowing the meanings, singing what they think they heard. The young adolescent and teenager are attracted to "hard rock"; the more mature adult seeks out jazz, the waltz, and melodies of nostalgia, of yesteryear. Interesting to observe is the appeal and tremendous growth of country music, which draws from all ages and groups.

However, as one truly listens to the *words* of most music today, a very traditional message is heard—that of man's struggle with loneliness, sadness, disappointment, love, human relationships—the age-old themes which reflect the entire society or cultural group.

In many societies music plays yet another role. Blacking (p. 23) comments that "music is an audible and visible sign of social and political groupings in Venda society. The music that a man can command or forbid is a measure of his status."

Status is measured in another way, as we are now seeing throughout the world, and particularly in the United States, England, and Japan, in the form of the tremendous financial impact of music and the huge sums of money commanded by singing stars both young and old and by the recording companies. Development of certain records for children has created "instant" millionaires. Also of some deep concern is the disappearance of many fine small production companies that find it no longer economically feasible to publish high-quality music for young children and have been forced out of business.

Music can mean many things.

Speaking of the values of a harmonious blend of music that children can bring with them, Pitcher et al. (1974, p. 45) add, "People from other countries and from different parts of our own all speak the common language of music, but each speaks it in a slightly different way: these differences add color and life."

SHARING OUR HERITAGE

Young children want to share the songs and music that are part of their heritage and enjoy hearing the melodies others have to offer. Children are the carriers of tradition. They have preserved a vast storehouse of games, songs, and rhymes. They add, revise, and interpret music according to how it "feels." Seek out the

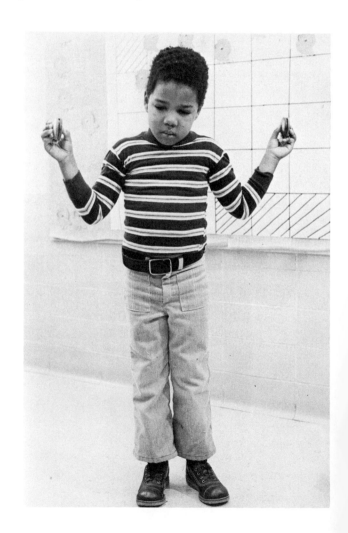

richness of the family groups represented by the young children who come together. Todd and Heffernan (1970, p. 501) remind us, "It does not matter whether a teacher [adult] provides experience with music that is primarily classical, modern, folk, or some other kind of music. But it is highly important that these experiences become increasingly more musical."

Music of the many ethnic groups also adds to the understanding of community. Children are a part of that larger community as they grow from infancy through childhood.

Diggs (1974, p. 581), making a plea for education across cultures, states:

> Our likenesses make us human and our differences make us individuals. Programs should be planned that provide children ample opportunity to learn about the lives and contributions of culturally different individuals who have achieved success.

Read (1971, p. 221) supports the use of music for deepening understanding:

> Some schools are fortunate in having children of different racial origins within the group. In schools that do not have children with different cultural backgrounds, the teachers can broaden the children's experience by bringing in visitors. There may be someone from Japan or from India who will come in native costume and share stories and songs.

Costuming, realia of all kinds, and dance add a distinctive quality to music presented to the young child. The child, too, enjoys "dressing up" as part of the singing.

Landeck (1961, p. 3) echoes similar feelings:

> Anyone who has ever enjoyed music with children or young adults knows that their enthusiasm is roused most readily by songs people have sung in the course of everyday living—folk songs, in the rough, so to speak, with none of the sharp edges toned down by quasi-sentimental performances.

Silberman (1976, p. 58) states it in another way: "The arts are the language of the whole range of human experience. To neglect them is to neglect ourselves and to deny children the full development that education should provide."

Family groups have long been a natural environment for sharing music. Relationships are enriched as grandparents, aunts, and cousins add to the lore of the family through songs shared with children. One of us (M. R.) knows well a woman who early found employment playing piano for the silent movies. Later in her teaching, children thrilled to the rigorous music of a bygone day. Witness also the popularity of the many folk music shows nationally televised, the folk festivals, and the nostalgic feeling of much contemporary singing. We need our musical heritage to make us whole.

Write family songs, play musical games, sing to children in the circle of the family, sing on long automobile trips, use certain songs to alleviate tensions, sadness, and disappointments—a song can be found to express the various moods of the child. Build your own "family" heritage of songs, whether in the home, the preschool, or other group setting.

FOLK MUSIC

Music presented to groups of children might include selections from Africa, South and Central America, and

the Caribbean, as well as from European countries. Oriental music, American folk songs and dances, New Orleans jazz, mountain songs, and Indian dance promise a wealth of richness, appreciation, and enjoyment to all of us.

Andrews (1976, p. 34), writing in *Young Children,* shares her conviction: "Musical experiences for both adults and children defy time limits, exacting goals and expectation. There is no recipe for musical expression. The time allotted for music is *all* time."

One music director, speaking of the music of his people (Neumann, 1975, p. 3), says, "Jewish music is an avenue to personal identification with the Jewish experience through the ages, the vitality, creativity, hopes

and aspirations of Israel today are expressed in its music." Other similar reactions are echoed from family groups around the world.

The songs and narrative of the Vietnamese that follow came to the writers in a very special way, shared by a young teacher (Griffith, 1977) as she came to know a family within her community.

Thuy Dang was a first-grader in my class. Her family were Vietnamese refugees who had just come to town in August. Only Thuy's father spoke a little English. Thuy was very attentive in class, but she never participated in Music. Of course, her speaking was *very* limited, but she usually shyly tried. However, whenever we sang, Thuy just sat. She didn't

even tap, sway, or move to the various rhythms. Because I wanted her to enjoy music and because I realized that in singing Thuy would begin to speak aloud, I decided to find a Vietnamese children's song and have *her* teach it to the rest of us.

My search for a song proved fruitless. One Oriental lady even told me that I wouldn't be able to find one because Oriental children were taught to be quiet and respectful. I just couldn't believe that this bright-eyed, happy child didn't sing! In desperation, I visited her home and discussed the situation with her father (who explained it to her mother). Thank, Thuy's dad, volunteered to tape a favorite children's song and encouraged Thuy to teach it to us. This began a lovely friendship between our families. Thank not only taped the song but wrote out these copies for us. He was both happy to help and very talented.

Thuy both played the tape and very hesitantly began to teach her cute little song. The rest of our class liked learning the foreign-language song that Thank voluntarily sent us, the Elephant Song. As Thuy taught us the song, we taught her a song about a dog—she began to sing, speak aloud, and participate in all the music. Music broke the ice and began a very warm and happy year for all of us.

Seeger (1948, p. 17), long known for her interest and development of American folk songs, writes:

> The fear of hurting a child through song and content came as somewhat of a surprise—a natural thing to sing of all sorts of living. Should we try to shield the child—he builds fantasies, can take action through songs—the deed is done in fantasy and the pressure relieved.

In other words, a child can better accept hurts, disappointments, and the problems of daily living by singing (or fantasizing) much as is done through the sharing of books that deal with life's realities.

We need to be reminded, too, that song difficulty is not always a factor. Children thrill to the challenge of the difficult, of big words. They do not necessarily learn the simple songs first!

Seeger (p. 21) also believes that we need to give early experience of democratic attitudes and values. American folk music has partaken of the making of America. Our children have a right to be brought up with it.

This participation in the making of America is reflected by the statement, "Negro folk music today is the largest body of genuine folk music still alive in the United States." Such is the strong belief expressed by

Harold Courlander in the preface of his valuable book *Negro Folk Music, U.S.A.* (1963). Speaking of the confraternity of young and old that has resulted in a cross-fertilization of youthful and more sophisticated song lyrics which remain to this day in the songs of black America, Courlander (pp. 27 and 147) discusses significant elements of such music:

—leader and choral response
—the patting and hand clapping
—the verbalization of personal feelings

Many of the ballads and folk songs of all ethnic groups provide the opportunity for total participation of lead singer and audience.

The singing of songs of Haiti, Jamaica, other West Indian Islands, and West Africa, as well as the old Louisiana Creole songs, spirituals and anthems, railroad ballads and work songs, melodic calls, and children's ring games, all evoke deep-rooted response patterns. It is as though each singer lives the experience of the other and echoes or affirms mutual feelings; a sense of community is established and shared.

"Patting and hand clapping also serve the purpose of being percussive and maintaining the rhythmic pulse and are used extensively in most children's ring games and 'play party' songs" (Courlander, p. 27).

This same need for communion of singer and audience can be noted in the popular "rock" groups of the day. Independent of these are the songs of the "blues," many of the mountain ballads, and the songs of the American West and the lone cowboy that speak of one person's view of life or the courage and exploits of a group.

"John Henry," "Casey Jones," "Frankie and Johnnie," and "Home on the Range" are legends sung and preserved through many generations and need to be a part of the lives of young children.

The humor, fun, nonsense, and vitality of folk songs and dances invite participation and pleasure and are never outgrown. Old and young alike can enjoy the old-fashioned square dance, the hoedown, the ethnic dances, the clog, and the Highland Fling. Travel the world and revel in native music and dance.

Most of the songs are intended to be sung simply, with simple accompaniment and at a fairly rapid pace. The guitar, ukelele, dulcimer, zither, and bells are favorites. The blood tingles and the foot stirs; smiles come easily. Often other words can be substituted, and improvisation becomes spontaneous.

Who has not thrilled to and savored:
"I've Been Workin' on the Railroad"
"He's Got the Whole World in His Hands"
"Down by the Station"
"The Bear Went Over the Mountain"
"Shoo, Fly"
"Yankee Doodle"
"She'll Be Comin' 'Round the Mountain"
"Home on the Range"
"Frog Went a-Courtin'"
"Blue-Tail Fly"
"Hush, Little Baby"
"Swing Low, Sweet Chariot"
"Go Tell Aunt Rhody"

From Germany:
"O, Christmas Tree"
"O Come, Little Children"
From England:
"A-Hunting We Will Go"
"Christmas is Coming"
"Go In and Out the Window"
"We Wish You a Merry Christmas"
"Hippity Hop to the Barber Shop"

The several songs included within this chapter and the resources listed in Appendix B are merely representative of the abundance of fine melodies available for garnering from the many family groups from which young children come. Our heritage is precious; music makes it live.

MARY HAD A LITTLE LAMB

SARA JOSEPHA HALE

Traditional
Arranged by K. BAYLESS

1. Ma - ry had a lit - tle lamb, lit - tle lamb, lit - tle lamb,

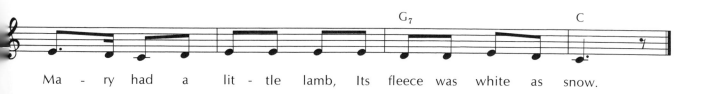

Ma - ry had a lit - tle lamb, Its fleece was white as snow.

	3	4
And ev'ry where that Mary went,	It followed her to school one day,	It made the children laugh and play
Mary went, Mary went,	School one day, school one day,	Laugh and play, laugh and play,
Ev'rywhere that Mary went,	It followed her to school one day,	It made the children laugh and play,
The lamb was sure to go.	Which was against the rule.	To see a lamb in school.

OVER IN THE MEADOW

South Appalachian folk song

Accompaniment by K. BAYLES

1. O - ver in the mead - ow in a nest in the tree Lived an old moth - er bird - ie and her lit - tle ba - bies three. "Sing," said the moth - er, "We sing," said the three. And they sang and were hap - py in the nest in the tree.

2. O - ver in the hol - low in a pool in the bog Lived an old moth - er frog - gie and her ba - by pol - li - wog. "Kick," said the moth - er, "I kick," said the wog. Then he kicked and he kicked him - self in - to a lit - tle frog.

148

HOKEY POKEY

Traditional U.S. game song

Arranged by K. BAYLESS

1. You put your right foot in, you put your

right foot out, you put your right foot in and you

shake it all a - bout. You do the Hok - ey Pok - ey, and you

turn your - self a - round, That's what it's all a - bout.

You put your left foot in,
You put your right arm in,

4. You put your left arm in,
5. You put your whole self in,

149

POP GOES THE WEASEL

Traditional

American folk tune
Arranged by K. BAYLES.

HUSH, LITTLE BABY

Alabama folk song

Arranged by K. BAYLESS

1. Hush, lit-tle ba-by, don't say a word, Ma-ma's going to buy you a mock-ing-bird.

If that mockingbird won't sing,
Mama's going to buy you a diamond ring.

If that looking glass gets broke,
Mama's going to buy you a billy goat.

If that cart and bull turn over,
Mama's going to buy you a dog named Rover.

that horse and cart fall down,
You'll still be the prettiest girl in town.

3
If that diamond ring turns to brass,
Mama's going to buy you a looking glass.

5
If that billy goat won't pull,
Mama's going to buy you a cart and bull.

7
If that dog named Rover won't bark,
Mama's going to buy you a horse and cart.

151

BOW, BELINDA

Traditional
Adapted

American game song
Arranged by K. BAYLESS

1. Bow, bow, Oh, Be-lin - da. Bow, bow, Oh Be-lin - da.

Bow, bow, Oh Be-lin - da. Please bow, Be - lin - da.

2
One hand out, oh Belinda,
  or right hand out, oh Belinda,
One hand out, oh Belinda,
One hand out, oh Belinda,
One hand out before you.

3
Another hand out, oh Belinda,
  or two hands out, oh Belinda,
  or left hand out, oh Belinda,
Another hand out, oh Belinda,
Another hand out, oh Belinda,
Both hands out before you.

JIM-ALONG, JOSIE

Traditional American folk game
Arranged and adapted by K. BAYLESS

Adjust the rhythm according
to the particular movement.

1. Hey, Jim a - long, Jim a - long Jo - sie, Hey, Jim a - long, Jim a - long, Joe!

Hey, Jim a - long, Jim a - long Jo - sie, Hey, Jim a - long, Jim a - long, Joe!

Look to the cen - ter, Hands on your knees, Stamp three times and turn a - round, please.

Go to beginning

Skip, Jim-a-long, Jim-a-long, Josie,
Tiptoe along, Jim-a-long, Josie,
Jump, Jim-a-long, Jim-a-long, Josie,

5. Run, Jim-a-long, Jim-a-long, Josie,
6. Hop, Jim-a-long, Jim-a-long, Josie,

THERE'S A LITTLE WHEEL

Spiritual

Arranged by K. BAYLESS

1. There's a lit - tle wheel a - turn - ing in my heart, There's a

lit - tle wheel a turn - ing in my heart. In my heart,_____ in my

heart,_____ There's a lit - tle wheel a - turn - ing in my heart.

Other verses that may be added to "There's a Little Wheel a-Turning":

2. Oh, I feel so very happy in my heart,
3. There's a little drum a-beating in my heart,
4. There's a little harp a-strumming in my heart,

5. There's a little bell a-ringing in my heart,
6. There's a little bit of kindness in my heart,
7. There's a little song a-singing in my heart,

---

*If the A is too low, sing middle C instead.

ALL NIGHT, ALL DAY

Spiritual

Arranged by K. BAYLESS

All night, all day, An - gels watch-ing o - ver me, my Lord.

All night, all day, An - gels watch-ing o - ver me.

SEE THE LITTLE DUCKLINGS

German folk tune

See the lit - tle duck - lings, swim - ming here and there,

Heads are in the wa - ter, tails are in the air.

TWINKLE, TWINKLE, LITTLE STAR

JANE TAYLOR

French folk tune
Arranged by K. BAYLESS

HOW D'YOU DO, MY PARTNER?

Swedish singing game

Arranged by K. BAYLESS

How d'you do, my part - ner, How d'you do to - day____?

Will you dance in a cir - cle? I will show you the way.

Children stand in a circle facing the center. One child stands in the center and skips to a child in the circle. They shake hands, then join hands and skip around the inside of the circle. Other children clap hands. The song is repeated with the two children choosing new partners, etc.

LES PETITES MARIONETTES
(Little Puppets)

English version by JUDITH GREEN

French folk song
Arranged by K. BAYLESS

Ain - si font, font, font, Les pe - ti - tes mar - ion - et - tes; Ain - si
1 and 5. See them go, go, go, See the lit - tle mar - ion - et - tes; See them

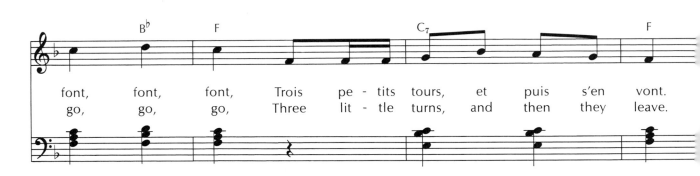

font, font, font, Trois pe - tits tours, et puis s'en vont.
go, go, go, Three lit - tle turns, and then they leave.

2
See them move their heads,
See the little marionettes;
See them move their heads,
Three little nods, and then they
  leave.

3
See them move their arms,
See the little marionettes,
See them move their arms,
Three little claps, and then they
  leave.

4
See them move their legs,
See the little marionettes;
See them move their legs,
Three little jumps, and then the
  leave.

LONDON BRIDGE

Mother Goose

English singing game
Arranged by K. BAYLESS

1. Lon - don Bridge is fall - ing down, fall - ing down, fall - ing down,

Lon - don Bridge is fall - ing down, my fair la - dy.

2. Build it up with iron bars,
3. Iron bars will bend and break,
4. Build it up with gold and silver,
5. Gold and silver I've not got,
6. Here's a prisoner I have got,

7. What'll you take to set him free,
8. One hundred pounds will set him free,
9. One hundred pounds we have not got,
10. Then off to prison he must go,

Two children are chosen to make an arch by raising their arms above their heads to make a bridge for the other children to pass under. These children secretly decide which one represents silver and which one gold. The other children then pass under the bridge as the song is sung. At the words "My fair lady," the bridge falls. The child who is caught is asked which he prefers, gold or silver. This child then stands behind the one who represents his choice. The game continues until all the children have been chosen. When all the children have been caught under the bridge, a tug of war can be played between the gold and silver ones.

THE MUFFIN MAN

English singing game

Arranged by K. BAYLESS

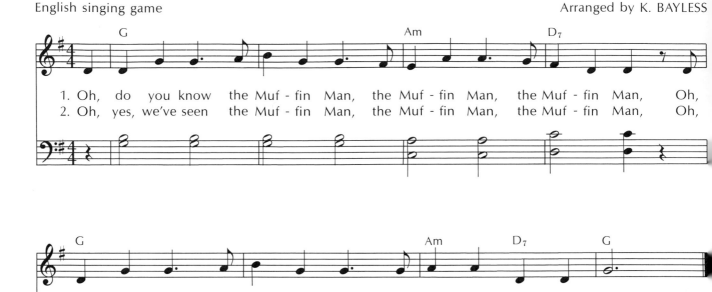

1. Oh, do you know the Muf - fin Man, the Muf - fin Man, the Muf - fin Man, Oh,
2. Oh, yes, we've seen the Muf - fin Man, the Muf - fin Man, the Muf - fin Man, Oh,

do you know the Muf - fin Man, That lives in Dru - ry Lane?
yes, we've seen the Muf - fin Man, That lives in Dru - ry Lane!

SUGGESTIONS

Form a large circle. With younger children do not join hands. Skip around the circle. One child stands in the center. On the words, "Oh, yes, we've seen the Muffin Man," the child in the center skips to the outer circle and chooses a partner. They join hands and skip inside the circle. Another child is chosen, and the game begins again. The actions to this game song may be adapted according to the age level of the children.

THIS OLD MAN

English singing game

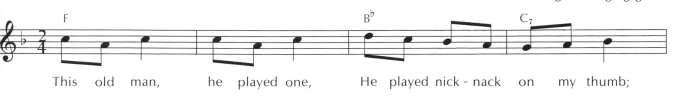

This old man, he played one, He played nick - nack on my thumb;

Nick - nack, pad - dy whack, Give a dog a bone, This old man came roll - ing home.

his old man, he played two,
le played nick-nack on my shoe;
Nick-nack, paddy whack, Give a dog a bone,
his old man came rolling home.

3
This old man, he played three,
He played nick-nack on my knee;
Nick-nack, paddy whack, Give a dog a bone,
This old man came rolling home.

his old man, he played four,
le played nick-nack on my door; (Point to forehead.)

5
This old man, he played five,
He played nick-nack on my hive; (Fight the bees.)

his old man, he played six,
le played nick-nack on my sticks; (Hold up index fingers.)

7
This old man, he played sev'n,
He played nick-nack up in heav'n; (Fly like angels.)

his old man, he played eight,
le played nick-nack on my pate; (Point to top of head.)

9
This old man, he played nine,
He played nick-nack on my spine; (Tap between shoulders.)

10
This old man, he played ten,
He played nick-nack once again;
Nick-nack, paddy whack, Give a dog a bone,
Now we'll all go running home.

LOOBY LOO

Old English folk game

Arranged by K. BAYLESS

Here we dance Loo - by Loo, Here we dance Loo - by light,
(go)

Here we dance Loo - by Loo, All on a Sat - ur - day night. I

put my right hand in, I put my right hand out, I

give my right hand a shake, shake, shake, And turn my - self a - bout.

2. left hand   3. right foot   4. left foot   5. head right in   6. whole self

SANDY MALONEY

English singing game

1. Can you dance, San - dy Ma - lon - ey? Can you dance, San - dy Ma - lon - ey?

Can you dance, San - dy Ma - lon - ey, As we go round a - bout?

2
Put both your hands on your shoulders,
Put both your hands on your shoulders,
Put both your hands on your shoulders,
And turn you round about.

Chorus
Here we dance, Sandy Maloney,
Here we dance, Sandy Maloney,
Here we dance, Sandy Maloney,
As we go round about.

3
Put your hands behind you,
Put your hands behind you,
Put your hands behind you,
As we go round about.

Chorus

(Continue to have children create additional verses.)

FIVE LITTLE BUNS

Traditional English song

Arranged by K. BAYLESS

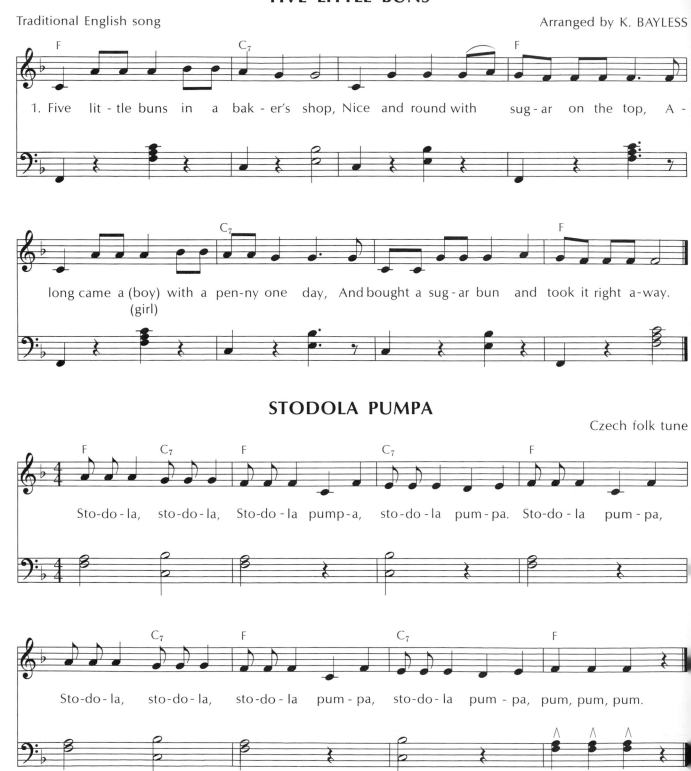

1. Five lit-tle buns in a bak-er's shop, Nice and round with sug-ar on the top, A-

long came a (boy) with a pen-ny one day, And bought a sug-ar bun and took it right a-way.
(girl)

STODOLA PUMPA

Czech folk tune

Sto-do-la, sto-do-la, Sto-do-la pump-a, sto-do-la pum-pa. Sto-do-la pum-pa,

Sto-do-la, sto-do-la, sto-do-la pum-pa, sto-do-la pum-pa, pum, pum, pum.

SUGGESTIONS
Slap each knee once for each "stodola." Clap twice for each "pumpa." Clap
for each "pum" at the end of the song.

BINGO

Scottish song

Arranged by K. BAYLESS

There was a farm-er who had a dog, And Bin-go was his

name - O. B - I - N - G-O, B - I - N - G-O,

B - I - N - G-O, And Bin-go was his name - O

SUGGESTIONS

Sing the song through as written. Then repeat it and clap instead of singing the letter "B" in "B-I-N-G-O." On the next repetition substitute clapping for the letters "B" and "I," etc. (This song is excellent for helping develop concentration.)

WE WISH YOU A MERRY CHRISTMAS

English carol

Arranged by K. BAYLESS

We wish you a mer-ry Christ-mas, We wish you a mer-ry Christ-mas, We

wish you a mer-ry Christ-mas, And a hap-py New Year!

2
Now bring us some figgy pudding,
Now bring us some figgy pudding,
Now bring us some figgy pudding,
And bring it out here.

3
For we love our figgy pudding,
For we love our figgy pudding,
For we love our figgy pudding,
So bring some out here.

4
We won't go until we get some,
We won't go until we get some,
We won't go until we get some,
So bring some out here.

CHIAPANECAS

Mexican folk tune

Arranged and adapted by K. BAYLESS

2. Come, let us stamp feet like this, (stamp, stamp)

For variation children may count 1-2 as they clap hands.

AḤ-SHAV!—RIGHT NOW!*

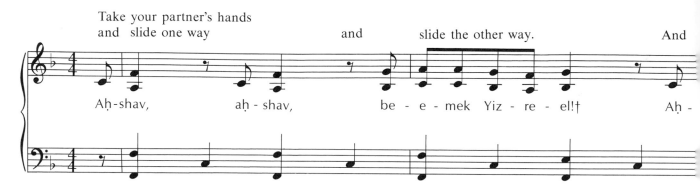

Take your partner's hands
and slide one way   and   slide the other way.   And

Aḥ-shav,   aḥ-shav,   be - e - mek Yiz - re - el!†   Aḥ-

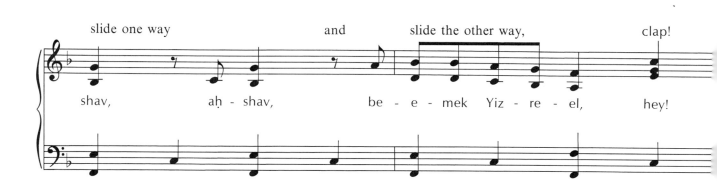

slide one way   and   slide the other way,   clap!

shav,   aḥ - shav,   be - e - mek Yiz - re - el,   hey!

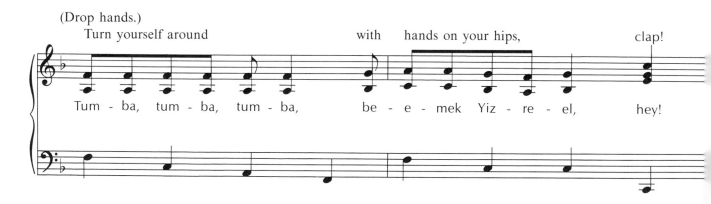

(Drop hands.)
Turn yourself around   with   hands on your hips,   clap!

Tum - ba, tum - ba, tum - ba,   be - e - mek Yiz - re - el,   hey!

*Reprinted with permission from *Songs of Childhood* by Eisenstein and Prensky, published by United Synagogue of America.
†"Right now in the Valley of Jezreel."

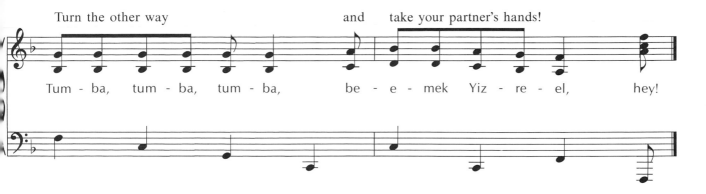

As you complete your first reading of the book, we suggest you go back to the beginning to the Statement of Beliefs and perhaps reaffirm with us that:

> Early education must provide the eye that sees, the mind that comprehends, and the spirit which leaps to respond. Art teaches and develops them all (Marshall, 1976, p. 88).

REFERENCES AND SUGGESTED READINGS

Andrews, Palmyra. Music and motion: the rhythmic language of children. *Young Children,* November 1976, **32**(1), 33–36.

Barkan, Emanuel. *Children's songs.* New York: Board of Jewish Education of Greater New York. Undated. (A collection of 21 simple Hebrew melodies about nature, the classroom, and the home. Each song appears in Hebrew. Transliterated Hebrew and English.)

Basho et al. *Japanese Haiku.* Mount Vernon, New York: Peter Pauper Press, 1956.

Berg, R. C. *Music for young Americans: sharing music.* New York: American Book Co., 1966.

Berman, Louise M., and Roderick, Jessie A. (Eds.). *Feeling, valuing, and the art of growing: insights into the affective.* 1977 Yearbook. Washington, D.C.: Association for Supervision and Curriculum Development, 1977.

Blacking, John. *Venda children's songs: a study in ethnomusicological analysis.* Johannesburg, South Africa: Witwatersrand University Press, 1967.

Choate, E. A., et al. *Music for early childhood.* New York: American Book Co., 1970.

Coopersmith, Harry. Music for the Jewish School. In Richard Neumann, *A song curriculum and teaching guide* (2nd. rev. ed.). New York: Board of Jewish Education, Inc., 1975.

Courlander, Harold. *Negro folk music, U.S.A.* New York: Columbia University Press, 1963.

Dallin, Leon and Dallin, Lynn. *Heritage songster.* Dubuque, Iowa: William C. Brown Co., Publishers, 1966.

Diggs, Ruth W. Education across cultures. *Exceptional Children,* May 1974, **40**(8), 581.

Eisenstein, Judith, and Prensky, Frieda. *Songs of childhood.* New York: The United Synagogue Commission of Jewish Education, 1955 (5716).

Foerster, Leona M., and Little Soldier, Dale. Trends in early childhood education for Native American pupils. *Educational Leadership,* February 1977, **34**(5), 373–378.

Griffith, Pamela. Personal communication, February 11, 1977.

Hanks, Nancy. The arts in the schools—a 200 year struggle. *American Education.* Washington, D.C.: U.S. Department of Health, Education, and Welfare. Office of Education, July 1975, **11**(6), 18–23.

Jay, M. T., and Hilyard, Imogene. *Making music your own.* Morristown, N.J.: Silver Burdett Co., 1966.

Landeck, Beatrice. *Children and music.* New York: William Sloane Associates, Inc., 1958, pp. 126–127.

Landeck, Beatrice. *Echoes of Africa in folk songs of the Americas.* New York: David McKay Co., 1961.

Marshall, Sybil. The ecology of education: the arts. *The National Elementary Principal,* January/February 1976, **55**(3), 88.

McLaughlin, R., and Wood, Lucile. *The small singer.* Glendale, Calif.: Bowmar, 1969.

Minturn, Leigh, and Lambert, William W. (Eds.). Mother of six cultures. In Kaoru Yamamoto (Ed.), *The child and his image.* Boston: Houghton Mifflin Co., 1972.

Newton, Marie. Let there be music in the home. *Music for primaries.* Nashville, Tenn.: The Sunday School Board of the Southern Baptist Convention, Second Quarter 1968, **3**(2).

Palmer, Hap. *Movin'*. Freeport, N.Y.: Educational Activities, Inc. (Album)

Pitcher, Evelyn, et al. Music for young children. In *Helping young children learn*. Columbus, Ohio: Charles E. Merrill Publishing Co., 1974, pp. 45–55.

Read, Katherine H. *The nursery school* (5th. ed.). Philadelphia: W. B. Saunders Co., 1971.

Reagan, Bernice. The sound of thunder. Atlanta: Kintel Corporation, 1200 Spring Street, N.W. (Record)

Seeger, Ruth Crawford. *American folk songs for children.* Garden City, N.Y.: Doubleday & Doubleday, Inc., 1948.

Shelley, Shirley J. Music. In Carol Seefeldt (Ed.), *Curriculum for the preschool primary child.* Columbus, Ohio: Charles E. Merrill Publishing Co., 1976.

Silberman, Charles E. The ecology of education: the arts. *The National Elementary Principal,* January/February 1976, **55**(3), 58.

Smith, R., and Leonhard, C. *Discovering music together: early childhood.* Chicago: Follett Publishing Co., 1968.

Todd, Virginia Edmiston, and Heffernan, Helen. *The years before school: guiding preschool children* (2nd. ed.). New York: The Macmillan Co., 1970.

Todd, Virginia Edmiston, and Heffernan, Helen. *The years before school* (3rd. ed.). Enjoying musical sounds. New York: Macmillan Publishing Co., Inc., 1977, pp. 511–538.

APPENDIX A # Musical approaches for young children

Music is such an important part of a child's total development, it has been shown to facilitate even skills not directly related to music. Obviously, the earlier we can assist children in the process, the easier it will be for them to feel comfortable and at ease with music. Therefore, educators have been keenly interested in employing a variety of techniques in the instruction of music. Many different approaches are being used in schools throughout the United States. Some of these methodologies are new and some are old. Many have common elements and differing philosophies, but all have the same goal: teaching children music early and exposing them to good musical experiences. Four significant methods of music have originated from outside the United States. These methods are discussed briefly for benefit of the reader.

The *Dalcroze method* was originated by Emile Jaques-Dalcroze, a Swiss composer and educator. Dalcroze believed that children could develop a feeling for an awareness of music through body movement. The child's body is used as a musical instrument to interpret sounds. This procedure is called *eurhythmics*. Rhythmic sense and voice and body coordination are learned simultaneously through the synchronization of body movement and music.

Listening to musical changes is thought to be important. For example, children listen to the piano and move their bodies along with what they hear. They do exercises, such as tiptoeing to music, freezing to silence, and stepping heavier to louder sounds and softer to lighter sounds.

There is said to be a coordination of brain, nerves, and muscles when the child responds with physical actions to musical stimuli. This then creates a greater depth of feeling and sensitivity to music.

This is accomplished in the Dalcroze system by component parts: body movement, ear training, and improvisation at the piano. The strength of this system is based on the integration of these elements.

Although this approach was originated in the early 1900s, it has gained a new popularity, especially through the energetic endeavors of Manhattan School of Music professor, Robert M. Abramson, who also believes that it is necessary to train good musicians, not just rote note players.

Willour (1969, p. 72) describes a program offered at the Cleveland Institute of Music, where training commences at age 4. The Institute believes that this instruction contributes to the child's total personality and encourages the development of creativity as well as that of large muscle coordination.

This approach could be employed in the public and private elementary schools easily, according to Spector (1972, pp. 19–21).

Another popular approach used for the young child is the *Kodály method*. The Hungarian composer-educator Zoltan Kodály is responsible for this educational philosophy, which proposes that a child's education in music begins when he starts to "make" his own music. Thus the child's voice is his first and most important instrument. Kodály differed from Dalcroze in that he did not believe the piano should be used for accompaniment. In fact, he thought it to be a distraction. The child should learn rather to appreciate music as a pure, unadulterated melody coming from himself.

He believed that this could be achieved through the

use of ear training exercises. The children would also learn to read musical intervals at sight in correct rhythm. Thus, he developed play songs, chants, and games to assist in this teaching of rhythm, meter, and accent. Hand signals were employed, one for each scale tone. The hand would move up or down according to the ascension or descension of tones. This served to reinforce what the child learned. In this methodology, the child learns music as he learns his language. He learns to read music as he learns to read words.

Kodály strongly believed that it was possible to bring music to the general public in this manner. His followers contend that this method could be part of the general school curriculum for the "average" child. With occasional consultation, the classroom teacher could handle this simple technique. Workbooks that include the structured songs and games are the only equipment required.

A recent study conducted by Harper et al. (1973, pp. 628–629) of the Kodály approach used in the kindergarten indicated very positive results. A comparison was made between the program and control children on the following criteria: auditory discrimination, visual-motor integration, and first-grade level academic skills. The children in the program displayed higher levels of skills in all areas, a better self-image, and a readiness for first grade.

The *Orff,* or *Orff-Schulwerfe, method* was introduced by Carl Orff, the well-known contemporary German composer. This musical approach emphasizes the use of specially designed percussion instruments for young children.

Rhythm is the primary element in Orff's style of musical composition, which depends greatly on contrast and variation of rhythm. Percussion instruments then would naturally play a primary role in his works. Thus he invented new percussion instruments to meet his demand for novel effects.

Orff was convinced that these melodic and fixed percussion devices would allow children the opportunity for creative improvisation and ensemble experience, since rhythmic responses are so natural to the young child. Thus the child memorizes pitch and rhythmic patterns with facility and lack of inhibition.

Despite the facts that the teacher must be fairly well trained in order to use this procedure and that the instruments are fairly expensive, this approach is used in many schools throughout the United States with much success and popularity.

A recent musical approach called the *Suzuki system,* or *Saino-Kyoiku,* was developed in Japan by Dr. Shinichi Suzuki, a Japanese teacher. The method received world wide recognition and acclaim when 3-, 4-, and 5-year-old children demonstrated their ability to play demanding sonatas and concertos on their miniature-sized violins.

This instruction employs a psycholinguistic approach, wherein the child's abilities are believed to be developed by being developed.

Thus he learns to respond to and repeat music in the same manner that he learns to speak his mother tongue. He learns to play first by ear rather than by reading notes.

The preschool age child plays the violin by ear as soon as he is able to comfortably hold the instrument and the bow. Prior to this stage, the infants practice physical exercises in preparation and learn "bow gymnastics" through games.

Suzuki believes that the most important aspect of learning music is the physical movement. The children, therefore, learn to walk, squat, balance on either leg, and so forth while holding the violin. It becomes like a natural appendage to the body. He believes that children do not become involved or learn as freely by remaining still and rigid.

In this approach, the mother becomes the active, involved partner. She has to learn to play the violin several months before it is introduced to the child. The child listens to the mother play and repeats what he hears after a period of first listening to recordings of the same musical pieces being played precisely and correctly. The child memorizes the first simple tunes. He enjoys rapid success through the use of simple materials and the encouragement of mother and teacher. Only after this success, as well as the proper fingering, bowing and positioning techniques, is taught are the notes of the pieces learned previously finally introduced and learned as note reading.

Suzuki has enjoyed the success of his students and feels that this instructional procedure can be used in all forms of teaching. Now many schools are employing the Suzuki method and the instrumental technique that relies on the human ear as a fine piece of natural equipment.

Obviously, each approach offers unique musical experiences to the young child. The most effective procedure will depend on the teacher employing this method. Whatever approach matches the philosophy with which she feels most comfortable will be the one that will be the most successful for the students.

REFERENCES AND SUGGESTED READINGS

Garson, Alfred. Learning with Suzuki: seven questions answered. *Music Educators Journal,* February 1970, **56,** 64–65.

Garson, Alfred. Suzuki and physical movement. *Music Educators Journal,* December 1970, **60,** 34–37.

Harper, Andrew, et al. Education through music. *Phi Delta Kappan,* May 1973, **54,** 628–629.

Markel, Roberta. *Parents' and teachers' guide to music education.* New York: The Macmillan Co., 1972.

Rubin-Rabson, Grace. A Kodály symposium. *The American Music Teacher,* April 1974, **23,** 14–16.

Spector, Irwin. Bring back Dalcroze. *American Music Teacher,* July 1972, **21,** 19–21.

Willour, Judith. Beginning with delight, leading to wisdom: Dalcroze. *Music Educators Journal,* September 1969, **56,** 42–43.

APPENDIX B   Resource materials

PROFESSIONAL ORGANIZATIONS, NEWSLETTERS, AND JOURNALS

ORGANIZATIONS

A.C.E.I.
Association for Childhood Education International
3615 Wisconsin Ave., N.W.
Washington, D.C. 20016

D.C.C.D.C.A.
Day Care and Child Development Council of America, Inc.
1401 K St., N.W.
Washington, D.C. 20005

ERIC/ECE
Educational Resources Information Center/Early Childhood Education
805 West Pennsylvania Ave.
Urbana, Ill. 61801

MENC
Music Educators National Conference
1902 Association Dr.
Reston, Va. 22091

N.A.E.Y.C.
National Association for the Education of Young Children
1834 Connecticut Ave. N.W.
Washington, D.C. 20009

U.S. DHEW
U.S. Department of Health, Education, and Welfare
Office of Child Development
Children's Bureau
Washington, D.C. 20201

NEWSLETTERS

ERIC/ECE Newsletter
805 West Pennsylvania Ave.
Urbana, Ill. 61801

Report on Preschool Education
Capitol Publications, Inc.
Suite G-12
2430 Pennsylvania Ave., N.W.
Washington, D.C. 20037

Today's Child
Roosevelt, N.J. 08555

JOURNALS

Childhood Education
Association for Childhood Education International
3615 Wisconsin Ave., N.W.
Washington, D.C. 20016

Children Today
U.S. Department of Health, Education, and Welfare
Office of Child Development
Children's Bureau
Superintendent of Documents
U.S. Government Printing Office
Washington, D.C. 20402

Child Development
Society for Research in Child Development
University of Chicago Press
5801 Ellis Ave.
Chicago, Ill. 60637

Music Educators Journal
Music Educators National Conference
1902 Association Dr.
Reston, Va. 22091

Merrill-Palmer Quarterly of Behavior and Development
Merrill-Palmer Institute
71 East Ferry Ave.
Detroit, Mich. 48202

Young Children
National Association for the Education of Young Children
1834 Connecticut Ave., N.W.
Washington, D.C. 20009

SONG BOOKS

Listings are alphabetized according to publisher:

American Folk Songs for Children
Ruth Crawford Seeger
Doubleday & Co., Inc.
New York, N.Y. 1948
Includes 90 favorite folk songs with guitar chording. The introductory chapters explain how to sing the songs, how to improvise on the words, how to use the songs at home and at school, how to use the rhythm and repetition, and how to use the humor and tone play of folk songs.

Eye Winker, Tom Tinker, Chin Chopper
Tom Glazer
Doubleday & Co., Inc.
New York, N.Y. 1973
Contains 50 finger plays. There are familiar finger play songs, and also familiar finger plays newly set to music, as well as some beautiful new songs and famous folk songs with brand new finger plays.

Pentatonic Songs for Young Children
Mary Helen Richards
Fearon Publishers, Inc.
Belmont, Calif. 1967
Songs have voice range of six tones or less.

The Big Book of Favorite Songs for Children
Dorothy Berliner Commins
Grosset & Dunlap, Inc.
New York, N.Y. 1951
Contains 29 favorite songs of early childhood.

Jim Along Josie
Nancy and John Langstaff
Harcourt Brace Jovanovich, Inc.
New York, N.Y. 1970
Collection of folk songs and singing games for young children. The book contains traditional singing games that involve the child in singing, dancing, and acting out words. There are many action songs especially suited to the youngest child. Included are piano accompaniments, guitar chords, and some optional percussion accompaniments for use with simple instruments.

Music for Fun
Music for Learning
Lois Birkenshaw
Holt, Rinehart & Winston of Canada Ltd.
Toronto, 1977
For regular and special classrooms.

Music Resource Book
Lutheran Church Press
Philadelphia, Pa. 1967
Contains many action songs that are sung to traditional melodies. Teaching suggestions and chording for Autoharp are included.

Wake Up and Sing
Beatrice Landeck and Elizabeth Crook
William Morrow & Co., Inc.
New York, N.Y. 1969
Collection of American folk songs with teaching suggestions, guitar chordings, and piano accompaniments.

Songs to Sing with the Very Young
Random House, Inc.
New York, N.Y. 1966

The Animal Song Book
Edward Fisher
St. Martin's Press, Inc.
New York, N.Y.
Includes songs about lions, porcupines, and other creatures that are excellent for creative movement.

Songs for Early Childhood
W. Lawrence Curry et al.
The Westminster Press
Philadelphia, Pa. 1958
Contains a wide variety of songs and music for very young children with simple piano accompaniment.

Wake Up Beautiful World!
Upstarts, Inc.
Sue Blum
2920 Eaton Road
Cleveland, Ohio 44112
A musical experience created by Upstarts, Inc. The songs in this booklet are arranged by concept, and each section is color coded. The booklet contains songs and ideas centering around language arts, numbers, movement, and self-image.

The following music books are published by Bowmar Publishing Co., 4563 Colorado Blvd., Los Angeles, Calif. 90039:

Singing Fun
Louise Scott and Lucille Wood
1961
All-time favorite songbook and record for preschool and primary grades. Original songs of farm, circus, seasons, etc. delight children. 64 pages, soft-cover.

More Singing Fun
Louise Scott and Lucille Wood
1961
A sequel to *Singing Fun,* with two records and original songs of the sea, Halloween, etc. 64 pages, soft-cover.

Rhythms to Reading Songbook
Lucille Wood
1972

A picture songbook that celebrates seasonal events. The songs are from the twelve records of the *Rhythms to Reading* program. The songs help the child make the transition from prereading to reading through action songs, rhythms, and singing games. Each song has a full-color informative picture. Suggestions for language arts and music activities are included with each song. 160 pages, hardcover, $12\frac{1}{4}$ x $11\frac{1}{3}$ inches.

Sing a Song of People Songbook
Roberta McLaughlin and Lucille Wood
1973

110 pages with 75 songs and 35 full-page original illustrations interpreting each of the songs in a colorful, childlike style extremely appealing to children. The artwork promotes language expression and develops motivation for musical experiences and interpretation through movement. Original and traditional songs are organized to develop cultural understandings and attitudes within the settings of holidays and seasons, home and community, and cultural neighbors, such as the Indian, Mexican, Oriental, and Black American. Included with many of the songs are teaching suggestions and Autoharp accompaniment.

The Small Singer Songbook
Roberta McLaughlin and Lucille Wood
1969

112 pages of 125 familiar and new songs of action, dramatization, relaxation, counting, echoing, stories, seasons, and holidays. Repeated patterns and simple refrains with percussion and bell accompaniments are ideal for prekindergarten as well as primary grades. Delightful full-color illustrations. 9-inch x 12-inch cover.

MUSIC BOOK SERIES, PROGRAMS, AND HANDBOOKS

Listings are alphabetized according to publisher:

Music Activities for Retarded Children
David R. Ginglend and Winifred E. Stiles.
Abingdon Press
New York 1965

An excellent handbook to assist parents or teachers in initiating a developmental music program for retarded children or young "normal" children.

Comprehensive Musicianship Program (kindergarten and first grade)
Dorothy K. Gillett
Addison-Wesley Publishing Co., Inc.
Menlo Park, Calif. 1974

Zone 1 of the Comprehensive Musicianship Program is intended for children in kindergarten and first grade. Activities emphasized include moving, singing, playing basic instruments, listening, improvising, and experimenting. An ensemble approach is featured: while some students sing, others play rhythm accompaniments, and the rest move to the music. Then all students change roles, providing opportunity for individualization and encouraging the experiencing of music as a whole.

This is Music For Today (kindergarten and nursery school)
Adeline McCall
Allyn & Bacon, Inc.
Boston 1971

Contents: Friends and Family, Animals, Singing through the Day, Eskimo, Cowboy, and Indian, Answer-Back Songs, the Sound of Words, On the Go, Movement, Around the Year, American Folk Songs for Children, Stories and Dramatizations with Music, and Learning to Play Instruments.

Music for Early Childhood
Robert A. Choate
New Dimensions in Music
American Book Co.
New York 1970

Resource collection for teachers and parents of children 2 through 5 years old. Music materials are organized into units. All the songs and related activities are based on children's interests and subject areas that are generally considered a part of the curriculum for this age.

Beginning Music
Robert A. Choate
New Dimensions in Music
American Book Co.
New York 1970

Same format as *Music for Early Childhood* with many additional songs for the preschool and kindergarten age child.

Discovering Music Together: Early Childhood
Charles Leonhard
Follett Publishing Co.
Chicago 1968

Teacher's book for kindergarten, integrating the areas of singing, playing, moving, and creating.

Music Round About Us
Irving Wolfe
Follett Publishing Co.
Chicago 1964

Contents: over 200 pages of songs about people, places, animals, games, seasons, holidays, etc. Book also contains piano music for creative rhythms.

The Magic of Music (kindergarten)
Lorrain E. Watters
Ginn & Co.
Boston 1965

> Collection of songs, song stories, and musical themes for appreciation. The collection is divided into the following sections: Music Makes Us Friends, Music Brings Us Wonderment, Music Helps Us Celebrate, Music of Home and Country, Music Tip to Toe, and Music in the Land of Make-Believe.

Exploring Music: Kindergarten
Eunice Boardman Weske
Holt, Rinehart & Winston
New York 1969

> Contents: Exploring Music Through Moving, Singing, Listening, Playing Instruments, Reading, and Music for Special Times.

The Spectrum of Music (*with Related Arts*) (kindergarten)
Mary Val Marsh
Macmillan Publishing Co., Inc.
New York 1974

> Organized to help the teacher plan and teach in the most direct manner possible. It is divided into four areas. In each area one broad aspect of music is emphasized:
> media—the voices and instruments that produce music
> components—the ways in which sound is used to create rhythm, melody, harmony, and expression
> structures—the ways in which the components of music are organized into musical forms
> perspectives—the role music plays in our daily lives—ethnic, patriotic, holiday music
> Each lesson employs a set of teaching strategies to enable the teacher to use the material most effectively. The book is oriented to the learner, and the text is written so that the children will learn as they explore the material.

Teacher's Guide to the Open Court Kindergarten Music Program
Betty Smith and T. C. Harter
Open Court Publishing Co.
La Salle, Ill. 1970

> The Open Court Kindergarten Music Program has a threefold purpose: [1] to provide encouragement and tools to enable the teacher to communicate a sense of joy in music to young children; [2] to provide a repertoire of traditional songs that children enjoy and on which they may build; and [3] to provide a wide variety of musical experiences so that each child may know success in some form of music. Each classroom unit includes a teacher's guide (containing music and lesson plans), a children's book for each child, and a set of four teaching records.

Growing with Music (Related Arts Edition)
Harry R. Wilson et al.
Prentice-Hall, Inc.
Englewood Cliffs, N.J. 1970

> The emphasis of the *Growing With Music* series is on the study of music as a significant learning. The intrinsic values of music and the contribution music makes to personality fulfillment have been given primary consideration in organizing these books. Contents of *Book One* include: Songs About Me, Mood In Music, Moving With Music, The World Of Sound, Melody In Music, Words and Music, Acting Out Songs, Playing Instruments, Song Patterns, Fun Songs, Songs For Special Days, and Music For Movement.

Silver Burdett Music (teacher's edition)
Elizabeth Crook et al.
Silver Burdett Co.
Morriston, N.J. 1974

> The *Silver Burdett Music* early childhood learning program consists of twenty-four Experience Modules. Each module is a unified set of lessons that involves the child with music through experiences of its sense and its expressiveness. Each lesson within a module clarifies a particular quality of music (tempo, tone, color, etc.) by involving the child in musical activity—singing, playing instruments, listening, moving, creating. The focus is never on the musical quality for its own sake, but on the experience of the quality through active musical exploration. The program also includes chart book for pupils, crayon activities, and sound stories, plus recordings that come in records or cassettes.

The Joy of Music
Roberta McLaughlin and Patti Schliestett
Summy-Birchard Co.
Evanston, Ill. 1967

> In addition to providing a large selection of songs for singing and listening, contains sections advising teachers on helping undeveloped voices, encouraging active response, learning through listening, measuring musical growth, experimenting with rhythm, melody, and harmony instruments, and many other essential phases of a child's introduction to music.

SOURCES OF RECORDS

A A Records
250 West 57th St.
New York, N.Y. 10019

Bowmar
4563 Colorado Blvd.
Los Angeles, Calif. 90039

Capital Records, Inc.
1290 Avenue of the Americas
New York, N.Y. 10019

Columbia Records
51 West 52nd St.
New York, N.Y. 10019

Childcraft
Education Corp.
20 Kilmer Rd.
Edison, N.J. 08817

Children's Book & Music Center
5373 West Pico Blvd.
Los Angeles, Calif. 90019

Decca Records
445 Park Ave.
New York, N.Y. 10022

Disneyland Records
800 Sonora Ave.
Glendale, Calif. 91201

Educational Activities, Inc.
Freeport, N.Y. 11520

Education Record Sales
157 Chambers St.
New York, N.Y. 10007

Educational Recordings of America
P.O. Box 231
Monroe, Conn. 06468

Folkways Records
43 West 61st St.
New York, N.Y. 10023

Folkways/Scholastic Records
50 West 44th St.
New York, N.Y. 10036

Golden Records Educational Division
Michael Brent Publications, Inc.
Port Chester, N.Y. 10573

Honor Your Partner Records
P.O. Box 392
Freeport, N.Y. 11520

Kimbo Educational
P.O. Box 477
86 South 5th Ave.
Long Branch, N.J. 07740

A. B. LeCrone Co.
819 N.W. 92nd St.
Oklahoma City, Okla. 73114

Lyons Band
530 Riverview Ave.
Elkhart, Ind. 46514

MCA Records
100 Universal City Plaza
Universal City, Calif. 91608

Phoebe James
P.O. Box 475
Oakview, Calif. 93022

RCA Music Service
Educational Department
1133 Avenue of the Americas
New York, N.Y. 10036

RCA Records
Educational Sales
P.O. Box RCA 1000
Indianapolis, Ind. 46291

Scott, Foresman & Co.
1900 East Lake Ave.
Glenview, Ill. 60025

Sing 'N Do Records
(Kimbo Educational)
P.O. Box 55
Deal, N.J.

Stanley Bowmar, Inc.
4 Broadway
Valhalla, N.Y. 10595

Youngheart Music Education Service
Box 27784
Los Angeles, Calif. 90027

Vox Productions, Inc.
211 East 43rd St.
New York, N.Y. 10017

RECORDINGS

The following list of recordings is only a small sample of the number and variety of recordings available for use with young children. Many come in both record and cassette form. Before purchase, it is best to write for catalogs to check for correct number and price.

SELECTED RECORDINGS FOR THE VERY YOUNG

Music for 1's and 2's CMS 649
Songs & Games For Young Children
Tom Glazer
CMS Records, Inc.
14 Warren St.
New York, N.Y. 10007

Lullabies for Sleepy-Heads CAS-1003(e)
Dorothy Olsen
Camden—RCA Records

Lullaby Time for Little People LB9312
Lyons Band
   Kindergarten–1

Nursery Rhymes for Little People
Lyons Band
   Prekindergarten–1

Nursery and Mother Goose Songs 007 and 019
Bowmar

SINGING

Nursery Rhymes—Rhyming & Remembering R 7660
Ella Jenkins
Folkways Records
   22 favorite nursery rhymes

Early Childhood Songs R 7630
Ella Jenkins
Folkways Records
   Nursery school youngsters singing simple songs that have
   been sung by generations of children

Counting Games and Rhythms for the Little Ones R 7679
Folkways Records

And One and Two R 7544
Ella Jenkins
Folkways Records
   Simple songs for preschool and primary ages

Nursery Rhymes for Little People KIM 0820
Kimbo Educational
   Preschool–first grade

Activity and Funtime Songs LP 200
Wonderland—Golden Records

Happy Times SG 1
Educational Recordings of America
P.O. Box 231
Monroe, Conn. 06468
   16 Singing Games for Young Children

Folk Songs for Little Singers 020
Bowmar

Songs to Grow On, vol. 1
Folkways Records

Singing Fun 001
More Singing Fun 003
More Singing Fun 004
Bowmar

Edgar Kendricks Sings for the Very Young FC 7556
Folkways Records

Little Favorites 007
Bowmar

The Small Singer 021 and 022
Bowmar

Singing Games 110 and 111
Bowmar
   Prekindergarten–3

*Burl Ives Sings Little White Duck and Other Children's Fa-
  vorites*
Columbia Records

Songs for Classroom Activity and Singing CM 1033
Classroom Materials Co.
93 Myrtle Dr.
Great Neck, N.Y. 11021

This-a-Way, That-a-Way R 7546
Ella Jenkins
Folkways Records

Songs and Activities for Children with Special Needs LP 0602
Kimbo Educational

Spin, Spider, Spin AR 551
Patty Zeitlin and Marcia Berman
Educational Activities, Inc.
   Songs for greater appreciation of nature

Folk Song Carnival AR 524
Hap Palmer
Educational Activities, Inc.
   An excellent collection of folk songs

Call-and-Response Rhythmic Group Singing R 7638
Ella Jenkins
Folkways Records

You'll Sing a Song and I'll Sing a Song R 7664
Ella Jenkins
Folkways Records

Kindergarten Record Library
RCA Music Service, Educational Department
   Over 40 of the world's greatest children's songs

Kindergarten Songs 015 and 016
Bowmar

Rainy Day Dances, Rainy Day Songs AR 570
Educational Activities, Inc.

Holiday Songs & Rhythms AR 538
Hap Palmer
Educational Activities

Birds, Beasts, Bugs and Little Fishes 7610
Pete Seeger
Scholastic
904 Sylvan Ave.
Englewood Cliffs, N.J. 07632

American Folk Songs for Children R 7601
Pete Seeger
Scholastic

Song and Play-Time R 7526
Pete Seeger
Scholastic

NOTE: Hap Palmer's *Learning Basic Skills Through Music*, vols. I to III, have been very popular in helping children develop many different skills through music. These records can be obtained from Educational Activities, Inc., and other sources.

MOVEMENT AND RHYTHMS

The Small Dancer 391
Bowmar
  Good collection for use with the young child

Finger Games HYP-506
Educational Activities, Inc.
  Rhythmic verses combined with hand motions

Easy Does It AR 581
Hap Palmer
Educational Activities, Inc.
  Activity songs for basic motor skill development

Counting Games and Rhythms for the Little Ones, vol. 1 R 7679 and vol. 2 R 7680
Ella Jenkins
Folkways Records

Simplified Lummi Stick Activities KIM 2015
Laura Johnson
Kimbo Educational
  Prekindergarten–2

Dances for Little People KIM 0860
William C. Janiak
Kimbo Educational
  Preschool–kindergarten

The Hokey Pokey and Other Favorites MH-33
A. B. LeCrone Co.
  Recorded slow for the very young and exceptional child, faster for the advanced; a fine record for the young child

Circle Games, Activity Songs, and Lullabies AR 547
Patty Zeitlin and Marcia Berman
Educational Activities, Inc.

Rhythms of Childhood with Ella Jenkins R 7632
Folkways Records
  Rhythms in nature, dance, and far away

Dance-a-Story
Anne Lief Barlin
Ginn & Co.
  Storybook-record combination for beginning dance technique, creative rhythms, pantomime, and dramatic motivation

Dance-a-Folk Song
Two 7-inch records
Anne and Paul Barlin
Bowmar

Childhood Rhythms
Ruth Evans
Lyons Band

Children's Activities to Music for Kindergarten FC 7563
Folkways Records

Sing a Song of Action LP 3060
Kimbo Educational
  23 progressive songs to act out rhythmically through finger play and games

Singing Games and Dances
Bowmar

Activities for Rainy Days MH-83
A. B. LeCrone Co.

Pretend AR 563
Hap Palmer
Educational Activities, Inc.
  Pretending with movement

Perceptual Motor Rhythm Games AR 50
Jack Capon and Rosemary Hallum
Educational Activities, Inc.

Honor Your Partner
Album 7
Educational Activities, Inc.
  Rhythms—skating, skipping, etc.

Movement Exploration LP 5090
Educational Activities, Inc.

Creative Movement and Rhythmic Expression AR 533
Hap Palmer
Educational Activities, Inc.

Dancing Numerals AR 537
Rosemary Hallum and Henry "Buzz" Glass
Educational Activities, Inc.
  Through music, games, and chants

Basic Concepts Through Dance EALP 601
Educational Activities, Inc.
  Body image

Movin' AR 546
Hap Palmer
Educational Activities, Inc.
  Collection of original music written for movement exploration and creative movement activities

Clap Snap and Tap AR 48
Ambrose Brazelton and Gabe DeSantis
Educational Activities, Inc.
  Designed for relevant activities in limited space

Fun Activities for Fine Motor Skills LP 9076
Kimbo Educational
  Activities designed to help children focus on developing fine motor skills

Sensorimotor Training in the Class AR 532
Linda Williams and Donna Wemple
Educational Activities, Inc.
  Kindergarten–3

Chicken Fat LB 6270
Lyons Band

Rhythms For Today HYP-29
Educational Activities, Inc.

Mod Marches AR 527
Hap Palmer
Educational Activities, Inc.

World of Marches 131
Bowmar
  A fine collection of well-selected marches for young children

Marches HYP-R 11
Educational Activities, Inc.
  No runs or frills to break rhythm

Altogether Songs and Marches K 7007
Educational Activities, Inc.

Patriotic and Morning Time Songs AR 519
Hap Palmer
Educational Activities, Inc.

NOTE: "Alley Cat," "Syncopated Clock," "Raindrops Keep Falling on My Head," "The Waltzing Cat," and many classical recordings are excellent to use for creative rhythms.

LISTENING AND APPRECIATION

Amaryllis (Ghys)

Ballet of the Unhatched Chicks (Moussorgsky)

Barcarolle from Tales of Hoffman (Offenbach)

Carnival of the Animals (Saint-Saëns)

Country Gardens (Granger)

Children's Corner Suite (Debussy)

Children's Games (Bizet)

Dance Macabre (Saint-Saëns)

Grand Canyon Suite (Grofé)

March of the Little Lead Soldiers (Pierné)

March of the Toys (Herbert)

Nutcracker Suite (Tchaikovsky)

Peter and the Wolf (Prokofiev)

Peer Gynt Suite No. 1 (Grieg)

Sleighride (Anderson)

Symphony No. 94 in G Major (*Surprise*) (Haydn)

The Dancing Doll (Poldini)

The Flight of the Bumblebee (Rimsky-Korsakov)

The Skater's Waltz (Waldteufel)

The Syncopated Clock (Anderson)

Toy Symphony (Haydn)

  The RCA Victor Music Service Basic Record Library contains exemplary volumes and selections for listening and appreciation.

The Small Listener 393
Bowmar

Bowmar Orchestral Library
Series 1 and 2
  The beginning, for students of any age, of a "listener's repertoire"; excellent source

Papa Haydn's Surprise and Toy Symphonies
Disneyland Records
119 Fifth Ave.
New York, N.Y. 10003

Sounds I Can Hear
Scott, Foresman & Co.

Introduction To Great Music
Golden Records Educational Division
Michael Brent Publications, Inc.
  A Child's Introduction To The Nutcracker Suite
  Peter And the Wolf
  Sleeping Beauty and Swan Lake
  Saturday Morning Children's Concert
  Music of the Great Composers
  Gilbert and Sullivan

INSTRUMENTS

Homemade Band AR 545
Hap Palmer
Educational Activities, Inc.

Instruments of the Orchestra
Education Record Sales
  National Symphony Orchestra for RCA Victor; illustrates each of the instruments of the symphony orchestra individually

Know the Orchestra
Bowmar
  An introduction to the instruments of the orchestra, musical form, and style storybook; recording, filmstrip with cassette, study prints, etc.

Modern Tunes for Rhythms and Instruments AR 523
Hap Palmer
Kimbo Educational Records

Perceptual Motor Activities Using Rhythm Instruments KR 9078
Educational Activities, Inc.

Play Your Instruments and Make a Pretty Sound 7665
Ella Jenkins
Folkways Records

The Small Player 392
Bowmar
  Music encouraging hesitant and musically inexperienced young children in free exploration and experimentation with rhythm instruments and movement

NOTE: Many excellent compositions can be used to illustrate various instruments. One such example is "Peter and the Wolf."

FEELINGS, AWARENESS

Getting to Know Myself AR 543
Hap Palmer
Educational Activities, Inc.

Ideas, Thoughts and Feelings AR 549
Hap Palmer
Educational Activities, Inc.
  Experience in discovery and independent thinking

Won't You Be My Friend AR 544
Patty Zeitlin and Marcia Berman
Educational Activities, Inc.
  Songs for social and emotional growth

I Like Myself LP 0800
Synovia Simms and Doreen Bellhorn
Kimbo Educational

Everybody Cries Sometimes AR 561
Patty Zeitlin and Marcia Berman
Educational Activities, Inc.

Free To Be You And Me Al 4003
Marlo Thomas and Friends
Arista Records
1776 Broadway
New York, N.Y. 10019

Know Your Body from Head to Toe LP 264
Golden Records Educational Division
Michael Brent Publications, Inc.

LANGUAGE AND READING

Dancing Words AR 539
Rosemary Hallum and Henry "Buzz" Glass
Educational Activities, Inc.
  A movement approach to language and reading

Feelin' Free AR 517
Hap Palmer
Educational Activities, Inc.
  A personalized approach to vocabulary and language development

Poems for the Very Young
Bowmar
  Related poems and music

Rhythms to Reading
Lucille Wood
Bowmar
  A multimedia program that prepares children for success in reading, with opportunity for purposeful listening, following directions, singing, and movement; twelve book-and-record sets, filmstrips, picture songbook, etc. The recorded narrative and songs from each book develop reading readiness and musical sensitivity.

Witches' Brew AR 576
Hap and Martha Palmer
Educational Activities, Inc.
  Songs for oral language development

Learning Basic Skills Through Music AR 521
Hap Palmer
Educational Activities, Inc.
  Vocabulary

BOOKS ON MAKING INSTRUMENTS

Music and Instruments for Children to Make (Book One)
John Hawkinson and Martha Faulhaber
Albert Whitman & Co.
560 West Lake St.
Chicago, Ill. 60606

Rhythms, Music and Instruments to Make (Book Two)
John Hawkinson and Martha Faulhaber
Albert Whitman & Co.

SOURCES FOR ORDERING INSTRUMENTS

Blocks*
330 North Dr.
Memphis, Tenn. 38109

Children's Music Center, Inc.
5373 West Pico Blvd.
Los Angeles, Calif. 90019

Lyons Band
530 Riverview Ave.
Elkhart, Ind. 46514

Magnamusic-Baton, Inc.
10370 Page Industrial Blvd.
St. Louis, Mo. 63132

Music Education Group
Garden State Rd.
Union, N.J. 07083
  Handles materials from various suppliers. Write for name
  of store nearest you.

Oscar Schmidt-International, Inc.
Garden State Rd.
Union, N.J. 07083
  Makes and distributes the original Autoharp.

Peripole, Inc.
P.O. Box 146
Browns Mills, N.J. 08015

Rhythm Band, Inc.
P.O. Box 126
Fort Worth, Tex. 76101

FILMS

The following films can be ordered and rented from the
Audio-Visual Aids Center, Kent State University, Kent, Ohio
44242:

Building Children's Personalities with Creative Dancing
Bailey Films 1955
Color (29 minutes)
  Portrays a creative dance teacher guiding a group of pupils
  in the development of individual styles in creative dancing.
  The initial awkwardness of a group of 5- to 10-year-old
  boys and girls gives way to more relaxed and rhythmic
  movements as the teacher encourages the pupils to express
  freely their inner feelings by suggesting word pictures to
  them and praising their efforts.

*When ordering, write name of instrument as first line of address.

Dance Your Way
Bailey Films 1961
Color (10 minutes)
  Shortened version of the preceding film. Children listen to a
  phonograph and dance their own way, sometimes with the
  group and sometimes alone, to the rhythm they feel
  and hear.

Learning through the Arts
Churchill Films 1967
Color (22 minutes)
  Catches the natural reactions of four 4-year-olds through
  experiences with language arts, response to music and
  rhythm, and imaginative use of paint and clay.

Movement Exploration: What Am I?
Film Associates 1968
Color (11 minutes)
  Shows children exploring movement, mimicking birds, ani-
  mals, and machines.

BOOKS ON SOUND

Borten, Helen. *Do you hear what I hear?* New York: Abe-
  lard-Schuman Ltd., 1960.

Branley, Franklyn. *Rusty rings a bell.* New York: Thomas
  Y. Crowell Co., Inc., 1957.

Brown, Margaret. *The city noisy book.* New York: Harper &
  Row, 1939.
  The country noisy book. 1942.
  The indoor noisy book. 1943.
  The seashore noisy book. 1941.
  The quiet noisy book. 1950.
  The summer noisy book. 1951.
  The winter noisy book. 1947.

Dawson, Rosemary and Dawson, Richard. *A walk in the city.*
  New York: Viking Press, 1960.

Frost, Marie. *Whispering sounds: a listening book.* Elgin, Ill.:
  David C. Cook Publishing Co., 1967.

Gramatky, Hardy. *Little Toot.* New York: G. P. Putnam's
  Sons, 1939.

Grifalconi, Ann. *City rhythms.* New York: the Bobbs-Merrill
  Co., Inc., 1965.

Grifalconi, Ann. *The toy trumpet.* New York: The Bobbs-
  Merrill Co., Inc., 1968.

Kaufman, Lois. *What's that noise?* New York: Lothrop, Lee &
  Shepard Co., 1965.

Keats, Ezra. *Whistle for Willie.* New York: The Viking
  Press, 1964.

McGovern, Ann. *Too much noise.* New York: Houghton Mifflin Co., 1967.

Showers, Paul. *The listening walk.* New York: Thomas Y. Crowell Co., Inc., 1961.

Skaar, Grace. *What do the animals say?* Reading, Mass.: Addison-Wesley Publishing Co., Inc., 1968.

Spooner, Jane. *Tony plays with sounds.* New York: The John Day Co., Inc., 1961.

Steiner, Charlotte. *Listen to my seashell.* New York: Alfred A. Knopf, Inc., 1959.

Summers, Sandra. *Bell sounds: a listening book.* Elgin, Ill. David C. Cook Publishing Co., 1967.

Tresselt, Alvis. *Rain drop splash.* New York: Lothrop, Lee & Shepard Co., 1962.

A practical approach in learning to play the Autoharp

CARE AND TUNING

The Autoharp should receive the same kind of treatment that one would give a fine piano or other instrument. Dampness and sudden changes of temperature will affect its playing qualities. When it is not in use, it is advisable to keep it in a box or case and to store it in a dry place of even temperature.

The instrument should be tuned frequently to keep it in perfect tune. This is not difficult to do if one has a good sense of pitch. It should either be tuned to a well-tuned piano, to some other instrument with a fixed pitch (such as an accordion), or to a pitch pipe. If one person plays the corresponding key on the piano while the other person tunes the Autoharp, the tuning can be done in approximately ten minutes.

Middle C should be tuned first, and the lower and higher octaves tuned in unison with it. In the same manner continue to tune the other strings. The tuning tool should be placed on each peg and turned *slowly* with either the right or left hand, either clockwise or counterclockwise until the tone produced by the string matches the tone of the corresponding key of the piano or other instrument. With the other hand, pluck the string with the thumbnail while turning the tuning tool. By turning the tool clockwise, the pitch of the string will be raised. Turning the tool counterclockwise lowers the pitch. The change in tone will tell you when you have the proper pitch. When one is first learning to tune the Autoharp, it is most helpful to have one person playing the note on the piano while the other person does the tuning. Continued practice in tuning the Autoharp should make one's ear more sensitive to changes in pitch.

When checking to see if the Autoharp is out of tune, press down the bars one at a time and slowly draw the pick across the strings. This will enable one to locate the string or strings out of tune with the chord. Usually, only a few strings will be out of tune at one time.

For optimum results it is extremely important to keep the instrument in tune. If one does not have a good ear for pitch, ask a music teacher or some other musical person for help.

VARIATIONS IN STRUMMING TECHNIQUE

Variations in rhythm or accent can be accomplished by strumming in different ways.

In order to strum rhythmically one must be acquainted with the time or meter signature found at the beginning of every song. Some of the more commonly used meter signatures are 2/4, 3/4, 4/4, and 6/8. The top number always indicates the number of beats or counts in each measure; the lower number indicates what kind of note or rest receives one beat or one count. For example, in 2/4 time the top number *2* shows there are two beats in each measure, and the lower number *4* shows that a quarter note (♩) receives one count. In 6/8 time, the top number *6* shows there are six beats in each measure; the lower number *8* shows that an eighth note (♪) receives one count.

Following are several suggested variations in strumming patterns*†:

2/4 time—One or two strokes per measure, depending on the tempo and style of the song. For one stroke per measure, strum on beat 1 and count silently on beat 2. For two strokes per measure, strum on both beats, 1 and 2.

3/4 time—One long, accented stroke or one long accented and two short strokes, depending on tempo and style of the song. Strum one long, accented, full stroke, and count silently on beats 2 and 3, or strum one long, accented, full stroke from the bass strings up and two short unaccented strokes on the higher-pitched strings.

4/4 time—One, two, or four strokes to the measure depending on the tempo and style of the song. For one full stroke to a measure, strum on beat 1 and count silently on beats 2, 3, and 4. For two full strokes to a measure, strum on beats 1 and 3 and count silently on beats 2 and 4. For four strokes to a measure, use short strokes on all 4 beats.

Banjo quality—Sharp, short strokes from the bass strings up or the higher-pitched strings down or stroking in both directions. The player can best decide on the desired length of stroke. A plastic pick is sometimes desirable to obtain the banjo effect.

Harp quality—Full, long strokes from the bass strings up using most or all of the strings. One may also achieve the harp quality by

strumming in both directions on the strings for certain desired effects. By strumming on the left side of the bars, one can obtain a realistic harplike effect. Play smoothly without accent and only fast enough to keep the rhythmic pattern flowing.

Broken rhythms—A combination of short and long strokes in either direction. If one can "feel" certain rhythmic patterns, it is usually not difficult with experimentation and practice to strum these patterns on the Autoharp.

When practicing the strumming patterns, press down firmly one bar button at a time with the fingers of the left hand. Strum with the right hand, using an easy, flowing action. Remember that the left-handed person may find it easier to reverse these positions. It is possible to obtain an endless variety of rhythm patterns by experimentation.

When playing the Autoharp, always try to strum and play it in such a way that it will help to create a mood that is appropriate to the song being played or sung.

PLAYING

A good approach in learning to play the Autoharp according to chord markings is to select a familiar song that can be accompanied using only one chord. An example of this kind would be the round "Are You Sleeping?" Place the index finger of the left hand on the G major bar and stroke with the right hand on the first and third beats of each measure. Notice the song is written in 4/4 time. This means that there are four beats to a measure, and a quarter note receives one beat. Hold the bar button down firmly while strumming. Strum each time the letter appears above the staff and note.

If the player finds that the song is too high in pitch in this key, place the index finger of the left hand on the F major bar button instead.

*Press down one of the bar buttons with the index finger of the left hand and strum with the right, using the suggested variations.
†Chord markings for the songs in this book, placed above the music staff, are changed when the melodic line requires it. Additional chords are to be strummed between chord changes according to the rhythm of the song and the strumming patterns desired by the player.

ARE YOU SLEEPING?

Key of G major

Are you sleep - ing? are you sleep - ing, Broth - er

John, Broth - er John? Morn-ing bells are ring - ing, Morn-ing bells are

ring - ing: Ding, ding, dong, ding, ding, dong.

Important: When using the Autoharp to accompany singing, always be sure to strum the beginning chord several times in order to establish the key feeling for a song. If desired, one may pluck the beginning note of a song on the correct string indicated by the letter name shown beneath it.

"Row, Row, Row Your Boat" is another example of a song that can be played using only one chord. Strum on the first beat of each measure or on both beats 1 and 2 if desired. Notice that this song has only two beats to a measure. Place the index finger on the C major bar.

ROW, ROW, ROW YOUR BOAT

Key of C major

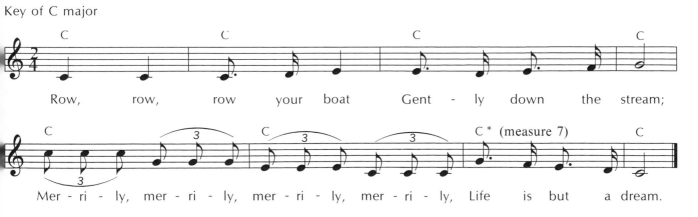

Row, row, row your boat Gent - ly down the stream;

Mer - ri - ly, mer - ri - ly, mer - ri - ly, mer - ri - ly, Life is but a dream.

---

*After the song has been played once, play it a second time. At the beginning of measure 7 use the G_7 chord instead of the C chord. This should produce a more pleasing sound to the ear. In the last measure return to the C chord.

If the key of C is too low, try playing the song in the key of F. Place the index finger on the F major bar. In measure 7 use the C_7 chord. Return to the F major chord in the last measure.

Other songs that may be played with the use of only one chord are "Little Tom Tinker," "Swing Low, Sweet Chariot," and "For Health and Strength" (sometimes called "Choral Grace").

Continued early experiences in playing should consist of using songs limited to two chords, in which the player should listen for the individual qualities of each of the chords used. Most songs having only two chords use a chord with the same letter name as the key in which the song is written, indicated by an *I* and called the *tonic chord,* and another chord that has the same letter name as the fifth tone of the scale in which the song is written, indicated by a V_7 and called the *dominant seventh chord.* The I chord gives the feeling of "completion" or "being at rest," whereas the V_7 chord has the quality of "unrest" and the need for resolution or completion, as was pointed out in the example of "Row, Row, Row Your Boat" (measure 7).

An example of a two-chord song would be "Mary Had a Little Lamb." Place the index finger of the left hand on the F major bar. The C_7 chord should be played with the middle finger of the left hand. Strum on the first beat of each measure.

The F major chord is the I chord, and the C_7 chord is the V_7 chord in this song.

MARY HAD A LITTLE LAMB

Key of F major

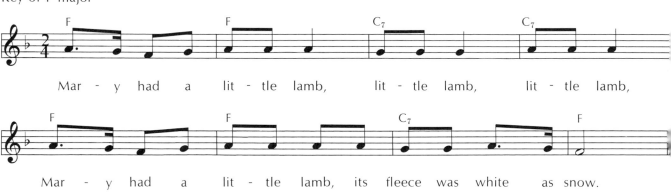

Other songs that may be played using two chords are "Polly Wolly Doodle," "Down in the Valley," and "Skip to My Lou."

After mastering two-chord songs, three-chord songs should be explored for the distinctive quality of the third chord used. This third chord has the same letter name as the fourth tone of the scale in which the song is written and is indicated by a *IV* and called the *subdominant chord.* The chord progression from IV to I sounds much like the "Amen" that appears at the end of many hymns.

An example of a three-chord song is "Twinkle, Twinkle, Little Star." Notice the song is written in 2/4 time. Strum on the first beat of each measure or on beats 1 and 2 if desired. Place the index finger of the left hand on the F major bar button. The middle finger should play the C_7 chord and the ring finger the B^b major chord.

In this key, the F chord is the I chord, the C_7 chord is the V_7 chord, and the B^b chord is the IV chord.

Other songs that may be played using three chords are "Jingle Bells," "Home on the Range," "Brahm's Lullaby," "I've Been Working on the Railroad," and "Jacob's Ladder."

TWINKLE, TWINKLE, LITTLE STAR

Key of F major

Twin - kle, twin - kle, lit - tle star; How I won - der
what you are, Up a - bove the world so high,
Like a dia - mond in the sky! Twin - kle, twin - kle,
lit - tle star; How I won - der what you are.

CHORDING DEFINED

In order to explain the chords used by the Autoharp, it is necessary to consider first a basic system of organizing musical tones known as the *scale*.

A scale is a series of eight consecutive tones ascending or descending from a given pitch according to a particular pattern. Pitches are identified by the use of letters. For this purpose, the letters A through G are used and repeated. Thus a scale beginning on the pitch of C would include the tones of C, D, E, F, G, A, B, and C.

A second technique uses a system of numerals from 1 through 8. Note the following example:

Songs are written in various keys. The key of a song is determined by the scale tones used. Thus a song in the key of C uses the tones in the scale of C:

Key of C

In this scale, the pitch of C is considered to be the key center or the pitch that begins and ends the scale series, and in this scale it is given the number 1. In the C scale the pitch of D is number 2, E is number 3, F is number 4, G is number 5, A is number 6, B is number 7, and C again is number 8, or the octave of 1. In the scale of C none of the pitches is either sharped (♯) or flatted (♭), so in a song in the key of C no sharps or flats are shown at the beginning of the song. Songs in other keys show key signatures that use sharps or flats because they are based on scales which have to use pitches either sharped or flatted. Thus a song in the key of G, the tones of which are derived from the scale of G, has to use a sharp (F♯) in its signature because in the scale of G this pitch (F) has to be sharped:

Key of G

This sharp is placed on the staff after the clef sign. In each case the key signature denotes the pitch considered to be the key center for the song. The pitch so considered is always given the number of 1.

In order to play or sing a song in its proper key setting, it is important to be able to tell from the key signature in what key the song is to be played or sung. The technique of determining the key from a given key signature is not difficult.

In songs having flats in their signatures, call the line or space of the staff on which the last flat (the one to the far right of any others shown) is placed "four" (4) and count downward each consecutive line or space of the staff until the line or space number one (1) is reached. The pitch for that line or space of the staff is then the key center (x), or key tone (keys of B♭, E♭, A♭, and D♭):

Key of F   B♭   E♭   A♭   D♭

In songs having only one flat in their signature, call the line of the staff on which it is placed "4," and count down to 1 (key of F above).

In order to find the key of songs with sharps, move up one line or space of the staff from the last sharp, which is the one to the far right of any others shown in the key signature. If the last sharp is located on a line, the key center will be located on the next space. If the last sharp is located in a space, the key center will be located on the next line:

Key of G   D   A   E   B

Before proceeding further it may be wise to point out that Arabic numerals (1, 2, 3, 4, 5, 6, 7, 8) are used to indicate scale degrees or pitches.

The next step in explaining Autoharp chording is a consideration of the structure of chords. A chord results from the simultaneous playing of a combination of pitches. A chord may be built on any step of a scale by placing three or more notes one above the other on alternate lines or spaces of the staff*:

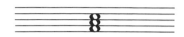

Three-tone chord

In any key the chord built on the first tone of the scale for that key is indicated by the Roman numeral I† and is called the *tonic chord*. In a specific key it also has a letter name, that of the key. Thus in the key of C, the chord built on the pitch of C is given the numeral I and is called the tonic chord and the C chord:

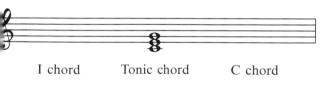

I chord   Tonic chord   C chord

The pitch of C is the root tone, E is the third of the triad and G is the fifth of the triad. On the Autoharp it is labeled the "C Maj." chord.

Most folk songs and songs for children may be accompanied by the use of three different chords. These chords are the ones built on the first, fourth, and fifth tones of a scale. They are given the Roman numerals I, IV, and V_7. They are frequently referred to as the *primary chords*.

The V chord, built on the fifth step or tone of the scale, is called the *dominant chord*. It is labeled with a Roman numeral V. In a specific key it assumes the letter name of the fifth degree or step of that scale. Thus in the

key of C the dominant chord is the G chord. *Important note:* On the Autoharp the form of the dominant chord used is the dominant seventh (V_7). It consists of four tones: a root (the fifth tone of the scale), a third (three staff degrees above the root), a fifth (five staff degrees above the root), and a seventh (seven staff degrees above the root):

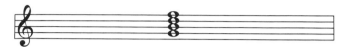

V_7 chord   Dominant seventh chord G_7 chord

The IV chord, built on the fourth degree of the scale, is called the *subdominant chord*. It is labeled with a Roman numeral IV. In a specific key it assumes the letter name of the fourth step of that scale. Thus in the key of C the subdominant chord IV is the F chord:

IV chord   Subdominant chord   F chord

Chords constructed in minor keys are built on the same degrees of the scale as in major keys and are also referred to as tonic, dominant, and subdominant chords. For example, a chord built on the first tone of the A minor scale is called the *tonic chord in the key of A minor* and is given the Roman numeral I. The minor chords provided on the Autoharp are for use not only in minor keys but often to harmonize a part of a melody in a major key as well. A common series of chords known as a chord progression making use of this is:

I	VI	IV	V_7	I
C	A_m	F	G	C

Note the difference in the quality of the chords as you move from a major chord to a minor chord and back again to a major.

On the twelve-bar Autoharp there are only three minor chords available—g, d, and a—but they are usually sufficient for accompanying the majority of songs sung in the kindergarten and grades one, two, and three. The minor chords are located on the upper row of buttons, and the fingers of the left hand are used in the same way as for the major chords.

The fifteen-bar Autoharp has fifteen prepared chords

---

* A basic type of chord is known as a *triad,* which is a chord of three tones, one of which is called the *root* (the scale tone on which the triad is built), another is called the *third* (a tone three staff degrees above the root), and another tone called the *fifth* (five staff degrees above the root).

† Roman numerals refer to the degree of the scale on which the chord is built. The letter symbol refers to the pitch name of the particular note on which the chord is built.

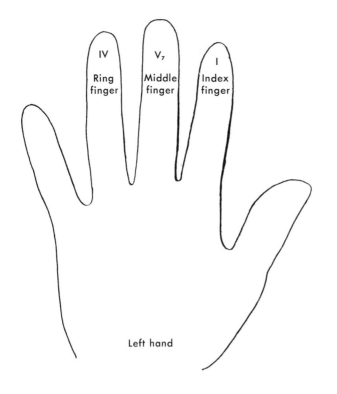

IV — Ring finger
V₇ — Middle finger
I — Index finger

Left hand

The chart below indicates the chord markings for the twelve-bar Autoharp, the system used in this appendix:

Bar label*	Chord produced	See note†
G Min.	G minor	G_m
B♭ Maj.	B♭ major	B♭
A Sev.	A seventh	A_7
C Sev.	C seventh	C_7
D Min.	D minor	D_m
F Maj.	F major	F
E Sev.	E seventh	E_7
G Sev.	G seventh	G_7
A Min.	A minor	A_m
C Maj.	C major	C
D Sev.	D seventh	D_7
G Maj.	G major	G

*On the Autoharp "Maj" stands for the word *major*, and "Min" stands for the word *minor*. In a song a chord marking followed by a small *m* indicates that the chord is a minor one. A chord is considered major if it is not followed by a small letter.

†The letters and signs shown in this column are the same ones that are generally found in guitar chords on sheet music.

instead of twelve. This includes three diminished chords and makes this particular model useful in the field of popular and folk music.

This chart indicates the primary chords as they appear in the various Autoharp keys:

Key*	Tonic I	Subdominant IV	Dominant V₇	Tonic I
C major	C	F	G_7	C
F major	F	B♭	C_7	F
G major	G	C	D_7	G
D minor	D_m	G_m	A_7	D_m
A minor	A_m	D_m	E_7	A_m

*Play the chord progressions in each key until you feel familiar with their individual qualities.

The primary chords on the Autoharp, the I, the IV, and the V_7 in any of the keys, are played in the following manner. When the index finger is placed on the I chord of a given key, the middle finger falls on the V_7 chord and the ring finger on the IV chord of that key. For example, place the index finger on the F major bar. This would be the I chord in the key of F. The middle finger would fall on the C_7 bar (the V_7), and the ring finger would fall on the B♭ major bar (the IV chord).

CHORDING A MELODY

There are many songs in the basic music series or in individual songbook collections that indicate the chord markings to use with the Autoharp. Many times, however, there are songs one wishes to use with the instrument for which chord markings are not given. It is not difficult to chord songs for the Autoharp if one knows the basic principles of harmony.

If a song keeps within a suitable singing range (from middle C to E above high C), and the song can be marked with the three primary chords, I, IV, and V_7, it may be accompanied on the Autoharp.

To write the chords for a song, a further discussion of harmony is necessary.

In any key the I chord is made up of the scale tones 1, 3, and 5. The IV chord is made up of the scale tones 4, 6, and 1 (or 8). The V chord is made up of the scale tones 5, 7, and 2. Since on the Autoharp the form of the V chord that is used is the V_7, the scale tones are 5, 7, 2, and 4. The V_7 chord is called a *seventh chord* because the top tone is 7 staff degrees above the root of the chord.

The scale tone numbers and the chord markings are given for the various Autoharp keys:

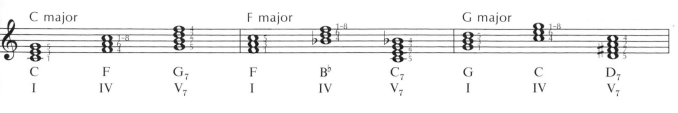

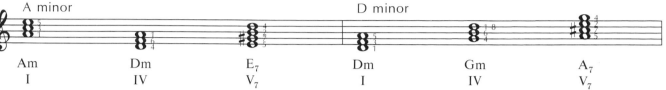

To determine the chord markings for a song, do the following steps:
1. Establish the key of the song.
2. Under each note of the melody, place its scale-tone number beneath the staff.
3. Within each measure look for a grouping of notes that are represented in a chord. (If piano accompaniments are given, this will often help the beginner chord a melody.)

"John Brown Had a Little Indian"

To illustrate the three preceding steps, the chorus of "John Brown Had a Little Indian" is used to show how a song can be chorded simply for the Autoharp:

As stated previously as step 1, *establish the key of the song.* Counting down each line and space of the staff from B♭—4, 3, 2, 1—it is found that the song is in the key of F.

Step 2, *number the scale tones in each measure.* The beginner will find that if he will number the eight tones of the F scale and write out the I, IV, and V_7 chords for that key, step 2 will be much easier to do. This can be done as shown in the following example:

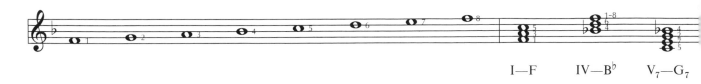

I—F   IV—B♭ V_7—G_7

After step 2 has been completed, *look for a grouping of notes that are represented in a chord within each measure.* In this instance, the primary chords in the key of F are F, B♭, and V_7. The harmony of some songs requires the use of more than one different chord within a measure; however, the song "John Brown" makes use of only one chord per measure.

Referring to measure 1, the melody consists solely of the scale tone 1 in the key of F. Looking at the chords that may be used, F appears both in the I chord and also in the IV chord. Since most songs begin with the I chord, it is safe to assume that the chord that should be used in this measure is the F chord. Mark the letter *F* above the first and third beats. *F* is marked above the third beat to show the proper beat position for strumming.

In measure 2, the melody consists of all three members of the F chord, and there remains no doubt as to the chord to be used. Place the chord marking *F* again above beats 1 and 3.

Measure 3 makes use of only the scale tone 2. Notice that it appears in the C_7 chord in the key of F, so this is the chord that should be used. Mark C_7 on both beats 1 and 3.

In measure 4, the scale tones 7, 2, and 5 can be found in the C_7 chord. Mark the chords as in measure 3.

Continue working with each measure in the same manner until the entire chorus has been chorded.

"Skip to My Lou"

Establish the key of the song. Using the same procedure as in the song "John Brown Had a Little Indian," the key is found to be F major.

Number the scale tones in each measure.

Look for chord groupings within each measure.

Measure 1 makes use of scale tones 3 and 1. Use F chord.
Measure 2 uses scale tones 3 and 5. Use F chord again.

Scale tones are 2 and 7 in measure 3. Use C_7 chord. Since this is the first chord change, be sure to mark it above the measure.

Measure 4 is scale tones 2 and 4. C_7 is used again.

In measure 5 the scale tones are 3 and 1. Use F chord. Mark chord change.

Measure 6 uses scale tones 3 and 5. F chord is used again.

In measure 7 the scale tones 2, 3, and 4 are used. The second and fourth tones in this measure are relatively unimportant for harmonic purposes and thus will not be chorded. Since they are not members of the chord used, they are called *nonharmonic tones* and are of a type known as *passing tones*. The other tones of the melody in this measure are members of the C_7 chord, and this chord should be used for the entire measure. Mark the chord change.

In measure 8 the melody is coming back to the tonic tone, and therefore the F chord (I) is used. Mark chord change.

Continue chording the rest of the song.

SKIP TO MY LOU

"London Bridge"

Notice that this song has no flats or sharps in the key signature. Therefore it is written in the key of C. For clarification and convenience, the scale tones and the chords for the key of C are given below:

Key of C

Number the scale tones in each measure.

Look for chord groupings within each measure. In measure 1, scale tones 5, 6, 4, and 3 are used. Tones 6 and 4 are passed by very quickly, and because a song usually begins with a tonic chord, the C chord would be a good choice in this measure. Strum on the first and third beats.

Scale tones 2, 3, 4, and 5 are used in measure 2. This measure is a good example of where *two* chords are needed within the measure to harmonize it correctly. Tones 2 and 4 represent the G_7 chord. The next grouping of tones 3, 4, and 5 indicates that a chord change needs to be made. Since 4 is a passing tone here, only tones 3 and 5 need to be considered. They represent the C chord. Be sure to change the chord marking at the top of the staff. Singing the words "falling down, falling down" as the Autoharp is being played will help one establish the fact that the G_7 chord cannot be used alone in this measure.

Measure 3 contains the same scale tones as in measure 1. Use the same chord, C.

Two chords will be needed to chord measure 4, also. The scale tones 2 and 5 are representative of the G_7 chord, and the tones 3 and 1 are members of the C chord. Be sure to indicate the chord change from G_7 to C in the measure. Again, if one will sing the words "My fair lady," the player's ear will be a good indicator of when the melody warrants a chord change.

LONDON BRIDGE

Singing game

"This Old Man"

    With the help given in the songs "John Brown Had a Little Indian," "Skip to My Lou," and "London Bridge," the student should be able to construct the chord patterns for "This Old Man." Follow the same steps used in the other songs. Notice that this song is written in the key of G. For the player's convenience, the scale tones and the chords for the key are given here:

THIS OLD MAN

This old man, he played one, He played nick - nack on my thumb;

Nick - nack pad-dy whack, Give a dog a bone, This old man came roll - ing home.

Index

Index

Index